I0766354

LANDCASTER PRESS

Gatsby

Thomas G. Jewusiak

Gatsby

(The incredible true story of the man some called the great Gatsby, as related by those who knew him personally, reported faithfully by his grandson)

Exploring Questions of Reality, Memory, Nostalgia, Identity, Race, Racism, Culture, Morality, the Self-made Man, the American Dream and Death

"Tell me your dreams and I will tell you who you are."
Francois Marichette

"Anyone turning biographer has committed himself to lies, concealment, to hypocrisy, to flattery, and even to hiding his own lack of understanding, for biographical truth is not to be had, and even if it were it couldn't be useful."   Sigmund Freud

"There is no such thing as real memory. There is only the fiction that we conjure to soothe our souls and turn down the heat of our brains. It is the duty of the state to mediate our memories for the preservation of ourselves and the state."   Wladislaw Gomulka

Jacket Design by Thomas Jewusiak

Back Cover Photo by Thomas Jewusiak

Cover Art and Design by Thomas Jewusiak

Printed by Hand on the Outer Banks

This is a work of fiction, a comedy, a parody. Any resemblance to any persons or fictional characters or any other works is entirely coincidental. This is a parody of The Great Gatsby. All-of the racist rants of Nick Carraway are quotes from the letters, books, stories and cited conversations of F. Scott Fitzgerald. Fitzgerald stepped far beyond the casual racism of his time.

First Hard Cover Edition
First Printing

Jewusiak, Thomas G.
Gatsby
ISBN: 978-0-9993587-5-7

Parts of this work were written in old growth ancient virgin forests. While the author was living in the woods, he hurt no old trees in any way. The paper in this book was made from the pulp of fallen trees. No live trees were cut-down. Only hand tools were used to cut and gather the fallen trees. Only horse and oxen drawn vehicles were used. The Humane Society monitored all animals, one monitor per animal. The linen fiber in the paper was recycled from the white linen suits originally worn by Spanish grandees in pre-revolutionary Cuba.

LANDCASTER PRESS
West Palm Beach
LandcasterPress.com
LandcasterPress@aol.com

Carraway at the Buchanans

Nicholas Carraway was invited to the Thomas Buchanan's at the desperate urging of an old mutual aunt back in Chicago, not yet demented. But it is Gatsby that hung or hovered over the event, like a ghostly presence that would not go away.

Carraway was broken and abandoned in a summer cottage out in Great Neck that he could ill-afford, hoodwinked into signing a lease by a coworker, a man called Outwater, who found that after only two days he couldn't stand to live under the same roof with Nick Carraway, or so he told anyone who would listen, and unceremoniously relocated to a cottage down the road.

In no shape to drive, they had Nick picked up and delivered to their door in neighboring Manhasset like a piece of cold meat covered with a thick brown coat of furry mold, resembling mutant peach fuzz. The outing would do him good; so, they were told.

It didn't. It was a fiasco. He kept making uninvited passes at the two women, Daisy, his cousin and Jordan, her friend. Most of the time he seemed out of it, answering questions no one asked, referring to Daisy as the "bewitching Morgan La Fay":

> "You look like a rookie witch with her pointed hat knocked off and her hair all messed up."

And asking if she had just gotten in from her flight around the house:

> "How was the view up there?"

For reasons known only to himself he thought this was hilarious and giggled like an ass-backward little girl; everyone else smiled in apprehension. Tom was pressed into physically guiding him, maneuvering him like a comatose oversized checker through a complex of nonexistent squares. Buchanan, massive and seething, dwarfed the hollow, androgynous Carraway as he pushed him around without enthusiasm. Carraway, shaken, unnerved, neutered by the enormity of Buchanan's physical proximity which guttered whatever little residual confidence persisted in Nick.

He kept wanting to see the "barns" and fancied Tom a polo player, like out of the slicks, fully conceived in full polo regalia, at the dinner table no less, no doubt reeking from the stables: horse shit, piss and sweat; or was he sanitized and deodorized in Nick's busted brain, a photographer's pristine model peeled straight off the page of the rotogravure lying indecently spread-eagled face down and fingered on the side-table, displacing the family bible which had been quietly interred in a mahogany box in the attic. This was an imitation of a life, a bad one that didn't work; skimmed hastily from a worn pile of popular magazines and pulp books.

Polo was a game for which the actual Thomas Buchanan, who invariably dressed for dinner, had utter and complete contempt. These incessant players of games were, in his mind, the inept, ineffectual destroyers of his own privileged class and he loathed them for it.

Nick kept repeating that he wasn't at all like a rose and none of them knew what he was talking about. They thought he might be trying to reference Shakespeare; but that wasn't it. It was he himself that he thought of as the rose.

It was an overwrought, high-strung afternoon, tension ballooning exponentially, everyone jumpy, jittery. Daisy only half succumbed complaining of "a bad case of nerves;" a phrase that in her secure inbred circle was applied with equal imprecision to anything from compulsive nail-biting to funny farm psychosis. Jordan frantically wrestled to make her getaway, to disentangle from the cotton candy, Carraway's sickly sugar-sticky delusions which affixed by the feeblest touch; soggy enshrouding Muzak, taffy clogging arteries, congealing the blood, asphyxiating the brain. In his own muddled mind, he was consummating a union with Jordan, twisting some innocuous remark of Daisy's about being set out in a boat together. Jordan cringed. There was nothing impersonal in her eyes and she was full of desire; she just had no desire of any kind for *Mr. Carraway,* as she insisted on calling him; the name rolling off her tongue, shot-out like an expectorated child's gumball.

It was as if they were all sitting around a keg of gun powder anticipating the inexorable ignition, never knowing what seemingly innocuous remark might set off the explosion. Little did they appreciate they would soon take turns tossing lighted matches at the ruptured drum, an out-of-time replay of a wicked children's game they once reveled in.

In an hallucinatory movie Paul Newman would be good for Nick Carraway. The perpetual boy excluded from proper society, a wounded, earnest, yearning outsider peering   in, a screen persona Newman tried to perfect in some of his early movies. Also, Matt Damon as he played *The Talented Mr. Ripley* but not so murderous or quite so pathetic.

Nick:

"Have you come east for good?"

Tom:

"I'd be a fool not to stay."

Nick, as if a wicked switch had been flicked:

"New York has its thousands of Real Folks... I grant you that... but it is cursed with unnumbered foreigners. We came too late... too late. It's not fit for any decent white man... nobody who loves his wife and children and likes to shake the hand of his neighbor. New York is no longer white, native, or Christian.

"There is, of course the Jew... the Jew, the incomprehensible alien, the corrupter. The Italians, the Poles, the Czechs, Scandinavians and Armenians all have the same remarkably ugly visages and that same smell. They all lack the symmetry of feature, which is essential to the true Aryan... The Jew when he's not intruding... shouldering... muscling in... he has his enclaves... the slow upward creep... always growing...   expanding...   consolidating...

moving... always moving... watching over his goods with his sharp hawk's eye and his bee's attention... insect attention to detail."

Nick, hyper, talking a mile a minute:

"Your Jew arrived as part of the great inundation... that's what it was... they had a boost... a head-start on your Micks, your Wops, your Greaseballs, even your Muffe or Heinie and your Pollacks... they fought with them all tooth and claw... and it wasn't an exceptional endowment of industry, sobriety, or ambition that pushed them ahead. No... No... Ya see... your Jew had for centuries been prohibited from owning land in Europe... the controlling powers erroneously believed that the land, the sanctified land was the source of all real wealth... that's how your Jew was liberated from being a mindless shit-kicker or clodhopper... they did him a big favor... they didn't mean to...Thomas Jefferson versus Alexander Hamilton and Hamilton triumphed hands down... no contest...

> Those who labor in the earth are the chosen people of God, if ever he had a chosen people.

So said Jefferson... a man so inept that he couldn't make money with a thousand slaves and thousands of acres of land and managed to pile up a crushing mountain of debt by shamelessly exploiting his position as ex-president. He built what he optimistically or delusionaly fancied a plantation on a mountain... an act of peculiar idiocy... there was little level ground, and the soil was poor. He fashioned a mere architectural curiosity as enduring testimony to his childish dilettantism... driving... whipping his slaves into an incessant commotion... pulling it down and building it right back up again like some mad Winchester widow or the crazy man up on the hill. He was intoxicated by a mad acquisitiveness predictive of twentieth century consumerism... an oniomaniac, ransacking Europe for silver, furniture, wine and fine comestibles, anything that struck his fevered materialistic fancy... this was no collector of art... mind you. He was petrified of speaking publicly. He did write exceptionally well, though.

The Jew's persecution had been the means of his own liberation... his elevation... his chains became his weapon and his tools... they herded him into cities with its trades and professions... his well-honed occupational skills served him well in America, with its urbanizing, industrializing... it's like they set the stage for him... ushering him in.

"And then they were money lenders, usurers... originally forbidden to Christians... They would take over the tables the Puritan Anglo-Saxon had so carefully set... beat them at their own game.

"This latest load of discharged Ellis Island cargo will worm their way like creeping bugs, make a cozy home among the neglected and abandoned residences of your own grandfathers and uncles. They'll step into the shoes of good solid Americans who won't be coming home, who died with their boots stuck in the mud, the perpetual quagmire which is Europe.

"These hordes we're letting in will poison our society... they are beaten men from beaten races, representing the worst failures in the ceaseless struggle for survival. We are interfering with a natural ineluctible process in which they have singled themselves out by their incompetence for necessary destruction. We must cull the herd or the weak and inept will bring us down with them like a sick man on our back."

Tom, interrupting him, trying to get him to slow down, afraid his train was going to leave the tracks; that he would blow with the least provocation:

"This may be the very reason to stay... East, I mean.

"I thought the Johnson Quota Act solved that problem."

Jordan, grabbing the microphone, so to speak:

"Why are we all coming East? Isn't this a reverse migration? What happened to the great promise of the West, the Promised Land, the last frontier? The American Dream is turned on its ear. Now rich men trek East from the Middle West and West... to splurge... their pockets bulging... bursting the seams with booty. The regular American law doesn't run here. It's a market place of commodities and everything but everything is reduced to bought-goods. Is there anything in New York that doesn't come out of money?

And poor boys from the farm instead of looking west look to the big city like a Mecca. There's a corruption here.

Maybe that accounts for the desperate debauchery we're drowning in. We are the first Americans sapped by our confrontation or lack of confrontation... with exhausted frontiers."

Daisy:

Oh, Jordan. You're beginning to sound like Tom. You're such a philosopher.

Jordan to Tom mostly, in a songful cadence, playfully:

"They came for baubles, bibelots and bows. The big spenders, the high rollers, the small-town boosters chomping down on the big sloppy wet cigars, gathered like a great host from the provinces, the backwaters and boondocks to get plastered on the distilled spirits of exhilaration... and faster and faster did the hucksters unload of their trinkets and slippers, so the factories strained to labor into the night, churning out more trinkets and slippers. Until a great roar arises from the mob swamping all peace and all quiet: 'More baubles. More bows. More trinkets. More slippers.'"

Daisy:

"What is that from?"

Jordan:

"I don't know. (pause) Where do you think it's from?"

Daisy:

"It sounds familiar."

Jordan:

"It does, doesn't it?"

Daisy:

"It sounds like the Bible."

Jordan:

"It's not the Bible, though. I think it's me but I'm not sure. I might have heard it somewhere. Ideas are in the air…. (whispering) The end is near.

"Every thought and act you have, owes its complexion to the acts of your dead and living brothers. Somebody else said that too. I forgot who."

Daisy:

"No, you didn't. You don't forget anything.

"What does it mean, though? The first part I mean, about the baubles and bows."

After a pause, Jordan:

"I'm not sure.

"New York... the East embodied... incarnate... Broadway... the façade of the American city... a false front... a cracking veneer beginning to peel... a set for a second-feature movie shot on the West Coast."

Picking up speed like a race car with its peddle stuck to the floor:

"The vaunted achievements of our material civilization... our hotels, our department stores, and our Woolworth towers are only symptoms of our spiritual impoverishment, papering over the vacancy of our manic acquisitiveness, the getting and the spending... as-a-consequence our existence is shallow, base and hollow, frittering our substance on worthless tchotchkes and flashy gewgaws... scatterbrained savages clawing each other over glass beads... We go gaga over wampum."

Daisy:

"We have to get you a church or at least a pulpit. We have to rent you a hall... that's it... or a big barn. You could speak on Balzac, Flaubert, Zola, Ibsen, Strindberg and Chekhov too. You just love Chekhov."

Nick kept trying to get off lame jokes that lay flat, crawled off, died and putrefied in the corner of the room; jokes that they felt compelled to anxiously laugh at; something about the women coming down from their balloons. He made some reference to a stop-over in Chicago and the town being in mourning with their rear wheels painted black as a wreath for Daisy. She gently reminded him she was not dead, yet. There might have been something funny in there deep down, but Carraway was so fractured, so inept and ill at ease that he couldn't pull it off. Re-rehearsed and re-spoken in the calm quiet loneliness of his overpriced rented bungalow these lines might actually come off as comical.

Tom expounded upon his favorite thesis: that ruling elites may maintain their power for a while through their exclusiveness but unless they have an avenue whereby, they admit new competent, fresh, worthy blood, their very exclusiveness will be the cause of their eventual doom. I think he purposely tried to calm things down, defuse the situation, by shifting the spotlight clear of Carraway.

> "This fellow Batsell predicts that this decade, the twenties, will mark the last decade in which members of the Anglo-Saxon establishment will hold sway. It is the beginning of their... our end. Up until now they have been safeguarded by countless caste barriers, from the rest of the people, and have had everything more-or-less their own way. This decade will be pervaded by a sense of impending loss of dominance, a sense of their own passing. Goldenhirst makes the

point that the Jews are perceived by the writers of this generation as a kind of vanguard, as the representative, par excellence, of the postwar assault on the upper social classes. And he does call it an assault. They are a stalking horse.

The American Anglo-Saxon privileged class is dumbfounding in its ill-conceived exclusionary clannishness. (Buchanan actually spoke like this.) They will wither and they will die for it and it will be their just desert... no one to blame but themselves. The English gave the Scots... regarded as an alien race... hated... land and titles and clutched them to their bosom. The Russians struck their deal and made the remnants of the Tartar chieftains into nobles. It has been estimated that ten percent of Russian noble blood is Tartar blood. You think this is because they loved the Tartars? They detested the Tartars. Expediency.

Who in the hell is this old-moneyed Anglo-Saxon elite... these people who dare to think of themselves as Patrician... of which I am a somewhat embarrassed member. They take themselves so deadly serious. They're nothing but the recent descendants of nouveau riche industrialists and merchants of the previous economic boom late in the last century... a pretentious... vicious mockery, a failed imitation of a defunct feudal regime... closed... violently egocentric and entirely un-chivalric. They assume all-of the pretentions but take none of the responsibility.

"America is backward, not forward thinking. Hosts of previous societies would have welcomed this Gatsby fellow… that nobody seems to be able to stop talking about … They would have welcomed him with open arms… would have married him off to their fairest daughters.

"The military has traditionally been an avenue for social advancement from the very beginning of history. If the term 'officer and gentleman' means anything it means exactly that. If you are an officer… you are a gentleman… period. This Gatsby was a Colonel for Christ's sake. What more do these bastards want? I'm told he was so covered over in medals you could hardly see the man. According to my sources the two major battles he fought in were the Battle of the Marne and the Battle of the Argonne Forest… both in 1918. Argonne probably the bloodiest of the war… involved more than a million Americans… resulting in over 25,000 dead and 100,000 wounded. These fools see him as the commoner in the king's chair while a legion of previous societies would have discerned in him the true and rightful king.

"I've done a little investigation of my own on this fellow… I've unearthed a rumor and it's only a rumor, mind you, that Gatsby was up for the Congressional Medal of Honor… they sunk it, shot it down… political reasons… he wasn't American enough… too German looking.… the blond hair, those killer blue eyes… the erect military bearing… the clipped, correct speech…

the quick step. You can practically hear the ghostly echo of boots clicking when he comes into a room; it shook them.

They say his mother was born in the Austrian... the Hapsburg Empire... Lemburg... On her citizenship papers she renounced allegiance to the Emperor of Austria... sounds like something out of a fairy tale... renouncing allegiance to the Emperor of Austria... but that wasn't good enough... spoke High German as everyone did in those conquered cities... who wanted to get anywhere.

"In any old society his military exploits alone would have conferred upon him vast estates and noble titles... Military prowess, after all, was the foundation of nobility... Thane of Cawdor... Forty acres in a former broken down fishing village, having to traverse the ash heaps of the Corona dump to get to the City, hardly does the trick... They forgot the damned mule.

"This Gatsby was born in the wrong country in the wrong century... the wrong millennium. If one of the most decorated officers... who has fought heroically for this country... a Colonel no less... can be referred to as a Mr. Nobody from Nowhere by a member of the reigning caste of this country... whose immediate progenitor founded his prosperity upon dry goods or hardware or... wholesale pork bellies... then that fool is not fit to occupy that seat and should be displaced by any means... any means... necessary.”

These remarks were met with deafening silence. Tom gave speeches... Daisy rolled her eyes... everyone’s mouth dropped. He was famous for his turgid conversation stoppers.

Jordan:

“And here I thought you were such a snob. I didn’t know you cared about these people.”

Tom:

“Care? I don’t care. I don’t give the slightest damn about these people... I care about me and mine... my own... my race. I care about survival. And we are eating ourselves up as a class. In fifty years, we may have the remnants of our money... some scattered enclaves... but our power, our control will be a fond memory, deliberated by historians and so-called ‘social engineers’, dissected and analyzed by the intellectuals... probably mostly Jews by then... who will supersede us. They will pick among our ruins like dispassionate archaeologists from a distant alien world.

“We have the dimwitted audacity to turn up our noses at those who want nothing more than to join and strengthen our ranks, to be our allies... confederates... collaborators... our brothers... to fight alongside us.”

Nick:

"This kind of nativism is only natural... the fear that the alien will not fit in... cannot become part of and therefore will disrupt the dominant social order and threaten it."

Tom, getting agitated:

"No... no... no... This isn't nativism... it is something far more complex and dangerous. Nativism is the fear that the new comer can't or won't adapt, that they are inferior and inimical to the existing structure... that identity is inherited, racially rooted and that this inheritance determines beliefs and customs.

"The fear of the ruling Anglo-Saxons is not that the newcomers will not be assimilated or that they are hostile or foreign but rather the very opposite... the fear is that they will become so identical to the privileged class as to be indistinguishable from it and so will pass... and I use that term very carefully... that these aliens can be excluded only by an exhaustive problematic tracing of roots. It's like the old aristocracy of Europe: 'Who is your father? What is your family?' or a crime family rooted in ethnicity... familia... to be accepted you need a rock-solid provenance... and a trusted crime member to vouch for you with his life."

Daisy:

"I married an athlete and wound up with a thinker. Yale men aren't supposed to be cerebral. What about that tremendous stupid energy they're famous for... the obtuse tough stamina of the Yale Bull Dog?"

Jordan, who was not hesitant about giving her own speeches:

"Have you ever noticed that even in the best American novels everyone sounds so brainless and speaks in these miniscule bites of sound while in foreign novels, especially the Russian ones, people give verbal expositions involving themselves in long protracted intellectual disputations... more accurately sequential monologues? You can't tell me those speeches are contrived or artificial. You take any stupid writing course and they tell you not to have your characters give speeches... but that's not reality. Give somebody just a little opportunity and you can't shut them up... you can't get a word in edgewise. I've heard Tom's brainier friends speak for an hour without coming up for air and what they say is sometimes actually worth listening to. Conversational speechmaking takes on the quality of an intellectual rant... trying ideas on for size. People say things they would hesitate to share with a larger audience or commit to paper. It's almost as if they're thinking to themselves out loud to hear themselves think."

Tom's mistake was attempting to undertake an intellectual colloquy, a Socratic dialectic which sadly but inevitably guttered into mudslinging matches, exchanges of juicy gossip or consumerist one-upmanship and posturing; mine is bigger than yours. The sedate social gatherings with intelligent conversation presided over by his powerful professorial grandfather had devolved with the years into wild jamborees, sexless orgies of drunkenness; leaderless, anarchic, and utterly useless.

Jordan:

> "Are American writers slaves to their editors who insist on short clipped dialogue? Or are too many American writers plain stupid, incapable of sustained reasoned philosophical discourse... or do they want their characters to appear stupid... as one of 'the people'... as if the people were stupid... which is itself a kind of intellectual arrogance... or is it that they are afraid to appear too intelligent... the bottom line... afraid that they won't sell books.

> "This Fitzgerald character calls many of his so-called heroes brilliant... He compensates for his own intellectual regrets and shortcomings by claiming for several protagonists a profundity they can't carry... he can't pull it off... His characters while supposedly highly intelligent sound like ignorant fools."

Tom, not exactly on point, which to him was entirely irrelevant:

> "There's a culture clash here...the Englishman... the Anglo-Saxon was always tight lipped... distrusting words and philosophizing... considering it a fool's-game, unbecoming...

unmanly even... shut your mouth and don't whine... as if words were inimical to action... a substitute for it and thus somehow cowardly... the American hero... like the cowboy... is a man of few words... they're brave... trustworthy not eloquent.

"Those who found fault are considered malcontents as if their psyche is fundamentally flawed... It's like accusing the doctor of spreading the disease he uncovers.

"Have you read this Irishman, this Joyce? The words practically pour out of him like whiskey out of a cracked jug. Nick... you write..."

Nick, seizing his chance to jump in and hog the whole show:

"Yes, I have. I certainly have as a matter-of-fact... and a muddy slovenly mess it is... no more than a monument of obscenity.... flashing phrase... calculating... even childish... limpid (sic) English... the pedantic scribbling of an eccentric... and this rubbish the intellectuals call literature. *Ulysses* suffers from an excess of design... he over-thinks it. Joyce has buried his story under the flair, flamboyance even, of his methodological technique. But there's a heavy suffocating weight to these sputtering pyrotechnics. He overruns the bounds of art into an arid ingenuity. He may be inimitable, but why would anyone want to imitate him in the first place. If writers try to imitate him literature as we know it will grind to a screeching halt... it will take decades to recover... He's also, possibly, quite mad".

"Personally... I didn't know enough Irish could read to sell a book like this... although it's not for sale in Ireland. How did you get a copy?"

Jordan:

"But not just the Irish are reading it. Actually, I think he's quite interesting. What about Eliot? Arthur Waugh compared Thomas Eliot to a drunken helot capable only of chastening the rising generation by his ignominious example ... or something to that effect."

Tom, ignoring the remark about Eliot:

"But the Irish I know... those that have what passes for intelligence, loath him... they see him for what he is... are overwhelmed by the pervasive body-stink the book exudes... They find the cloistered, insular atmosphere oppressive... the appallingly closed religiosity... Oh, he may claim to be irreligious but he's obsessed by it, entwined in and strangled by it... the small-mindedness... deathlike. One Irishman who writes tells me that this portrayal of middle-class Ireland depresses him, gives him a sort of hollow, cheerless pain... makes him feel appallingly naked... because his ancestors came from just such an Irish stratum. And this Joyce has not a clue as to how narrow-minded ... how claustrophobic and nauseating this prison house of the mind... this peculiar city of his is.

What did he say...? "For myself I always write about Dublin, because if I can get to the heart of Dublin, I can get to the heart of all the cities of the world. In the particular is contained the universal." But not when it comes to Dublin... no... not Dublin... definitely not Dublin, my friend. I, myself, have walked the streets of that foul grimy slum. Have you ever heard such arrogant solipsistic bullshit in your entire life? He's got his head so far up his dark ignorant ass he thinks he can pluck universal truths from a shithole."

Nick, back on his stage again:

"Yes... Yes... Joyce while claiming to reject this priest-ridden unholy Catholicism can't escape from it... he's mired in it... as much its prisoner as the most mindless true believer. I don't see why anyone else but the Irish would read this rubbish. Let us slay, as we would dragons, Wells, Joyce and Anatole France... so that the creation of literature may resume.

"And for chrissakes they're even imitating this bog Irishman. I'm in mortal fear of the latest spud in what's becoming a potato tradition."

This dropped like a lead balloon.

Trying to lighten things up Tom mentioned how much he and Daisy enjoyed Europe, that he was able to spend time in the museums, after hours. But the mere mention of Europe seemed to flick a switch in Nick's sick head, unleashing a withering, fanatical tirade... Nick, holding forth at the seized podium.

Nick:

> "God damn the continent of Europe... God damn it to hell. It is of merely antiquarian interest. Rome is only a few years behind Tyre and Babylon.
>
> "The Negroid streak creeps northward to defile the Nordic race. Already the Italians have the souls of blackamoors. Raise high the bars of immigration. Let only Scandinavians, Teutons, Anglo-Saxons and Celts enter."

It was Jordan who made the mistake of answering this hogwash.

Jordan:

> "You remind me of Negroes who hate other Negroes or Jews who hate Jews. You want to ingratiate yourself into the company of those who can't tolerate you... who despise you. There is something sick about that... full of self-loathing. You cozy up to the Anglo-Saxons without being one of them. It's self-defeating. You're paving the road to your own ruin.
>
> You're in love with the idea of your own failure. You plan for it. You wallow in it. It is grist for your mill. You will it, in-spite-of all your paeans to your dream of success. You prophesy your own doom. Yet while you have this conviction of the inevitability of your own failure you persist

in this talk... this narcissistic determination to 'succeed'".

Nick, interrupting her abruptly:

"I don't understand how any of this applies to me. What are you implying? Not one of who? What are you saying?"

Jordan, interrupting Nick, stepping on, crushing his words as if he didn't exist or shouldn't:

"German was an often heard second language in this country until the War... then they started shrouding their ethnic background en mass... changing their names... to English sounding ones. Even in the past Germans were often lumped together with other non-Anglo-Saxon people. Benjamin Franklin considered them inferior... a swarthy people who shouldn't be allowed into the country... who were too stupid to learn English. Back then they were overrunning the good 'white' English stock in Pennsylvania.

"Just this year the Reader's Digest reprinted 'America for the Americans,' condensed from The Forum. They celebrated the passage of the Johnson Act. They want to shut the doors against everyone except the so-called Nordics. The article argues not only against the admission of black or yellow peoples but against Germans who they don't consider true Nordics... What did they say: Our institutions are Anglo-Saxon and can only be maintained by Anglo-

Saxons and other Nordics... or something like that?

"During the War thousands of German-Americans were forced to buy war bonds to prove their loyalty. The Red Cross barred people with German last names from joining... they were afraid of sabotage. There was a Minnesota minister who was tarred and feathered because he was overheard praying in German with a woman... the woman was dying for the sake of God. Over 4,000 were imprisoned in 1917 through1918 for allegations of either spying or supporting the German war effort. In Iowa...the so-called 1918 Babel Proclamation... the governor prohibited all foreign languages in schools and public places. Nebraska banned instruction in any language but English... aimed specifically at the Germans. This is all a slippery slope.

"And the Germans in Germany hate other so-called Germans... this idea of a unified German Reich is a great lie... a myth incubating, impatient to be created by some dangerous crank. Arthur Moeller is in dread of the 'corrosive encrustation', as he calls it, of mixed blood... But the blood he fears is the tainted 'Latin blood' of the South Germans. Of course, he hates the Jews even more. When intellectuals conspire to undermine what they call vulgar liberal democracy in favor of some rarified dream, it is entirely reasonable to condemn them for the subsequent and inevitable horror they fail to foresee.

"The Dutch traditionally despised the Germans, regarding them as racially inferior... In the late 16th century, the Netherlands were the richest country in all Europe, and these people of what is now known as East Frisia and Emsland and also of Western Lower Saxony were extremely poor and a source for the prosperous Dutch of cheap slave-like labor. These Germans were regarded as unsophisticated, surly, stupid rubes... racially subordinate."

Ignoring this, as if in a daze, thinking back to what Nick had said previously, in a bit of a muddle, Daisy:

"I don't understand. How come all-of-a-sudden, the Scandinavians have become acceptable? Didn't you explain how you used to drool over the beautiful Swedish girls on their front porches in Saint Paul but that you couldn't even think of courting them because they were not socially acceptable? How did you put it? They weren't emerged enough economically to be part of what was then... 'society'... some society.

"Ha! Of course, maybe they wouldn't want you... would prefer big... big rugged Swedish boys who had actually graduated college... State College maybe, but college nonetheless... who would appreciate them for who they were."

They invited him to comfort him, console him and here they wound up attacking, with the fury of piranha fish.

He drew out the worst in them and made it fun... fun for them.

Nick:

"Oh no... no... no... that was because I was engaged to Ginevra."

Jordan:

"Engaged? Maybe to Ginevra Benci... in the painting... on the wall... in your head"

Nick, entirely ignoring this:

"But her parents broke it up, her father mostly... because I didn't have money."

Daisy:

"Is that so? Money, you say? Was that the issue? Really? How convenient for your elevated self-regard.

"Wasn't it because they thought you were weak... that she needed a strong, reliable husband... that you were unstable... that you hadn't graduated from college, had no career and drank too much.

"When you asked her father for her hand in marriage, he was dumbfounded more than outraged:

> 'How can you ask for my daughter's hand in the condition you're in... your drunk? You're always drunk.'

"Money had nothing to do with it. That's your excuse. You make believe you're a lady's man but you're a lady man. You affect a kind of dandyism but as you yourself admitted... after the war when dances and automobiles were prime fields of feminine conquest, you were a poor dancer and a worse driver... not to speak of your other short comings. Yet women... your inept, pathetic pursuit of them, are your obsession. You insist on playing a game with a losing hand... a game you can't possibly win."

Jordan, interrupting the interruption to Nick's relief:

"I notice you include the Celts in your superior group... those who should be allowed entry to this exclusive club of yours. If by Celts you include the Irish then you are performing intellectual acrobatics... more accurately contortions. The Irish were... are more loathed... by some... than these other groups. Some of my father's older friends wouldn't have Irish servants in the house.

"I would have thought that being Irish you would have more sympathy for these other groups instead of hating them the way you do."

Nick:

"That's a lie. That's an absolute bald-faced lie... a damnable lie. I don't have one iota, not one single, solitary drop of Irish blood in me.

"Who told you that? Where did you hear that? What have you been saying... my god...oh my

god... what have you been telling these people...
Daisy?"

Daisy:

"Only what I thought everyone knew. On your
other side, your mother's side.... didn't you
yourself describe your mother as straight 1850
potato famine Irish? I don't know if you were
drunk or not... sometimes I can't tell... but
then... you're almost always drunk. Molly, that's
what they call her, isn't it? 'Black shoe, brown
shoe Molly'... the one that says whatever comes
into her head... no interlocutor between brain
and mouth. One of our meaner relatives called
her the most awkward and the homeliest woman
she'd ever seen. That's why you're not invited to
the family functions. I always thought that was
so very stupid and bigoted. That's why I've
always made a particular point of inviting you.
You used to sob uncontrollably about how
unjust it was, that the Irish were treated like
subhumans... that the Irish were in fact 'whiter'
than anybody else. But I think you
misunderstand the criteria... colorlessness of
complexion really has nothing to do with it and
justice in this case is irrelevant. They may have
been pasty-faced, unpigmented and ashen, like
the untouchables of the hobo camp called
Walden Woods, who Thoreau reached out to; but
these fellow derlicts weren't "white" white; they
were Irish."

Nick:

"Well, you are sadly mistaken, sadly misinformed. My mother's name is Gertrude, not that ridiculous name... you said. There was some Scotch-Irish... who aren't Irish at all... pure, solid, Protestant stock. They loathe the Irish Roman Catholics more than the old American-English aristocracy does."

Jordan:

"I didn't know this country had an aristocracy, of which, you are, of course, a dues-paying member. Did they issue you an identity card, or a secret badge, maybe? Do you flash it at opportune moments? Do you have one of those silly hand-shakes?

This is a theme that's haunted American writers... how a society without an old established class structure, where the whole notion of a privileged class comes from mimicking inane British models. How does an individual compete with the descendants of so-called 'old money' which isn't old at all and might derive from nothing more than the hardware business or wholesale pork bellies... who fabricate a royalish ancestry to fit into an artificial structure that money from the nineteenth century boom created which finally devolves down to race and religion.

"But I notice that the hillbillies, southern white trash and the old ruined Southern Planter class so purposely, ruthlessly impoverished by the mercantile Puritans... who are all as Protestant and Anglo-Saxon as the best of the elite… aren't included. There is an irony in that… this… this Southern class with its traditional flamboyance and elegance reminiscent of the English Cavaliers is… or at least was far more 'aristocratic' in its trappings… its manners and mores… then their tight-assed, tight-fisted, stiff-necked Anglo-Saxon cousins from the North who would plunder and murder in the name of good, clutching a bible with blood dripping hands, spouting scripture.

"This was the true noble, imagined south of your father which remains a symbol for you even if you don't recognize it, of an idea of life, destroyed not only by industrial urban civilization but by the Anglo-Saxon Puritan who had been its initial driving force, who gleefully ground that beloved South of yours into the dirt and slavery was only the excuse… the pretext. So, what is this ineffable quality that makes them so exclusive and makes you want to become one of them? Not only are you a traitor to your race and class, you're a traitor to your father and your father's family. Your father, no matter what you say, remained an icon, a representation for you of a concept of life, a code of honor that disappeared, especially after the War, with its fast forward acceleration of industrial urbanization.

"You have this harebrained dream that the ever-eager parvenu will be allowed to join the debauched scions of this old money. You will never be allowed to join, never, no matter how useless and dissipated the moneyed Anglo-Saxons become... supplant...? Yes... replace...? maybe... conquer even... but join?... never... no... not ever. That's the tragedy of it all.

"You so often speak like a crazy man, being drunk is no excuse... as if no one is listening... and that no one will remember or care to remember what you say... that the poison you spew has no consequence... people die and will continue to die for the words you so carelessly give vent to. There is a kind of Karma... it's called memory. There are people writing down what you say and I guarantee... I guarantee... you will rue the day. These people you so despise will positively catapult into positions of power more quickly than you can conceive... positions of power in which to make or break you. While you're wasting your time ingratiating yourself to the fast-declining Anglo-Saxons, these people will make it on their own... create a universe of their own... apart from your beloved Anglo-Saxons and although they would invite you to join that world, your own words will come back armed... like an unjustly dismissed retainer... to haunt you. Your life would have been so much easier, so much better if you had made common cause against the Anglo-Saxon. You don't seem to understand that this is war. I assure you that whatever fame you reach... by some miracle... if posthumously, it would serve you right... no matter the beauty of your prose... what fame it finally attains... these words... most of all...

these indelible words of your hate will be forever engraved as your epitaph... even if living men armed with chisels have to descend upon your grave stone in the middle of the night.”

Jordan, in the heat of her peroration forgot who she was or rather who she was supposed to be; she was speaking words that might have lodged in her beloved father’s rended heart, that he never would have dared to let out.

Nick, oblivious:

“You don’t know anything about my father.

“Who are you calling a parvenu?”

Jordan:

“I’m not calling anyone anything. I’m simply making an observation.”

Daisy, finally getting to the subject in the back of everyone’s mind:

“Let’s change the subject. This is all getting very confusing.

“I understand you live right next to that absolutely gorgeous extravaganza of a house out on Great Neck, the one built by the mysterious and illustrious Mr. Gatsby... the one who heads up the American Legion.”

Nick, after a long pause, trying to collect his wits:

“Yes... I live in his shadow... so to speak, almost... a cottage. He tried to buy it but they won't sell. They rent it to undesirables... to spite him... I was told... I don't mean me... not me. I didn't rent it... not personally... this fellow from the office... but that's another... I guess they couldn't find an undesirable to rent it to."

Jordan:

"What about Gatsby?"

She was teasing now.

Nick:

"I've only seen him from far away. He's waved to me, almost like a formal salute... even from the distance I could catch his smile... like he knew me, like he had met me before... like he knew who I was.

"I have to be careful, though.

"He has fierce looking men with ferocious dogs straining at the leash patrolling the perimeter of his estate.

"He's remarkably Nordic... in appearance... but I was told by my housekeeper whose friend says that he might be a secret Jew. That would explain a lot.

"Your Jew is a ferocious competitor. When a Jew is interested, he has the strong sense of the track that we other races don't even know the sprinting time of.

"Your Jew is the vanguard, the stalking horse... he'll open the gates... in the night... while we sleep... let the other strangers in."

"But he's not like the others... Gatsby... the other Jews I mean. With the Jew, money and power are falling into the hands of certain of these people, who compared to the leader of a village Soviet would be a goldmine of judgment and culture."

Jordan:

"Gatsby's not a Jew. He's the Great Silkie of Sule Skerry ... who's seized command of the ship... while we were otherwise engaged below deck playing roulette."

Jordan, talk-singing very softly:

"'And thou shalt marry a proud gunner, And a very proud gunner I'm sure he'll be, And the very first shot that e're he shoots, he'll kill both my young son and me'."

which everyone, puzzled, ignored.

Nick:

"Did you notice how old Jews look like melted candles, like they're getting ready to waddle?"

Apropos of nothing.

Jordan to Nick:

"You've been to the Soviet Union?"

A question which was again ignored.

Jordan, again:

> "Didn't Gatsby's friend Belasco disguise his Jewish roots with the costume of a Catholic priest?"

Daisy:

> "I thought Belasco was dead."

Tom:

> "He didn't quite pretend to be a priest though... he just dressed up like one... a black suit with a stiff white Roman collar... the getup gave him the look of a Roman Catholic priest."

Daisy:

> "Yeh... I remember, now... They nicknamed him: 'The Bishop of Broadway.'"

Tom:

> "He's the fool who produced hokey melodrama and insisted it was a mirror of real life. He swore his preposterous stories were based on hard fact... that he himself knew they were true."

Jordan:

> "But isn't it the truest stories that make bad fiction because they are so bizarre, so unbelievable. Though a good deal is too strange to be believed, nothing is too strange to have happened. Who said that?

"No, no, now that I remember, I think he purposely took on the affectations of a priest. He concocted some preposterous cover story about being whisked off to a monastery for five years by a Father McGuire... who took him under his wing... his mentor... they became 'best friends'... but I'm not sure the benevolent priest McGuire existed except in his own head. His whole personality was his own invention like one of his overwrought scripts."

Daisy:

"His studio in the theater took on all the trappings of an old cathedral crypt. I think he was trying to relive old memories or trying to expunge them. I was in it... it was spooky... No, he's still living... I think. But I don't think they're friends."

Jordan, caught up in the enthusiasm of the subject, breathless:

"Yes, yes, they are... or were, at least. Belasco helped with his magic tricks... before the war... in the circus.

He helped with the floating houses, too... Him and the aviator... the one who broke the records. They met in the theater where Gatsby directed and acted."

Daisy:

"Whose magic tricks?"

Tom:

> "What circus?"

Jordan, composing herself:

> "Don't pay any attention to me. I just prattle
> on... and on. I have no idea what I'm talking
> about."

Tom, too full of himself, unable to shut up; letting slip
a potential goldmine of information:

> "In Elizabethan England actors were forbidden
> to wear their aristocratic costumes anywhere
> but, on the stage, ... and if they did, they were
> subject to flogging. I guess the fear was that they
> would pass themselves off as those they
> pretended to be, move into their great houses
> and take over, and the whole structure of society
> would come crashing down around their ears. In
> many old societies, classes distinguished
> themselves by the dress they wore... which they
> were required to wear... they couldn't violate the
> prescribed dress of their own class."

Daisy:

> "Did you make that up?"

Tom:

> "Would I do that?"

Jordan and Daisy together:

> "Yes."

Tom:

"And the King of England, James the First, used actors, his own King's Men to pretend to be aristocratic courtiers to wait upon a visiting foreign dignitary... I think it was a king. They managed to pull it off..."

Daisy, interrupting Tom:

"Where do you get all this stuff from?"

Tom:

"Books. Books. They call them books."

But Jordan wasn't through with Nick:

"You are obsessed. You're afraid of him. It's mixed up with your fear... your race anxiety, if I can call it that... that identity itself might be a performance... an act... a magic trick loosely linked to some imitational reality and not to a rock-hard definable reality based on something like family, blood... race. If Gatsby can create an identity out of his own imagination, his own accomplishments, possibly a bag of tricks, then it makes the whole concept of identity as physically based unstable. If he is the perfect simulacrum of the American Patrician ... what is the basis for his exclusion? Are not the manners and effects of that group... after all... no more than a well-rehearsed, well-schooled show... isn't all such schooling just a matter of being taught how to act? And if they won't let him... invite him in... isn't he even more of a threat?

"Gatsby... the unassimilable alien...? one of the foreign hordes who will overwhelm your closed tight privileged few... who closed you out... make it disappear before you have a chance to become one of them.

"You are aspiring for right of admission into a self-extinguishing clan... banging on the doors... trying to break into a quarantine hospital.

"You're being distracted and insulted by an uppity ticket clerk who won't let you book passage on the Titanic and puts you on a waiting list that waits forever.

"Are you really so incredibly dense or do you see it and are rendered impotent by your knowledge, like that man on the Titanic with haunting premonitions and icebergs in his head."

"Your dream transmogrifies into a lewd caricature of itself, struggling to hurdle into a decaying caste which is not only destroying itself but destroys all those who come into contact with it or seek to become a part of it."

Daisy:

"Enough... my head hurts."

Nick:

"What the hell are you talking about? They never closed me out. You are very confused... very confused.

Jordan:

"Doesn't your father run a hardware store?"

Nick:

"I beg your pardon. My father is in the wholesale hardware business as was my uncle before him."

Jordan:

"Oh, now I get it: retail hardware is déclassé... wholesale is crème de la crème."

Nick, shoots in:

"Do you personally know Gatsby or are you like everyone else just shuffling hearsay around, making things up as you go along?"

He thought this would fix her, finally shoot her down, shut her up good.

Jordan:

"Do I know him? Why... I'm his... I... I work for him. We're as thick as thieves"

Jordan regretted this outburst almost immediately. The carefully kept secret was out.

Flabbergasted, Daisy interrupted, violently, jealously, never suspecting that Jordan worked at any thing:

"You work for Gatsby? My god.... in what capacity... would you please tell me that... please?"

Jordan:

"Social secretary… mistress of etiquette… doyenne of doilies. I make sure the rules of social intercourse are minutely and scrupulously observed. We don't want any unrefined deadbeats, no riffraff sullying our hallowed halls.

"He's had you investigated if you live so close. I could guarantee it.

"It seems everybody is having everybody else investigated… they won't accept anything at face value… but who's investigating the investigators… that's what I'd like to know… maybe they exchange notes or make it all up…at the kitchen table at night… like some scribbler gone bonkers… formulating dossiers… they create our phony lives for us over ale and cold chicken… saves a lot of leg work.

"One art critic said that the biggest fraud of all is provenance… it's all nonsense… If the work is great and original it will reveal itself… it must stand on its own. Its history… its background… genealogy, if you will… by itself is meaningless… a diversion… the easiest thing in the world to fake.

"If a lost work of Shakespeare shows-up we will know instantly that it is genuine simply by reading it… it will be its own proof. No one, but no one could have written Shakespeare except Shakespeare… no one who left a written record came close… they were all illiterate dunces in comparison. What galls all those that hoist up a pathetic pretender is that they cannot accept the miracle that is Shakespeare... who rose-up out of nothing... thereby accusing them of their own inferiority... what excuse have they got... he was neither a Lord of the Realm nor University educated... the quintessential self-made man... and no one... no one has even come close in four hundred years. Why even bother?

"Probably only one in a thousand knows good writing from bad. The critics prove it, heaping exorbitant, orgasmic praise on unadulterated bunkum."

Jordan delivering the coup de grace:

"Gatsby knows more about you than you do about yourself."

She had read the file. She had read all their files. She was enjoying herself now. She couldn't help herself. A stunned silence all around.

Jordan:

"Gatsby... he's incredible... absolutely unbelievable."

Daisy:

"What... what on earth does that mean?"

Jordan with perfect aplomb, to Nick in particular:

"You must watch me play."

Nick:

"Uh...golf, right?"

Jordan:

"No, tennis, actually.

"Have you been to France, lately? We just got back."

The mere mention of France seemed to crack open the floodgates.

Nick:

"France? ... France? ... France makes me so sick. Its' silly pose as the thing the world has-to save. I think it's one goddamned shame that England and America didn't let Germany conquer Europe. It's the only thing that would have saved the fleet of tottering old wrecks."

Jordan:

"But you fought in the war, didn't you?"

Nick:

"Yes, I did. I most certainly did. Yes... I was.... I was... wounded... sent home before I got a chance to really mix it up."

Jordan:

"Didn't you say something about having a sporting...? I did hear you correctly... a 'sporting interest' in the German dash for Paris but that it didn't thrill you... that you had hoped the whole thing would be bloody and long?

"But why would you want to 'mix it up', as you say, against your favorite heroes, the Germans? Couldn't you send a substitute, I mean to the war, or don't they do that anymore? You could have paid someone to impersonate you, which is the same thing. There's a lot of that going around... impersonation... I mean. Then you could impersonate your own wife and collect your own widow's pension. Give you a chance to dress-up, like at Yale.

"But you stayed in France... after the War I mean?"

Nick:

"No... I came home then went back... I lived in France for a year. I know the country intimately... I know its people as only a writer can."

Jordan:

"But that's just the point... you don't know the country at all... not at all.

"From listening to you, you resided in France without ever living there... without having any real connection with the country. The only French you came in contact with were servants... who hated you and grew rich cheating you. You met few French writers and had no interest in the intellectual avant-garde. Even your friend Dos Passos made the point that you never saw any of the architectural landmarks... never went to the museums or the great churches... cared nothing for art or music or great food or great wine even and never bothered to learn the language. You inhabited a Europe of displaced Americans with money... ugly ignorant Americans... the habitués of hotels, nightclubs, bars and beaches. You remind me of why the English are so despised by their neighbors for their tourism... What a decadent concept... tourism... which looks down upon the natives as if they were an alien inferior species. These 'tourists' have all the manners of gawkers at a zoo.

"Your beloved Murphys, who you wasted so much time with, wallowed in hedonistic extravagance and squandered whatever money they inherited on the trivial perfection of frivolities."

Before he had a chance to counter this frontal attack Daisy chimed in:

"This is all getting much too complicated. Besides, Nick missed my wedding because of that silly war. Isn't that the reason? Isn't that why? Didn't you Nick?"

Daisy, revealing the ultimate solipsism of her ignorant, ridiculous self-absorption.

But Nick wouldn't give it up:

"I believe in the white man's burden. We are as far above the modern Frenchman as he is above the Negro. Even in art!

"We have to assert ascendancy being of the superior Nordic race. It is our duty, our destiny.

"Civilization is going to pieces."

But by some subtle intimation he didn't fully incorporate the women under the protection of his racialist umbrella.

Jordan was about to burst, when Daisy gently touched her shoulder as if to say: be still, child, this too will pass.

Jordan:

"When you say civilization is going to pieces what you really mean is white civilization... meaning that only white people are truly civilized. More particularly you mean the Anglo-Saxon or Nordic power structure... as if only the Nordics were the true keepers of the flame... that civilization's continued survival is dependent on the maintenance of that Nordic superiority. The very term 'civilization' is a politically and racially charged term used as a cudgel... much as the term 'culture' is used."

Before Jordan finished her last word Nick had passed out, almost as if the air had been let out of him; he buckled at the knees and collapsed at Tom's feet, a soused supplicant.

But this didn't slow them down; they continued to drink far into the night. The more Tom Buchanan drank the more sober he appeared, at least to those who didn't know him. He grew more grave and more correct, and knowing he was drunk, stingier with his words, which he knew would make little sense; assuming a demeanor emulating his dead grandfather whom he had worshipped as a child. If he could, when half in the bag, he would resurrect that life style, the generous frugality, the friendly sobriety, discretion, and restraint; strict adherence to a moral code that raised a glass only on occasions of great moment; a vanishing world, in which the defining characteristics of good taste were, balance, proportion, appropriateness and understatement, a lack of ostentation. Nothing should be noticed. Intoxicated on illegal hard liquor furnished by bootleggers, he became burdened by obsolete obligations, a reticent reserved style that used to be called 'breeding' but was reduced like so much else to a poor old shattered word by the nouveau riche. For Thomas Buchanan's father's father it was considered "vulgar", his grandfather's word, to give anything expensive in the way of "eatable or drinkable" at the evening or afternoons entertainment. He would have been appalled equally by Gatsby and what his little grandson had swollen into.

It is a blessing in some ways that this grand paterfamilias did not live to see the day that his beloved privileged class, his particular tribe, dripping its invisible war paint, would be disparaged by their déclassé successors, the "ethnics", the despised interlopers, the loathed bounders, heady in their exultantancy, triumphant over the remnants of his Anglo-Saxons, particularized and marginalized as: a Whartonian social ilk, the hereditarily rich American, as if they were some over-the-hill decayed untouchable, retreated to their fetid mountain lair, retrogressed to donning animal skins and telling stories, lies around the fire about the imagined days of empire; Solomon and his 700 wives, princesses of royal birth and 300 concubines.

The Buchanans had hired a car for Carraway just for the occasion; Tom being stingy in the use of his own car and driver for such circumstances, feeling that it was an imposition on his own man and not included in the unspoken terms of the man's employment:

> "I don't run a taxi service for every Tom, Dick and Harry who visits."

The hired driver waited patiently in the area designated for such help, it being considered inappropriate to allow him to mingle freely with Buchanan's own personal servants who were more privileged in Tom's eyes. But by 3:30 AM the driver, groggy and exhausted had the temerity to enquire gently at the servant's door whether Mr. Carraway would be leaving any time soon or staying the night, in which case he could return in the morning. Nick, informed of the driver's query, lashed out with a withering drunken barrage of billingsgate and had to be physically restrained by Tom from attacking the man with a large wooden object which came to hand nearby, an irreplaceable museum piece, which looked like an antique ornamental truncheon but would better be described as a fasces. Nick often acted under the misperception that his professed superiority in social status would protect him from any backlash from what he looked upon as the cheeky lower orders crying out for the discipline of a stern hand. The driver, composing his wits was not falling for it, ran around his car twice, like in some children's game or cheap movie comedy, something with Chaplin or *The Keystone Cops*, chased by a tripping Nick getting tangled up in his own feet and when he had the chance the driver jumped into his own seat and simply drove off with Nick clinging to the running board precariously, screaming obscenities and stumbling after him half way down the drive. Nick was not so lucky in other similar instances, and was beaten bloody and insensate by a taxicab driver over a fare dispute in Italy and dragged in by the police and beaten further and more methodically at the station house.

Buchanan, not wanting a loose cannon rolling around his house, guest wing or not, in the middle of the night, refused to invite Nick to spend the night; to hell with his condition. At 4:00 AM, a taxicab for some reason being unavailable, he finally had his own driver rousted, assuring the driver personally that it was exigent circumstances. With the typical faux egalitarianism of an asinine classist Nick insisted on sitting in the front seat although the car was obviously not designed for such an accommodation.

> "Sir, I believe we both would be more comfortable if you sat in the proper seat."

Nick:

> "Wouldn't dream of it. What da ya think I am?"

They all knew what he was. The driver knew enough to hold his tongue.

Nick, however, had forgotten his own street and number, while at the same time swearing, he knew exactly where he lived. The one driver who knew the address for sure was long gone. Tom's driver knew Great Neck and yet could make no sense of Nick's directions, and so they drove around in circles for two hours with Nick shouting out incomprehensible commands and non-existent landmarks. It is only with the sun risen and Nick approaching closer to what passed for sobriety that he regained the presence of mind to shout out in a moment of epiphany, an act of self-discovery:

> "Gatsby... right next to the great Gatsby...

> "The little house next to the big one."

Thomas Buchanan, unable to go to sleep, stumbling up his own steps, leaning on Daisy, who almost tripped him up, remarked mockingly, as if the gathering had been an imperfect success:

> "At least he didn't expose himself... But then again, the night was young and spring was in the air."

Daisy:

> "But it's summer"

Tom:

> "Exactly my point"

Daisy:

> "I guess I missed it, the point that is."

Tom:

> "Don't you always?"

Daisy:

> "Nice, very nice."

I Loved My Grandfather

I loved my grandfather. My grandfather was a great man. Some said he was a gangster, a bootlegger, a gambler, a "womanizer": that's a quaint, old fashioned piece of cant, but then, he was an old-school kind of fellow. If he was something of a conman, he was one short of pretentions; none-the-less always in the process of relentless, ruthless self-invention. But there are those who say that my grandfather didn't exist at all, at least not as I portray him. Of course, how can you prove someone's existence? Could I prove my own? Would you like me to take the testimony of proven liars? What footprints in the sand are ever recast in concrete?

They said he'd killed a man, maybe a great many men. But then they had it coming. He was in the war you know; still called the Great War when he came marching home, in one hard piece; a war hero they said, with medals to prove it, which he carried with him (around his neck) to his death. The rest of his life was an extension of hostilities, only, with less apparent blood. It was a war in which he exhibited such a superfluity of bravery, and for which he was exulted with such intemperate praise, that the remainder of his life appeared a postscript in soft lead pencil, the muted colors of pastel chalk, an indistinct afterthought.

Courage, he objected is overrated as virtue, if virtue at all:

> "Our highest crimes are begotten by our audacity; courage: the mother's milk of notorious corruption. Hell is bursting with heroes, prison slopping over with monsters devoid of fear."

The war may have been his; notwithstanding, he did not relish the excursion. If he had blood on his hands, he gave as good as he got and more and nursed no regrets.

I loved my grandfather. A day does not go by that I do not miss the dominion of his smile. I will never lay eyes upon his like again. I would hang on to his every word for hours on end and time stood still while I listened transfixed as he weaved his story. I write, long after it can make any difference, because of my father.

Not being, a bookish-man, he did not want his own father identified with a man in a book, no matter the fame of the book; neither anecdotal nor Dostoevsky; however, he found it not a trivial book, but thought it trivialized the man, his father; put down in words by Nick "Castaway," which is what he called him, a fool not equipped to try to depict the very different man, that was my father's father.

My grandfather was more generous in his judgment... he watched over Nick to the bitter end; sent out agents to the drunk tank to bail him out, to run him home in the middle of the night; counted him his friend and never called him Castaway, because he never was, not while James Gatsby lived.

Carraway titled one of Gatsby's hired toughs, his angel, guardian perhaps, his oblivious acolyte... for simply being there... always, showing up... whisking maggots off his still sentient flesh with a footman's brush... posting vigil at the lockup door as John Law bundled him in, beaten, humiliated, bloodied and bruised; tanked-up, stumbling in, in tight bloody cuffs digging into wounded flesh.

If it strikes you as childlike that I refer to this man repeatedly as grandfather, it is from a wealth of affection. From now on like everybody else, I'll call him Gatsby, J. Gatsby, that's who he was; the initial not the name and not ever, no never, Jay. He signed himself that way, with a grand magisterial flourish. Only Carraway called him Jay... never to his face... dense to the arrogance of calling anyone by other than the name they gave themselves; the supreme usurpation, the arrogated intimacy, the rechristening granted without a blessing, of best friends and even then. Nick was Gatsby's best friend though Gatsby hardly knew it at the time.

I always found it odd that Nick projected his own weaknesses on to my grandfather, imperfect as he was.

We want our heroes vulnerable, even those, especially those, we worship. We want them to be godlike but damaged, injured, unfinished, incomplete, alienated; plagued and crippled by kryptonite hidden in strange, undiscoverable places; lesser gods trapped on an even lesser planet; they deserve better; they're in a purgatory which they haven't earned; a superior entity serving hard time for a crime they've not been charged with and are ignorant of.

Carraway Mostly Loved Himself

Carraway mostly loved himself or his ideal or not so ideal self that he thought he saw in Gatsby or injected into him. He was an unembarrassed and embarrassing hero worshipper:

> "When I like men, I want to be just like them. I want to lose the external traits that give me my individuality and be like them. I don't want the man. I want to absorb into myself all the qualities that make him attractive and leave him out. I hang on to my own guts."

This is the kind of statement no heterosexual male makes today for fear of being accused of homoerotic inclinations. It got worse; at a basketball game he said of himself, how:

> "...he fell madly into admiration for a dark-haired boy who played with melancholy defiance."

We can't understand Gatsby or rather Nick's Gatsby without understanding Nick's purposeful and not so purposeful misrepresentation of him, and why he should bring forth such an erroneous story. These characters are all tied together. Thomas Buchanan analyzed Carraway's work, extensively and voluminously years later for reasons unknown; well, they're not entirely unknown.

Thomas Buchanan, uncatalogued archives, undated, untitled, unnumbered:

> "The writer can do nothing that the hero does; he can only admire, love, and take pleasure in him.... He is memory's genius. He can do nothing but recollect what has been done, can do nothing but venerate what has been done ... so that all may admire the hero as he does.... This is his calling, his self-effacing task; this is his faithful service in the abode of the hero...
>
> "Therefore, no one who was great will be forgotten, and even though it takes time, even though a cloud of misunderstanding takes away the hero, his lover, the writer, will nevertheless come, the more time passes, the more devotedly he clings to him.
>
> "A young lad falls in love with a princess, and this love is the total essence of his life, and yet the relation is such that it cannot possibly be realized, cannot possibly be translated from the ideal to the real. Of course, the slaves of the finite, the frogs in the swamps of life, scream: That kind of love is foolishness... Let them go on

croaking in the swamp. The knight of infinite resignation does not do any such thing; he does not give up the love, not for all the glories of the world. He is no fool."

This sounds like a bad translation of Kierkegaard.

For Carraway the history of the universe no less was the history of god creating himself. The ultimate self-made man is a god-man, spilling genuine blood; the American dream made flesh in Gatsby, finally shattering himself like blown glass against the hard malice of a ruthless world oblivious to his glorious incarnation.

This is the profound drivel that gives poignancy to Carraway and prevails upon us to take notice of this particular-man. The fact is that Gatsby never cracked while Carraway withered and crumbled.

Gatsby was astounded by the book:

"I never said ten words to the man and this. Maybe if I spoke more to him, acknowledged him, thought whether he existed or not, he would never have written it."

Ten words is not true; this was Broadway sounding off, holding forth in a mock unassuming manner, shifting speech patterns that belied his meaning, utilizing words like unobtrusive time bombs that self-detonate, mines consigned to a dying sea from a long-forgotten war.

A self-serving plagiarist once insisted: good writers borrow furtively from other writers while great writers steal outright, which is total bullshit as most quotable quotes are. Whoever said this was an inveterate, unembarrassed word thief.

However, I do believe in 'omage, that ridiculous word with the dropped H, of the soi-disant cognoscenti: to echo back previous authors or auteurs, to praise or mock them; or have a little fun with them, or just to signify that you too know the terrain, have lost and wasted scouts in the badlands, exhausted your horses to early, unnecessary deaths and dismemberments, leaving only your sturdy pack mules standing but half dead; have trekked the barren ground until your poor feet bleed, leaving footprints from the rain dance in inhospitable towns.

Carraway lifted some of his best lines from Gatsby, laid claim to them as his own, a mortal larceny in the minds of both men who knew the magic dwelt in the word itself; the spirit was not called forth by the word but existed in the word, reincarnated with the invocation.

We have in the book the borrowed splendor, the precision of a great lyric poem; the ritual incantation creating the godhead. It is no fluke that Nick never touched these heights either before or after. The fundamental proof is the man's body of work. There is only one piece. He rose once and only once, as if by enchanted proximity, to the wellspring.

Fitzgerald left more trash in his wake than a garbage scow on its watery way to the Staten Island dump, more than any other author of equal gifts. He was lethally smitten with the inauthentic cello throb of

Colliers and *The Saturday Evening Post,* purveying
with slick effrontery the fancies Horatio Alger never
woke up from, in his wet homoerotic reveries; poor
boys latching on to older men. He crooned pedestrian
music to the hoi polloi with pretentions; pandering to
a tin ear; a muzzled, beaten, blood and feces caked
circus bear droning agonizingly, painfully to a plastic
ukulele, strummed by a stumbling clown crying make-
up tears.

Gatsby loved neglected clichés, which by anachronistic
use he infused with immaculate significance. One
oblivious wag supposed that Shakespeare just
exploited the platitudes, the worn old saws of his own
day, which achieve a sharp awakening only by the very
fact of having their soiled context overlooked.

Gatsby never met an old cliché he didn't make love to;
he danced with all the old dowagers in the ancient
ballroom and they adored him for it, and they crooned
neglected ditties from another world in his good ear,
which he committed to a perfect memory.

Carraway Takes the House

It is by an inexplicable confluence of calamities that
Carraway laid hands on Gatsby's papers, an imperfect
storm of missteps, of stepping away when they should
have stepped in or up. On the day of the killings, the
police (there was no one left with a wallet thick enough)
emptied the house of witnesses, protective custody for
the butler, the footman, and the cooks. The chief of
police was there with his hand out, left waving in the

wind, which incensed him. The chauffeur left with the silver and the upstairs maid (surprised weeks later in his girlfriend's lair by Wolf's men who took back the silver and exacted interest); the phalanx of hired dicks hopped the first train in a limp panic.

But Gatsby had been in no position to stake his claim; boxed into a corner, a tight coffin. His proud castle was, for a transitory moment, an abandoned ship, adrift, ripe for salvage, land pirates crawling all over it.

Even Wolf kept his distance; the great fixer couldn't fix this. The place was crawling with newspapermen, like roaches scurrying wildly in the light, when he showed up, forcing his driver to back-up down the endless drive of Gatsby's citadel at a reckless speed, losing a back wheel.

And it was a citadel, a castle, an exact replica of a late medieval fortress perfected in the concrete dreams of a master architect. Just like Mad King Ludwig, who was not so mad that he couldn't fabricate his wildest imaginings in the forests of Bavaria. To this day it is Ludwig's masterpieces that grace the tourist posters beckoning foreigners into the visions of a dead daft king with perfect pitch.

But it was Wolf who finally did step in, storming the battlements, with the slick connivance of an actor acquaintance, a degenerate gambler deep into debt, who couldn't stomach the vig; with forged credentials, a denizen, habitué, he liked to say, of Broadway, a cornpone genuine character, who could slip into Shakespeare like a well-worn kid glove. He adlibbed Gatsby's concocted father to riotous effect, reduced the audience in-on-it to rolling in stitches on the floor. He assumed the permanent persona of the "shiftless and unsuccessful farm person;" part of his repertoire, the myth, the back-story; the back-story is just that and seldom true.

Protean Man

This Wolf-procured "vaudevillian" assumed the mantle, possessed the house.

The son was not amused by the pulp factory that was Wolf's mind. Gatsby bristled at Wolf's self-serving wisecracks:

> … an exotic man directing a protean man.

Was Gatsby the protean man? Did Wolf think of himself as exotic or did he read this shit somewhere? Wolf was always quoting someone, pretending he had forgotten who, assuming a mock ignorance but really quoting ironically, attempting to blow up both the quote and quoted with it.

Modern psychiatry thinks it has discovered something new, proclaiming:

> The protean style is distinguished by continuous shifts in identification and belief which results from such dynamics as the accelerating rapidity of historical transformation (fancy talk for things are changing more quickly than ever) and the revolution in mass media.

In this cocoon of self-serving involuted bullshit the "self" is no longer regarded as fixed and the jargon "self-process" is substituted. The emphasis is now upon change and flux usurping the old nomenclature "character" and "personality." This is intellectual gobbledygook. These terms never suggested fixity or stagnation.

The personality of any intelligent aggressive human has always been a process, a composition in development, an act of creation. Ever since the rise of the cities has facilitated a man's opportunity to liberate himself from the strict psychic confines of the village or small town, the self has been a work in progress; no longer cast by entrenched opinions, bad and good, by people who have always 'known' us and our family, from the time we crawled in the dirt and soiled our diapers. Every time we encounter a new person or group, we can debut a new play; we are given the opportunity to recreate ourselves, to grow and evolve. In stories old and new the characters that grab us are multifaceted, complex, tortuous, evolving and often contradictory and confused. Who was it that said?

> There never was a good biography of a good novelist. There couldn't be. He is too many people if he's any good.

There are good writers who make convolution and disorder the core, a molten, magnetic hot swirling core, of their best characters?

I will make my hero laugh when sensible people think he ought to cry.

Gentleman from another World

Gatsby:

> "Wolf's an older gentleman from another world... strangely naïve in some respects."

But Gatsby often found it difficult to overlook Wolf's condescending utterances.

It was Gatsby that said of Wolf:

> "I made him...I raised him up out of nothing."

Out of the grave is harder. Did the son create the father or the father the son? Are they coequal or were each the others doppelganger? Are they the arrivistes commanding entrance like the barbarian at the gate who hollers up undisguised in the stolen uniform of Rome? Is it capital they have sliced out of their confined peripheral worlds by the bluff, bravado and sheer swagger of their self-transformation, fashioned into the compelling devices that will thrust them into the upper crust which they pierce like a dagger, ousting the old moneyed Anglo-Saxons?

But was it Wolf who crowed of Gatsby:

> "I could use him good.

> "So thick like that in everything... thick as thieves... all the time allied together."

Was this a false rumor spread to sow discord? It was always a subtle question of exactly who was using who.

Gatsby loathed Carraway's bit where he was forever turning him into a girly bootlicker. Wolf was decidedly Gatsby's man. As for Dan Kodi, Gatsby reserved a particular distaste from the old dead debauchee.

Kodiac

Young Gatsby was minding his own business trekking the white, fine sand beaches of the Long Island Sound, his family had a beach house there, when Kodi, that's what he called himself, Kodiac to be exact, half sloshed, enquired whether he knew the hour of the receding tide; Gatsby did. Kodi whined that he was in a "terrible bind"; that "one of my crew jumped ship"; that he needed a replacement "pronto". Gatsby was only surprised that he wasn't looking for his little lost dog. The old fart offered him "triple the usual rate"… "would train him on the job as First Mate"… "was desperate to weigh anchor without delay." Kodi called the spot "Little Girl Bay" which was no doubt his own private sick joke; little girls, little boys, it didn't seem to matter much which to Don Kodi on the prowl.

Gatsby would soon enough find out. A few days later Kodi, docked at a Hudson River pier, took him to New York City and bought him two navy blue blazers, six pairs of white duck trousers, unplaited, and a yachting cap with an inappropriate scrambled egg brim; looking like he stepped off the pages of some imaginary

"Yachting Life". In his own mind he looked like a ding-dong, a fancy-pants dipshit on a fashion runway traipsing through Kodi's warped mind. He didn't like the way Kodi looked at him, didn't like the way he asked him to turn around so he could admire the fit; didn't like the way the other crew members, mostly good-looking young men, eyed him like fresh meat or competition. After only two weeks he confided in one of the boys, a handsome boy about his own age that he intended to jump ship the first chance he got.

> "But you can't quit. Don't you understand? If you ask to leave, he'll throw you overboard in the open sea with buckets of chum for the trailing sharks; if you jump ship, he'll report you as a thief.

> "In one-half hour we'll be rounding Sandy Hook. It's a short swim but the currents are vicious. This may be the last chance you'll get. It's worth a shot. Kodi's got his eye on you. If you jump now just before the open sea, he'll think you fell over-board and drowned. He'll never report it. He'd be scared to."

This sounded wild, like he was being suckered by a tall tale; but for some reason he believed him, just a little. Maybe he was just trying to get rid of the competition. This boy seemed quite content, in his own way, in his privileged position; he showed great personal deference toward Kodi in his presence. Gatsby swore that Kodi never made a pass at him. But then he would never admit something like that, not in those days; it would be a blot on his personal honor; somehow, he would be responsible. That's how boy-rapists stayed in business. Even those victims who manage to fend off their advances are often afflicted with disgust, guilt and self-loathing, an unholy transference, of which feelings the guilty perpetrator is immaculately free. So, there is a double crime; not only the crime itself but the guilt that should accrue to the offender which is thrust instead upon the victim.

He cut the picture of Kodi out of a photogravure years later and kept it on his dresser as a warning or was it a sign, a talisman of his enduring luck. Kodi had given him one hundred dollars as a signing bonus, although they didn't call it that in those days: "walking around money", a very pretty penny in 1906. He jumped ship with the money carefully wrapped in oil cloth but would definitely have drowned if not for an old tug pulling an over-laden barge seeming to sink from its load, that just happened to be passing by.

Kodi named his big yacht the Tuolomne, which he pronounced "To All o' Me", with a silent N and which he translated Straight Up Steep or as he would sing to himself when narcissistically drunk: to all of me straight up steep. The yacht was lost crossing the Atlantic with all hands; no trace ever found. Gatsby would sometimes mention the possibility of a mutiny but then the crew seemed so inexpert, so jarringly handsome, decked out in their fine pretty clothes. Advertisements can be treacherous in their propaganda, in their self-defeating lies. There were not enough experienced old weathered tars below deck. The Atlantic was wracked by ferocious storms that year. An extra hand that actually knew the ropes might have made all the difference.

But being a drunk Kodi did leave at least one enduring, positive legacy by way of example; for himself Gatsby formed the habit of letting liquor alone. As for the millions, as far as Gatsby knew they might as well have gone down with the ship.

Gatsby Was Not Dead

Most believed that Gatsby was not dead, that he could not die. The others were more afraid he was still alive.

He was waked in a closed mahogany casket in the early Fall of '22.

A second player intoned the 23rd psalm with a deep vibrato baritone as he slipped into the warm, sandy Long Island earth. Carraway couldn't stand to see the dead man's face or his hands for that matter, overcome as he was, which spared his life; the monkey wrench in the works.

Gatsby became a story, a myth, the legend before the book. But it was a very different story. Like any good story, in it, Gatsby lives:

> "He couldn't be killed so easy by a crazy man… he was always rung round by body guards… troopers … three… at least, who never left his side."

These loyal Tontos, all a crack shot:

"...would'a took a bullet for the Colonel."

"They would'a shot that bum down like the dog that he was, in the street, before he got to fifty feet of the boss."

They were his soldiers, men who had trudged behind him, in the mud and blood, of war, into the proverbial canon's mouth and lived to tell the tale; the tale was horror and death; the imperceptible salute, the stand-to of staunch ex-troops overstepping the threshold, invariably addressed him as Colonel, always Colonel.

And Gatsby himself was no paper pusher, no mere map gazer, no General on the hill:

"...a gunman, a pistollero, armed to the teeth with three hidden revolvers and a knife in each boot."

However, for the life of me, I don't remember the boots. They ached to have him live, like Kennedy or Elvis.

The Sightings

Then there were the sightings, the avowals and denials: Palm Beach, Switzerland and always Paris.

Some claimed that he secretly owned the casinos in Monte Carlo with ancient, old Grimaldi as his front man:

"They couldn't tie their shoe laces without Gatsby".

that he was:

> "...three times the king that Grimaldi ever was".

> "Grimaldi... that plump little frog... was just window dressing, an empty suit with a rotten ancient name".

Some claimed that Gatsby lived openly as himself in Geneva, that he travelled freely through the Soviet Union, procuring the late lamented Tsar's secreted treasures; that he carried letters of transit signed by Lenin, irrevocable; a ridiculous fiction; that he spoke Russian and German like a native and could pass; that he assumed preposterous poses like an actor playing parts:

> "...Fooled all the rich swells."

No, that was neither Gatsby's voice nor his style.

Gatsby had no prejudices against the old-moneyed rich; in fact, he liked their air, their style, the way the old ones carried themselves; the younger ones he pitied. In small irrelevant things he imitated the old ones. He, also, found something woeful about what they had become; even then they showed signs of passing like a sad old inbred race refusing to transfuse new blood. (The Romans confronted with the Ostrogoths.) They had what so many wasted their lives trying to get; those that were self-deceived, distracted, sidetracked; chasing a prize that inevitably proved empty to them.

Gatsby knew money as freedom, power, the power to create. He grasped that one could not be even a lesser god without money, a boat-load of money. The luxuries were beside the point, a distraction, irrelevant tchotchkes, toys for the brainless. He kept an original painting of Benjamin Franklin prominently on his wall and a bust on his desk. For Franklin money was not an end-in-itself, but a means to independence, liberation, time for the pursuit of creative knowledge and good works. For Gatsby it was the toys that helped devour the Anglo-Saxon rich like some Darwinian imperative making way, felling a wide, clear swath for the bold New Man.

The Irish Bootlegger

I know that Gatsby was comrade-in-arms with "old man Joe", the Irish bootlegger. They ran a pipeline out of Canada together. Why do people find it hard to believe in that storied pipeline, a mere 8 inches in diameter; that it was somehow beyond the ingenuity of a man who could float mansions up and down Long Island Sound and pitch them up like a circus tent in the middle of the night, a charmed caravansary, appearing like a vision made manifest in the morning vapors rising off the Long Island Sound?

Gatsby, like his predecessor was mysteriously seen along the shores in places which amazed the people. The fine scotch whiskey gushed like spring water through the astonishing pipes and made them both more moneyed than story book potentates.

They say Gatsby in later years was a secret caller at the White House; that he never logged in, that he swept through security without a pass like a privileged apparition, that he was a maker of presidents because he could never be one. Thrice the kingmaker never the king.

These were stories, stories of a distinguished, commanding gentleman at state dinners, a mesmerizing raconteur with a studied clipped manner of speech, and an accent that modulated with the company he chose to keep. If he called you old sport it would be best to dive quickly for the exit. It was an epithet employed with biting irony.

> "Oxford"?

they would ask.

> "Yes"

He would hesitate, wavering.

> "I took my degree in literature and stayed on to teach. I studied architecture privately, designed a home for Lord Heathrow... school connection."

"Too much personal information" he would later think. "Less is more. Less is more. Keep it mysterious."

He kept the photographs at home in a drawer; never on the wall.

He was married to a movie star, two movie stars, they say; not at the same time. He made movies, bought a studio, to meet beautiful woman they say; as good a reason as any.

Married My Grandmother

I know for a fact that Gatsby married my grandmother or rather the woman who would become my grandmother; a young tennis player, recently graduated, (Radcliffe, Smith? I forgot which), with family money and impeccable manners, irreproachable credentials.

She spoke four languages perfectly, by a strange coincidence, the same ones Gatsby spoke; enough to get her a plum job as a concierge's assistant in a second-string European hotel or the chairmanship of the linguistics department of an American university. She would slip into the embassies on her "shopping" trips to the city to earn her own money, translating. She was thrown together with Gatsby at the French embassy; there for a presentation ceremony, for Gatsby.

> "I understand that you are their ace translator. It would be a pleasure for me to practice my French on you"

opened Gatsby in nearly perfect French.

Her grandfather had made his mint in haberdashery, feigned a new adherence, changed his name; disappeared during the high holy days, rose to become a bastion of Charlestown society. But her pedigree was secretly suspect and subject to purposeful slights. She cringed at the word Kike, clutched these slights tightly to her bosom, gestating to bear a wombfull of toxic fruit.

Gatsby took her on in the summer of '22 to enlist with his squad of "social secretaries". She became his head fishermen, an authentic whaler with a hungry eye for the kill, hounding down the big fish, methodically, culling, combing, sifting the social register, the society columns, the financial journals, the Broadway rags, and the tax rolls to fashion a "guest list", which is what they euphemistically called it, an inspired amalgamation of old and new money with the common denominator being money, money, lots of money; also, a certain talent on the new money side.

For these nouveau-riche, admission required more scrutiny than a poor boy's scholarship to the Ivy League, all with an eye to the prize. Accommodations could be made for the Cophetua complex. The field was sown with the more than willing amateur lovelies for the likes of Tom Buchanan to pluck from.

Gatsby had a force of his own confidential erstwhile Pinkertons who sifted the truth from authorial fancy, composing thickening dossiers; a job more for minor deities than gumshoes. What man is not the sorry author of his own dumb biography, re-scribbled in a spilled pool of warm, stale beer, or chilled champagne poured in his hair?

Son of the Last Tsar

There is a family account that Gatsby is the out-of-wedlock son of the last Tsar of Russia, the murdered one, who, in fact, was mostly German. This tenacious rumor is outlandish, without a scrap of genuine hard evidence. He called himself pure Rus when the light spirit moved him, (unremembered in more sober moments, though he did not drink), the scion of a vanished empire.

He looked like a lost Viking, barreling down Main Street in a Brooks Brothers suit and a wide grin, claiming all he could survey in the name of the forgotten king; tall, blond, with the cheekbones of a Finn, the guts of a burglar and the manner of a king.

The Tsar connection is grounded on cracked, glass plate photographs, uncanny resemblances, and lost letters suspiciously rediscovered. But we all know that photographs lie and so do letters.

Calls in the night can easily be bogus, asylum internees with surreptitious access to an open line for a trifling bribe to an inexperienced orderly.

The real Anastasia reached out and settled for a time in the new wing.

There was an ancient woman with elegant manners and a suggestion of a Russian accent in her English, when she wasn't speaking perfect French, sequestered in her own cottage, incommunicado on the Long Island grounds with direct access to the Sound. She handed him down her rubies and the Rembrandts; reputed to be bogus, which charge incensed her. She insisted that it was the phonies, that's what she called them, that hung in the museums and the great houses of Europe, and that hers were the "real" thing; that is painted by Rembrandt himself. She personally knew the forger, commissioned him, married him; who she swore stood heads over Rembrandt, just unrecognized. She insisted that the so-called fakes in the museum were actually a cut-above the originals.

Gatsby hung them openly, the Rembrandts, attempted to have them authenticated. But no art expert would stand up to make fools of the museums and their procurers and their carefully nurtured provenance. They risked being ruined, hooted out of the field, never to labor in the sphere again.

Her priceless Persian rugs were looted during the interregnum when Carraway held sway. He meant no harm but couldn't keep the keys straight.

Gatsby longed to return to a homeland that was no longer there, if it had ever been; locked out in a diasporic expulsion.

I Know He Worked the Circus

I know Gatsby worked the circus before the outbreak of the War, a high wire walker, aerial illusionist, billing himself: "The Great Gatsby", hence the moniker which stuck; ironic that he should attain undying fame in the name of a forgotten circus act which folded in a year or two. His specialty was vanishing while striding the tight rope, dancing the wire in the lingo of the carn. He executed the high flip backward summersault, the salto mortale and never touched down; "plucked by an angel, a bird taking flight", intoned the hokey script; a quick trick minus trap doors; diversion and distraction, distance and height, pulled by a catapulting wire through a painted cloud on the canvas ceiling sky, in the merest puff of white, smoke, and a sound effects whoosh which blew hats off on the ground followed by a ground shaking thump which shook the patrons off their seats. The thumper, as it was christened, consisted of a contraption which lifted, by means of pulleys, hauled by three men, a two-thousand-pound weight, up a track, like a guillotine, timed to hit the ground the split second of the explosions, the blast of air and the white puff of smoke; all coming from different directions and never perfectly timed; the effect disorienting and profound.

A historian of magic informed me in no-uncertain-terms that no such trick had ever been performed in the whole history of magic; that the logistics were impossible. Yet Gatsby had the posters pronouncing himself the Vanishing Magus, "The Great Gatsby", carefully conserved. I had them hanging on my office wall. The historian insisted that the posters in themselves were insufficient evidence, not proof; publishing substantiatcs nothing. Like any good shaman Gatsby never divulged the tricks behind his miracles, as he was adamant in calling them. After all, he billed himself a wizard.

He turned water into wine, fine wine, the best that money could buy, Bordeaux, the best vintage year;

that was the real trick. Cheap "winers" were a dime a dozen. He was picketed by angry Anabaptists, with their shiny impeccably crafted horse carriages boldly blocking the motor car congested street. Anabaptist, an epithet which they themselves rejected and refused to recognize, who carried signs calling it a blasphemous trick, upstaging "the Lord", making fun of miracles. Nothing could be further from the truth, Gatsby insisted. The wine trick was a hands down cinch.

High on strong wings to perceive all kingdoms, eyes to outstare the sun, he disappeared up, the audience searched down, mumbling in awe that it was "no trick". "He vanished". They felt cheated; they wanted him back. They paid for a trick, prestidigitation, entertaining artifice, convivial conjuring, not cold hard reality. For some reason they dreaded his death. They yearned for resurrection. Masses thronged the gates. He did the magic only once every stop, to further the illusion; departed under cover of night. His knack was knowing when to stay dead.

He would be hailed on the street by travelling strangers as if he had come back from the empire of the dead with tales to tell. They yearned for the story. He pleaded ignorance. He had to stop. It was a matter of time. His number was up.

He took to the trapeze but had to give that up; lost faith in his catcher who eyed him cagily and his young pretty wife. He was saved by the Great War.

Carraway's War

I speak of Carraway's part in the war only because of his bizarre drivel about Teutonic migrations. Carraway ran so fast to the rear in such a state of blind screaming hysteria that he had to be tackled by two soldiers who feared he might sow further panic. He was restrained in a strait jacket mumbling incoherently, court martial unthinkable in his raving state. It is easy for cowards to make light of carnage. He sank into soothing amnesia, erasing inconvenient memories of the "war interlude", as he called it.

Strings were pulled from above and he managed a less than honorable discharge. His record was expunged, including in his own head; so, he never existed, not to the War Department at least, and he slumped whimpering home, broken, hollowed, and abused.

Gatsby recognized him instantly as the lunatic who had run him over, imaginary Huns screaming at his heels. He had tried to console him. It is the secretly terrified who especially despise the weak at heart. In the coward they spy themselves.

Though not an accomplished killer or any killer at all, Nick was not untouched by the slaughter. He never shot his gun. It remained secure in its tightly buckled holster; less than standard Government Issue for his lighter more delicate hand; none-the-less the stench of death would lodge ceaselessly in his broken head as he succumbed nightly to fitful, terrifying torpor. As he was known to remark: You never really get the smell of burning flesh out of your nose entirely, no matter how long you live.

Gatsby's Lover, Tom's Wife

It is Carraway who was obsessed with Gatsby's lover, Tom's wife, and his own true love, such as she was; he fantasizes that he has a chance with her. She flirts with him, mercilessly, toys with him. There was in Carraway the insuperable, uninitiated boy, habitually spurned or ignored by women and who, yet, keeps coming back for more, plodding annoyingly on, in love with the punishment.

He plays the go-between, intermediary for his stand-in, to quench his own thwarted desire. It is his vision of Gatsby and not Gatsby who drowns in the blue lakes of Daisy's eyes and is strangled in a tangle of her golden hair, slogging through the morasses sparing not his horse or sword; the fustian porter robbed <u>him</u> of his treasure and broke his little sword. The fact he refuses to face: she was never a princess and had no wish to be freed, was in fact enraptured by her slavery; her eyes stagnant, dark, drowning pools, her tower not of ivory but broken rubble stone and not so high; she loved to play the strumpet, her siren voice devoid of all but the chinks.

The irony is that Carraway, in the piece, is the obliging panderer, warming to the calling, happily divulging her impostership, unceremoniously unrobing, uncrowning the king's flaxen daughter, standing picket outside his thatched peasant's cottage while Gatsby, the imagined king, fucked Daisy inside, partaking as only Carraway could, listening, deriving vicarious satisfaction from the sounds of ecstatic orgasm emanating from within.

Some idea of himself had gone into loving Daisy and when she rebukes him; to save himself he projects it onto Gatsby. He becomes more confused and disordered; he shatters, breaks down, runs away so fast that even the hounds couldn't catch him, just like in the War. Writing the book, telling his story, pinning his trauma on Gatsby, externalizing his devouring demons allowed him to persist as best he could. The poor son-of-a-bitch.

Intricate Web of Make-believe

Carraway's life as he recounts it is an intricate web of make-believe; the yarn he whispers in his own ear to lull himself to sleep. He needs to set it down in the book to keep the lies straight; the playbook to document, legitimize his dream of himself, the paper pages to prop against his ruin.

If his family were prominent, well-to-do people once, they are no longer; his father once formidable, crutched by impeccable courtly manners, a ruin of a man, alcoholic, launching his son to oblivion with pathetic, high-flown platitudes, all that his poor, alcohol sodden brain could summon. He made it to Yale with handouts from a maiden aunt in her dotage who mistook him for the favored cousin.

Thomas Buchanan Was a Scholar

Thomas Buchanan was a scholar, plodding away doggedly at his doctoral thesis at Yale, interrupted permanently by his shotgun wedding to Daisy, although I doubt shotguns were anywhere to be found; more likely a civilized deliberation among the families, or what remained of them, in the library; the conversation suddenly hushed when the coffee is carried in, care of the servants, no finger sandwiches to be found, not appropriate, under the circumstances. Money was no doubt discussed.

Tom prided himself on his mastery of language, his learning, always meaning to come back to his thesis at Yale, whittled away as the years wore down; mocked by Daisy for reading deep books with "big words", he finally succumbed completely.

Thomas Buchanan had been a big man with a big practiced voice, a deep base echoing from the bottom of an oak barrel bursting the staves. In an imaginary movie Charlton Heston would have been a good choice to play him; Gregory Peck with blond hair; Bruce Dern was all wrong; Barry Sullivan was just okay. The looks but not the mannerisms or voice of Richard Denning or Peter Graves; the voice and accent of Kelsey Gammer or the voice of Paul Frees, of god writing checks or the voice of Alexander Scourbey with only a touch of the demonic presence of the over-the-top character Mike Lagana in Fritz Lang's *The Big Heat,* but with the sound and speech patterns of his famous King James Bible recorded for the blind.

Daisy:

> "You bully me with your big words... you big brute. I have no idea what you're talking about half the time. It's rude to use words that nobody understands".

She consumed him, busted him, plundered his season. She was a wastrel, a destroyer. She pulled him under with the seductiveness of the irrational, the common, the plebian. He was born into the wrong class. It was he that said that his fellow idle rich thought every day had to be a fiesta and that he was ruined by it. The celebrated writer whom he had grandly feted quoted him without attribution. That was his story; he would die without attribution. It is the same Buchanan who abandoned his own notes to storage praising the other writer.

Closeted, Schooled Pet

Buchanan craved work, yearned, ached for it. Daisy reduced him to entertaining a closed circle; a closeted, schooled pet, probing for an exit, propelling him in desperation to wagering, prostitutes and beggar maids. It was Daisy that got him started gambling; she "just loved the casinos." It was his manic concentration, his defiant perseverance, his best traits that militated against him; pitted him against an army of his own clones. He couldn't stand to lose which made him lose more. He couldn't do anything half-way. He bet and lost a king's ransom in the gambling halls of Monaco, which set him up as a permanent mark. He was being dressed to kill or better, dressed for the kill, the Eternal Tailor, the Universe's Pervert, taking intimate measurements at the inseam with impunity and he didn't have a clue. By the time Daisy left there was nothing left to leave; he was a spent shell; an egg sucked dry with only the shell left perfectly intact; the night's work of an egg-sucking possum; he shot his load at a moving target that wasn't there.

Gatsby Was in Business

Carraway never understood Gatsby, that Gatsby was in business, a businessman. It was an elemental misunderstanding, profound, even.

Gatsby didn't throw parties; he conceived events; a producer of his own life's theater, not host but impresario, a master of ceremonies staging extravaganzas to lure in life's plungers, risk-takers, high rollers; at least that's how they flattered themselves; Las Vegas before its time. His house gained fame as the only honest game in five states. When Rot-Gut Ferret was cleaned out it was the result of Ferret being both drunk and stupid, a money guttering combination. But there was much more to it than that. What might seem a huge gambling haul for a night was small potatoes for James Gatsby; something else was afoot, something bigger.

He was tired of constantly pulling up stakes; of floating the big boat down the never-ending lake.

The Saint Paul Girl

Carraway was induced to leave Saint Paul because of a series of ugly incidents involving the harassment of some poor young girl. He had gotten it into his head that they were engaged. The family intervened and agreed not to pursue it with the police if Carraway would get out of town, go east, far from their daughter. He had relatives in New York; Daisy it would turn out. But he continued to write the poor girl every week.

Things got worse. There were rumors that he used to roam the New York City streets at night and had been detained by the police for following young women home to their apartments. As far as anyone could tell nothing ever came of it. But then he loved the City, like a young girl does, with a crush that made her heart beat fast with excitement. He would moon about the vast, breathless bustle that was the City.

Friends had seen him peering into restaurant windows searching, searching for god-knows-what; lurking, as if he were a poor boy without the price of a meal or as if there were a party inside that he had not been invited to. I think he lived his life as if there were some fabulous party going on somewhere from which he had been purposely excluded, and if only he searched hard enough he would find it and if he jumped through the right hoops, made enough money, he would come up with the entry fee; that they would reconsider and let him in.

Gatsby's Merry Men

Years later Carraway was brutally beaten with a billy-club, a policemen's truncheon, back in the day when cops gloried and got away scot-free with such savagery. Ham-fisted meat-faced ape with badge and gun:

> "Ya like followin young girls around the street, do ya? Ya like lookin, do ya? Ya like scarin 'em, do ya?"

In a brogue which thickened to the cracking beat: "Do ya? Do ya?" like an obscene ditty to a tune by Stephen Foster from a vicious drunk more drunk than he.

He had been following the cop's sister for weeks in some drunken romantic reverie and kept screaming to the club as it came down relentlessly, mercilessly upon his bloodied head. The cop broke his nose, his left cheek bone, his jaw, four fingers in his right hand, his writing hand, and broke the drum in his left ear:

> "She smiled at me. You don't understand; she smiled at me."

She may very well have smiled at him. She was no beauty. She could have done a lot worse and did, often. No, Nick had long since stopped courting beauty. He had forsaken her entirely; it was fickle beauty that had cleaved his heart in two.

It was Gatsby's merry men who paid the cop a quiet late night visit he would not soon forget; to-be-sure he would not likely use his billy-club again in such-wise-fashion, or any fashion at all.

Innate Longing for a World Fairer

Nick's Carraway, that is Nick's portrayal of himself, is at odds with the real Carraway. The real Nick always carried the guilt for the murder of Gatsby although he never acknowledged it. He was an accessory before and after the fact. If he had revealed Daisy's guilt in the slaughter of Tom's lover to the police, he would have saved the lives of both Winslow and the putative Gatsby.

The fact that he proclaimed himself an innocent, an honest man, does not convince us that he himself believed it. Run when anyone insists how honest they are. Could he be so deluded? His life is nothing but a series of facile compromises. Despite his protestations, even as he describes himself, he is a man without a moral compass much less a moral anchor. He is irresponsible, careless, a moral bankrupt. Carraway, self-obsessed, self-consciously writing auto-biographically:

> "His boyhood passed more given to contemplation than to action. Less prosperous in fortune than at an earlier age he had every reason to expect; he retreated into the realm of the imagination and became a kind of idealist fabricating the world for himself from within through his formidable meditative power. He had an innate longing for a world fairer than the one outside of himself. "

What thinking man does not?

This would as well describe Gatsby, with-the-exception-of the arduously acquired worldly riches which exacted its own inestimable price. They were not the polar-opposites they might appear. They were brothers under the skin. Gatsby made manifest the fictions of his mind. But Carraway's dreams came to being in the word, the book. Carraway mercifully died in a real way on that day of death. It is Gatsby who lived on, his protector, his guardian, his doppelganger.

Gatsby's Resurrection

Gatsby held Nick accountable for the carnage that inauspicious day, for his own needless sacrifice and suffering. He longed, if not to punish him, to reprove him; to make him see.

But, even so, Gatsby revealed himself, made his presence known to Carraway years later; that he was still alive or back from the dead; he refused to explain which.

But Carraway denied him, refused to believe in him, thought he was an impostor or a ghost.

Gatsby:

    "Don't you recognize me, Nick?"

Nick:

"Recognize you? Why should I recognize you? I've never laid eyes on you before in my life. What is this? What are you trying to pull? Who are you, anyway?

"Get away from me. I don't know you. What do you want from me? Do you take me for a fool?"

Years before in 1922, at one of his own extravaganzas Gatsby came up to Nick, unassumingly. Everybody knew him... everybody it seems, except poor Nick, the bungling gatecrasher who stuck out so conspicuously.

Gatsby:

"Don't you recognize me, Nick?

Nick:

"No, I'm afraid..."

Gatsby:

"You almost knocked me over, once. Do you remember?"

Nick, visibly shaken as if he is talking to a ghost:

"No... of course...

Long pause, Nick:

The war... the war. How could I forget? You helped me... the one who...

"Yes, Yes. Yes, of course, the Colonel... Colonel Gatsby! My god... the hero. The man himself...

The conquering hero... They told me you died... in battle... in the war.

"You're that Gatsby? I mean... you... you own this place? You... built it? You're that man? The man... My god... you're alive... back from the dead."

Gatsby ignored the clumsiness, the inappropriateness of Nick's remark.

Nick, unnerved:

"What on earth are you doing here?"

Gatsby:

"I might ask you the same thing."

Nick:

"Well, you see... you see... I live just next door... in that bungalow way over there... you can't see it... not now... its hidden...obscured by the house, this house... It seems to shrink next to it... but it's there... and since there are no fences... well, not very big ones anyway and so many people... I just thought... I thought... well... why not?"

Gatsby:

"Well, you have-to be careful... old sport. In this neck-of-the-woods trespassing could get you shot or permanently lost."

Nick:

"But it's so crowded. Why does it... How could they...?

Gatsby:

"They've been watching you for quite-some-time... shadowing you ever since you slipped in. It seems you've eaten enough for a party of guests. How did you like the caviar?

"Listen, if I can be of any service... any help at all..?"

Nick:

"No! Oh no. No. I'm fine, just fine."

Gatsby:

"They didn't want to create a scene. I thought you looked familiar so I thought... I'd...

"The next time I'll send you an engraved invitation, hand delivered by a uniformed messenger in robin's egg blue. In the meantime, you're welcomed to stay as long as you like. Enjoy the show. We'll wrap some of the food up for you so you can take some home. If you eat any more now, you'll get sick.

"Do you know anyone here? Do you recognize anyone? Someone to talk to?"

Nick:

"I thought I saw my cousin Daisy's friend but she disappeared when I got close... into thin air."

Gatsby spoke to Nick the way a parent would to a clumsy child, not because he thought he was stupid but because he perceived in him the child that he was, and in some ways always would be.

And with that Gatsby dematerialized as was his custom only to suddenly resurrect in the far distance among another group of guests. The butcher in town said that his delivery boy insisted Gatsby was a shape-shifter but I'm not sure the delivery boy was smart enough to know what a shape-shifter was, exactly, or understand its implication.

All the Private Dicks

All the private dicks, all the lawyers, bail bondsman and literary agents, all the legions of hired intermediaries couldn't save Carraway from himself.

After the deaths and an interlude in Europe, Gatsby came back to America; he would always return; hid in plain sight, found it unnecessary to change his name, a name common enough. He was tired of creating names for himself. He always expected history to catch up with him, the infernal revenue to come knocking at his door, or the demoniac off-spring of some long dead desperado with an imagined score to settle.

Through mutual friends Gatsby formally made the reacquaintance of Nicholas Carraway, who bought whole heartedly into the pretense that he was someone else entirely. Carraway, after the denial, approached him warily, with trepidation, as if he were a real spirit this time, a genuine holy ghost. Carraway exploited this perceived friendship, would telephone him, late at night. But Gatsby got the distinct impression that Carraway was unhinged, thought he was talking to himself or part of himself and would carry on the most intimate soul-searching conversations. Nick sometimes imagined that it was Gatsby himself, the dead one, that he had somehow managed to reach, calling out to him into the nether regions beyond the grave. For some reason that I don't understand Gatsby recorded these conversations; it may be that it was just because the equipment was already in place. The early voice recorders were hooked up by his Serbian friend, his distant cousin. They weren't really conversations, more like confessions or ravings; he had them transcribed and bound, but with time the binding disintegrated, the heading pages with dates dislocated and scattered.

Gatsby Not Westinghouse

Contrary to popular belief it was Gatsby not Westinghouse who paid his cousin's hotel and restaurant bill, to the bitter end. He managed to keep Edison at bay as best he could, who he regarded as an ignorant gangster and racketeer, with disgustingly dirty personal habits. Gatsby had his own private bitter experiences with Edison and his so-called Trust, which sent in its hired goons to break up his very expensive custom-made, custom perfected camera equipment, which Edison alleged or imagined he had a patent on, having stolen the idea fair and square from the French. It was Edison's thugs that drove Gatsby into his first acquaintance, and then alliance with Wolf. But Gatsby could retaliate just so far. Edison possessed a certain unique immunity because of his undeserved status as a revered public icon; sacred societal idols were safeguarded, untouchable, whether criminal or not.

Edison (his father, Samuel Edison, was thought to be of Dutch extraction) and his cohorts, Anglo-Saxons or what passed for them, didn't grasp that this was war, that the battle was generational, cultural, philosophical, and religious. For them it was protecting business, movies a novelty. For Gatsby and the Independents who were ethnics, mostly Catholics, Jews and non-patrician Protestants, it was a struggle for the soul of a nation, for possession of the country itself. Although Edison was a truculent agnostic who thought all religion bunk and all bibles man-made fairytales, he listened in silent, if unvoiced acquiescence to his illiterate friend, Henry Ford, who harbored particular-loathing for the Jews, as the source of all evil in the world.

Recorded Everyone Who Mattered

In fact, Gatsby recorded everyone who mattered; he had an in with the phone company; he owned controlling interest, voting stock. There wasn't a phone in the country he couldn't listen in on. It's been alleged that the telephone was invented and funded at the behest of a secret, secret police force, to more effectively spy on people; but it wasn't the FBI.

Gatsby had a file drawer on J. Edgar, including pictures, which granted him immunity, of sorts. He knew where the bodies were buried, literally; he had detailed maps with pins.

Hoover stayed up nights with his good buddy Tolson, listening to phone calls rerouted, amended, custom tailored for his predilections; some of them out and out fabrications voiced by actors. Gatsby employed a solid corps of voice imitators, to skillfully elicit information and sow confusion among his adversaries.

Gatsby told me that although it was great for business it tended to be destructive of personal relationships. He knew too much, everyone's secret, what they thought of him; no, I take that back, what they said about him which is very different, full of empty posturing and not at all close to the truth. This almost omniscient knowledge in some ways crippled him, isolated him. He had a small army of transcribers, readers, recapitulaters, condensers and abridgers. He had virtual mystics combing for diamonds in the sewage, like listening for alien intelligence from the static emanating from deep space which you answered at your peril. He wasted too much time reading digests to learn that people mostly lied.

Under the Freedom of Information Act

Under the Freedom of Information Act certain files were released which purport to be transcripts of the telephone conversations of Carraway with a personage identified only as J. No further information or conjecture is offered about the identity or possible location of this "J" individual. There is a note that his location could not be traced but no reason is given for this failure. The files are also heavily redacted without explanation for what is being redacted or why. There is no reason given for the wiretaps except the broad umbrella title of "Subversive" which is stamped across the covers where the covers are intact. Since all good writers should be subversive, it is not explained if all writers of note are being bugged. There is also the possibility that this J person is the target of the tapping or at least the reason why Carraway is being tapped.

There is also the troubling anomaly: the recordings of Carraway continue until 1944, four years after his death. There is the possibility that since these bugs were for technical reasons always manned that the continued recording represents a boondoggle, a deception on the part of individual agents looking for a cushy assignment, a gold brick with little danger of being shot dead in the street by bank robbers. Since from their own scribbled notes, accidentally left in the file, it is evident they regarded the Director as a pompous ass, or worse, this would have been a great joke on him. The agents were always looking for ways to mislead or deceive the Director, "do a dance on his head", which lead to some interesting case files.

The agents seemed to have been well schooled in Carraway, since he was at times under continual surveillance. They may have known him better than he knew himself, a circumstance which seems to repeat itself. They could thus concoct the record of the so-called "postmortem" tapes at their leisure at night seated at the kitchen table, over ale and cold chicken.

There is also some obscure reference in the file that a previous agent had been suborned by the mysterious J character, became a friend and accomplice; opening the possibility that they all sat down together and fabricated the entire file; it could therefore be regarded as a literary construct, a production, fiction; something the Director could read late at night for his titillation. Some of the events described are wildly improbable, and must be a joke. Many of the Bureau files may have been in fact fabricated entirely for the Director's "entertainment" or befuddlement, unbeknownst to him, made up especially, to appeal to his prurient taste for intrigue and dark conspiracy. One agent reading the transcript said: "It's not like bullshit; it's more like poetry, bad poetry or lady pornography." The Director was called the little lady by his men.

There is an unsubstantiated story in the Bureau that one of these gumshoes created a brand-new identity for himself and became an early biographer of Carraway, mining the wiretap transcripts as a primary source. He became a professor at Princeton, counterfeiting a doctorate for himself, teaching freshman English while formulating his book; through this infiltration getting a better feel for the exact bullshit required.

However, the most plausible and simple explanation is that these are clerical errors on the part of some low-level typists. However, there are what seem to be oblique references to happenings after 1940 which would make the dates correct or implausibly, in the alternative, that those speaking could foresee the future or more implausibly still, could create it.

Carraway Didn't Die in 1940

The other explanation is that Carraway didn't die in 1940; which I grant you is farfetched. His death was plastered all-over the newspapers; the publicity was widespread and there was an open casket. My grandfather went to the funeral and said that he was dead, or at least it seemed that he was. But Gatsby had a friend who made a good living creating "corpses" for those wishing for reasons of their own to fake their deaths or attend their own funerals incognito; he did special effects in the movies and life-like masks and waxwork figures. It got to the point where a glass dome wasn't required on the open casket; the "remains" felt real dead to the touch.

This movie special effects artist was also in partnership with the New York City medical examiner who grew exceedingly rich signing death certificates and rigging autopsies. He spread the money around which was prudent. The Examiner had a summer mansion on the gold coast, just down from Gatsby; he claimed an inheritance from his wife's fabulously rich family in Argentina, which clan seems to have been extinguished in one fell swoop leaving every cent to poor dumb Mildred; which puzzled those who actually knew Mildred McGuire's people, penniless, shiftless boozehounds from the Lower East Side. The Examiner also lectured at City College about Retributive Justice. Being a medical examiner, a scholar in forensics and crime scene reconstruction, he had a lucrative sideline faking suicides and "accidental" deaths for an early Murder Incorporated with the consummate skill of an impresario constructing a stage set.

There are also transcripts of the Gatsby voice recordings of Carraway that seem to indicate that at times there was no one on the other end of the line even though the line was open, live, connected, whatever you call it when the electricity runs through the wire. But even these "exchanges" partake of what seems to be an active dialogue, a give and take. One cannot necessarily assume that Carraway was entirely crazy or hallucinating. Good writers, after all, conceive very real characters out of their own minds. Carraway might have used these "conversations", the telephone, as an imaginating device, to help bring forth, midwife, the life he was creating.

But at other times the person on the other end seems quite real; they step on each other's lines and finish each other's sentences, falling all over themselves, stealing the punch lines. There is also the real possibility that Carraway was "imitating" the voice of this J character and talking to himself like a deranged ventriloquist.

The calls start in 1923, continue, on an intermittent basis spanning twenty-one years. Many of the files are undated, out of order, and some are so badly water and mold damaged they are currently unreadable. Someone with deep pockets and the aid of a battalion of forensic document experts will no doubt be able to extract further precious gems, someday.

I've compared some of the Bureau's files with Gatsby's files where the dates still exist and match-up. Some of the subjects are the same but the words are entirely different which could be the fault of the transcribers. If you have ever given testimony before a court reporter and later read a transcript, you know that these are often the work of the reporter's imagination only suggested by the sworn testimony or enlivened by a bribe.

Gatsby with his Power

Gatsby, with all his limitless wealth and inexhaustible power, will live on in the written-down make-believe of others, as recreations, recollected mistakenly, if innocently, sifted through necessarily alien psyches, funhouse mirror images in unquiet pools; unless of course by some miracle I manage to set the record straight. Although as-yet unheard, I am to a very real extent the very last man standing. But then there are the other accounts: Thomas Buchanan's voluminous unsifted record, of which I have only begun to touch the surface, and then of course Jordan, my grandmother, the wildest of wildcards.

Can we not quite possibly invent the future by means of our dreams, our delusions made substantial?

My father insisted that I romanticized my grandfather, that after all he sometimes operated outside the law; but what law would that be? He took the law into his own capable hands where there was no possibility of justice. Weren't they all criminals in their own way, a rotten crowd, the whole damned bunch of them?

To Be a Great Criminal

From the James Jacob Gatsby archives, dated 1949, numbered document 5,652, untitled, catalogued by the executor's staff:

> A couple of kids sitting in the front row of a Saturday movie matinee were overheard saying that the greatest line in "literature" occurred in Arsene Lupin, a series of pulp novels about a gentleman thief and master of disguise, usually a force for good, while technically working independent of the law to overcome with Gallic panache those truly criminal who work inside the law:

> "If one can't be a great artist or a great soldier, the next best thing is to be a great criminal."

Someone described the Jazz Age hero as both murderer and saint.

Sometimes it's hard to tell one from the other.

Letter from the Catholic Harvard

November 2, 1913

Dear Father,

You have to save me. I just can't stand it any longer. I've made such a terrible mistake.

I'm sorry I didn't tell you sooner but I just couldn't. I know how you feel about the "stinking Papists". I just didn't see that I had any other options.

Aunt Sally called it the Catholic Harvard, which was ridiculous and was willing to foot the entire bill including a preposterously generous weekly stipend and I just didn't think I could turn her down. I've saved almost all of the allowance money. I've saved it for you, Dad. How is the new job? I'm so proud of you.

I sometimes feel I've died and gone to hell. This place is a looney-bin with the inmates as trusties.

You wouldn't believe the stuff they talk about: the shroud of Turin, the sighting of the Lady by some uneducated peasant girls in a dump and when they're going to reveal the predictions she made to them. They go on about whether Mary Magdalene was really a prostitute. They talk about the Trinity, the Immaculate Conception, the virgin birth, that the Eucharist becomes the actual, the actual body and blood of Christ and that even a mass murderer who tortures and rapes little children could go to heaven if he was really, truly sorry, and made a good confession thereby proving God's infinite mercy; but an innocent child that wasn't baptized couldn't get in, neither could anyone who died before the atoning death of Jesus, neither could John the Baptist, because he wasn't baptized, not by Jesus anyway and that's the only way that counts. They take this stuff deadly serious. I thought at first that it was an elaborate put on, some sort of a lame initiation. They consider this nonsense intense intellectual conversation. Those who can make you believe absurdities can make you commit atrocities. Anybody who believes crap like this is capable of anything, any crime.

And it's not like they are all stupid. That's the frightening part; they're not. It's like some essential part of their brain has been removed, all critical capacity burned out with sulfuric acid poured into precise holes drilled into their skulls. Either that or they're born slaves or they have somehow been reengineered into thralldom. These are all geeks who have formed a tight clique; a union of girly boys dribbling spit, panting like beaten bitches in heat, sucking up to the wolfish sissy priests; Catholic school boys jostling in line to lick the asshole of these ersatz holy men. I was told that the admission standards are somewhat exclusive. But they are looking for a particular type; then there's the self-selection. Who else would want to come here but the kind that are here? The term Catholic University is an oxymoron. To call a Papist a Catholic is an absurdity, buying into their big lie; there is absolutely nothing "catholic" about the so-called Roman Catholic Church; it's like surrendering the field before the battle has even begun. It just proves that by corrupting the language we corrupt our souls and surrender even the possibility of conveying reality.

And they all have bad skin. And they're all fat, not necessarily overweight but fat, soft, even the athletes; like they lack muscle tone, hardness; they all look sick, like they do filthy things, gorge on putrid, maggot infested meat. They dress badly and eat like pigs and speak in these heavy low-class accents, not English, really.

And they're the most self-important group of people. The fact that they don't know how to eat, don't know how to dress, don't know how to speak, are ill-educated doesn't bother them in the very least. They're too pig-headed to hang their bloated pig heads in shame. They're Catholic: God's chosen ones, with their own exclusive back door into heaven.

There's a careful selection process at work here. It's like wheat gone rotten that's been sifted and resifted again and again until all the iron is out, all the grit, all the germ with nothing left but a fine worthless white dust devoid of nutritional value puffed into an insubstantial breeze to eventually vanish into nothingness.

The worst thing about it is their priests. I learned very early-on never to be alone with one of these. But it's like all the students and their parents are in on it. It's like this is the way the game is played and if you don't know the rules you'll be locked out. I haven't seen an overt nod and wink but it's there, just beneath the surface or a quick nod when you're not looking. This is their club. They are all collaborators, just as guilty, guiltier than the prime perpetrators. Let them have it. Let them have each other. They deserve it. Let them send their sons off to be buggered, send them off like lambs to ritual slaughter for an empty pocket full of change.

Evil in high places is an incubator of evil; it infects and spreads the pestilence like a medieval plague house. The predator priests run rampant unembarrassed by their boy-rape. And if the minds they infect are locked shut, it does not inoculate them against the infection; these voluntary internees are incapable of any sense of smell, they carry the infection with them like shit on their shoes spreading it as they go about the world. And what do they become: fifth rank attorneys thieving and padding their rates, prosecutors mercilessly entrapping the merely avaricious, college professors as dumb as a post thoroughly demoralizing their charges by the impenetrable depth of their stupidity?

Also, I found out that cousin Eddie, Doctor Eddie is a big imposter. His really nice-guy routine is a racket to suck you in. By never making any waves, by bending over backwards, never disagreeing, he's avoided scrutiny. His whole life is a fraud, volunteer doctor for all the sport's teams, the CYO, Boy Scouts; team doctor, isn't that what he called himself; ready supply of boys is what it is; to play doctor with. He's part of it; one of them. They must have some sort of spy network, scouts looking out for prime meat. I've had two of those come up to me grinning like idiots, wanting to know if I went in for the same things as Eddie, wanting to give me their number, wanting mine. When I told one of them Eddie was married, he almost busted a gut and said: "You're not serious" and then "I thought he was going to become a priest. His priest buddies must be broken hearted. I guess he made a deal. Maybe she likes to watch." I guess his wife is in on it too. I made the mistake of telling this to Eddie when he came up to see me. He wanted to make sure the shackles were good and tight. Maybe he thought it was time to make his move. I ruined it for him, rained on his parade. I don't know what possessed me to tell him, to stick it in his face like that; it was a wicked, reckless thing to do. Maybe I was trying to get back at him.. I got sick when this all happened, sick in the pit of my stomach. I had to vomit. You have-to remember that with my mother and Aunt Margaret, Eddie was propped-up on a pedestal, a paragon of virtue and hard work, to be admired and imitated; no, someone to emulate. The earth had shifted off its axis, which is ridiculous; I'm embarrassed to say that, embarrassed that I made myself vulnerable, that I'm not made of tougher stuff. These people are worse than murderers; they are devourers of souls; they eat you up. I know I haven't been in war, that I haven't been hunted down in the streets like an animal or tortured on a rack. But this is in some ways worse, more nightmarish. This is the demons in disguise as saints. Where do you turn? Who do you tell? Satan had more dignity, was a Prince of the realm compared to these lowlife pigs.

I don't know if Uncle Mike knows, whether he's in on it. But how could he not know? From what I was able to learn, when Eddie was president of the student body at Regis, which made him General, or whatever stupid name they called it, he preyed upon the younger boys with the collusion of the priests, offering his choice picks to them; softening them up for the kill; schooling, grooming, priming them; he was one of the elect, singled out for special privileges, their private pimp; the priests were crazy for him... because of his huge physical attributes, that's what they say. I'm sorry to talk like this; it's very embarrassing. But I'm desperate. I can't take it anymore. Now it all comes together, makes peculiar crazy sense.

Everything is topsy-turvy, upside down, helter-skelter; I'm stuck down the rabbit hole. The Irish who are the lowest of the low everywhere else reign like tin-pot-despots here; the sons of pipe-laying contractors, ambulance chasing lawyers and crooked politicians, lording it over the Italians and Poles who they treat like their inferiors, calling them Wops, Guineas and Polacks; the Germans stand on the side laughing. But they all hate each other; the Poles, Italians and Germans think the Irish are scum. I have-to get out of here. This is a crazy house.

Please come and get me. I'm afraid they'll try to stop me, call the police if I try to leave by myself. They know the police; they're all "devout" Catholics; they keep the priests well stocked, pick-up boys in off the street for them, for "counseling and mentorship". In the future I will run like hell if I even hear the word mentor or protégé.

Please, I've learned my lesson. I've had enough. This is it. I am so sorry that I didn't listen to you. I was so wrong.

I love you and think about you often.

Your Devoted Son,

Nicolas

Who Knew Hell Could Be Bucolic

A day after sending the letter Nick stopped going to classes and tried his best to guardedly untangle any knots, extricate himself, and waited for his father. He packed his suitcases and waited. He left the school books piled on his desk and would not touch them, as if they were contaminated.

During the day he waited by the iron gate at the entrance to campus; who knew hell could be bucolic. As the sun set, he watched from his dormitory window like a young boy, though he was already sixteen, his face pressed and distorted against the window glass.

And on the third day, as if by some miracle, a massive black car pulled up just under his window. It was as big as a tank and might as well have been.

Nick could not have been happier if his father had galloped up on a pure white charger in full armor and flicked off all the predator priests like bowling pins in a dark alley or picked gorging flies off his wounded body struggling to stay alive; thrown open the doors to the cathedral and marched his high-stepping stallion, with a crunch of leather and the sparkle of silver spurs, straight into the sanctuary of evil and plucked his son up as if an enchanted eagle, from the high altar an instant before the obsidian dagger plunge and away from the priest with the filthy hands who would thrust in and rip out his still beating heart and bite out a bleeding piece of it with his teeth to eat.

An enormous man exited from the driver's side, walked around and with much fanfare opened the door for Nick's father. Maybe he, too, understood the portent of this moment: the father coming to rescue the son or was it the other way around, the son redeeming the father.

Nick's father looked rejuvenated, just like the old days, full of his old confidence, his essential drive, his immaculateness of purpose, as if the South would rise again out of the ashes.

Nick met his father half way.

Nick:

> "I've been waiting for you... at the window... by the gate. I've been in hell."

Father:

> "I left as soon as I got word."

Nick:

"You look wonderful, dad.

"But how could you know... so quick?"

Father:

"The miracle of the United States Post Office."

Nick knew this was one of his father's little jokes but thought there was more to it, as if his father knew, had another way of knowing, another source. But there would be time enough for that, he thought.

Father:

"We're leaving, now, right now, this very minute."

Nick:

"But don't we have to sign out."

Father:

"We don't have to sign a god-damned thing. They won't give us a refund... they're thieves."

Nick:

"But don't we have to fill out some forms? Won't they stop us?"

Father:

"I don't see any chains. Where're the armed guards? Where's their fucking army?"

Nick, shocked, his father never spoke like this:

"Dad?

"We have to get my clothes".

I think deep down that his father had the same irrational, visceral fear as the son, that once the Papists got their hooks into you, sunk their teeth deep, that there would be no escaping them.

Father:

"Buster, will get your personal stuff. Stay out here. Don't go near that place."

A nod and a smile from Buster as if he were a co-conspirator with the father and the son, in on the happy enterprise from the beginning.

Nick:

"My clothes? I have-to get my clothes."

Father:

"Are they the same clothes you left home with?"

Nick:

"Yes."

Father:

"Leave the clothes. Leave the books. Leave the old luggage.

"This hell-hole just happens to be in New York City, son.

"We're going to buy you new clothes and new books. We'll get the stink of candle wax and incense out of you. Have you exorcized by a genuine bible thumper from Missouri.

"You can spend Sally's blood money on yourself. Celebrate. What kind of motor car would you like?"

Not waiting for an answer, he continued:

"You can start Yale next fall... if that's what you want... that's what you wanted all along, your dream. They have your application from a year ago. You're accepted. You've been accepted. You can spend the rest of this school year reading and writing your stories."

Not appreciating it at all at the time, Nick would come to cherish this brief period as an almost enchanted interlude; he practiced his writing unhindered and would look back upon the spell with deep nostalgia. He would never be so happy and yet at the time he seemed not happy at all, not happy in the least when it was all happening.

Father:

"I talked to Dean Michaels. They're not going to recognize any credits from this shithole, so you'll have to start all over, fresh, a new beginning, a true commencement. My sister is going to help and I'll manage the rest... somehow, I'll do it. I promise you that, if it's the last thing I do."

The Old Priest Tried to Bugger You

Seven years after the cataclysmic event, the hit and run, Nick and Daisy met for lunch at the Plaza seemingly reconciled to a past that bound them like prisoners chained together, who might make their escape but never from each other.

Nick had confessed something to Daisy and made her swear to never tell another living soul; Daisy, his lady love, who he infused with a depth her shallowness could not begin to encompass. But Nick understood at some level that at its most degenerate and decadent the corrupted American Dream is personified by, becomes one with the American Debutante's Dream, young undeserving girls with the chinks, pluming themselves like bright birds with their brains extracted, embodied by Daisy's vapidity, an object of deadly, deathly, materialistic meaninglessness. To this woman, who he referred to as a ninny at times, he bared his soul in moments of supreme, if drunken, truth.

He confessed that no woman had ever loved him the way Sigourney Fey had. I think she was personally affronted, sincerely nauseated by the tawdriness of it all, which is a hoot.

Nick:

> "No woman ever loved me or will love me the way Monsignor Sigourney Fey did. He was my best friend in the whole world."

Daisy:

"Isn't he the old priest who tried to bugger you?"

Nick:

"Who told you that? I never said any such thing."

Daisy:

"Yes, you did. You most certainly did…. Just like now in one of your moments of inebriated truth… your moment of well-oiled crystalline clarity.

"You have these epiphanies… these awakenings, as you call them.

"You were sloshed… just like you are now… a little more so.

"You said you would never have become a successful writer if it hadn't been for Fey".

Nick:

"I never said any such thing. You made that up… to get back at me. You blame me for Gatsby when it was all your fault. I protected you. I… I lied for you. You might have gone to jail and Tom would have left you.

"I lost my soul for you."

Daisy:

"Uh, you're what? That's a joke. I'm not sure you ever had a soul to lose …. or worth losing. You'd already sold it. You made your pact.

"Your father didn't come quick enough to save you."

Nick:

"What do you know about my father...? You don't know my father."

Daisy:

"You read me the letter you wrote to him... the one you found with his things when he died... that he saved with his most valuable personal belongings. If only you had listened to him, confided in him... if he had come sooner. You loved your father, in your own crippled way. Going there was the ultimate betrayal... it wounded him to the quick... he hated the stinking Papists. Sometimes "hate is a saving grace". Are they your words or were you quoting your father's...? You soiled the letter when you found it... weeping into it... the ink running.

He took you out of hell but you remained in communion with one of its principal demons. The tentacles struck deep. You left your luggage but packed up hell in a suitcase.... Or is it a hand basket...? and took it with you. The fiend found its way to your belly, worming its way, making itself a cozy home. You already made your pact.

"You said that Monsignor Sigourney Fey, the perfume reeking dandy, loved you and mentored you and told you you would become a great writer... that he believed in you when no one else did... that he would read your work over and over... editing it, help you polish it... that's when you were writing junk... he helped you gild the turd... he brought you to the mountain top and showed you the world waiting for you.

"Sigourney Fey... a 'fin-de-siècle aesthete and dandy'... Isn't that what you called him...? who just 'adored' and turned you on to Decadent authors like Swinburne and Oscar Wilde.

"It's hysterical if it weren't so obscene... the self-proclaiming Right Reverend Monsignor bragging that his vestments are too gorgeous for words:

> 'I look like a Turner sunset when I am in full regalia.'

"He was a profligate nightmare. Didn't he squander most of his inherited family fortune on antique, mostly Renaissance, priestly dress. He would show it off with the least provocation and perform one man fashion shows, pirouetting foppishly like a peacock in a tutu.

"He celebrated high mass for a private select audience in the resplendent apparel of an ancient Borgia cardinal, hands shuddering as he elevated the jewel encrusted communion chalice skyward. Didn't he switch to Catholicism because they'd put up with his wardrobe predilections, which earned him the violent hatred of his previous Episcopalian bishop... who practically chased him out... calling him lewd.

Nick:

"My god! You are positively evil, the garbage you cook up."

Daisy:

"How could I know enough to make this up? My imagination isn't squalid enough. You're the writer.... Not me. Besides, all your so-called revelations are marred by an obvious suppression. You always lie to yourself and call it honor.

"Let me explain the pattern... you get drunk, in vino veritas, confess your mortal and venial sins, experience an epiphany, forget the epiphany come back drunk again, sense a breakthrough, deny the confession but know in your heart of hearts it is true"

Nick:

"You've taken all the bits ...the pieces, all my soul-searching scraps and regurgitated this crap. You've extrapolated?"

Daisy:

"I don't even know what that means. I'm the dummy. Remember calling me that?

"'How could I love such a dummy'? Your very words... Well, this dummy doesn't forget.

"You told me how your Monsignor loved young boys... unembarrassedly... that he would plant these young dainty sweet little things in front of the classroom facing it... he was so proud... as if they were trophies and stare and swoon over them and positively melt... during class... like he couldn't stand to be away from them."

Nick:

"Yes, he may have been a pederast but it wasn't like that with me. He was capable of pure, unreserved love. He loved me"

Daisy:

"He was a full-blown narcissist, a mean bastard when he didn't get what he wanted. Isn't that what you told me? He made a gross physical pass, misunderstood the signals, tried to kiss some boy or felt his crotch or something like that and the boy lashed out viscerally without thinking and the little priest fell to the floor, mostly with wounded pride. And that your little saint got his revenge, hounded and humiliated this boy, who had the audacity, the cheek, to reject him... drove the boy to drop out of school.

"Don't give me this saint crap. The picture you paint is of a monster among monsters who inveigled, cajoled and intimidated to have his way with them. He paid you off with attention and gross flattery and bought you like a cheap whore.

"I may have filled in some of the blanks but you painted the big picture for me. I may be dumb....

But I'm nowhere near as dumb as you think I am.

"You told me you wheedled an invitation for him to some of Gatsby's shindigs so that he might develop an interest in older young men. But he was spoiled by easy prey. He didn't know how to make his move, didn't know the signals, didn't know who was who and incensed by his high-pitched girlish giggles they got together, lured him and took turns beating the crap out of him.

"And that one time he showed up in a byzantine cardinal's get-up. He looked like a pontiff in drag... they wouldn't let him in ... said it wasn't a Halloween party or a masquerade ball.

"Then there was the time he started performing the Catholic mass in Gaelic. Isn't that anathema, forbidden?"

Nick:

"That's another often repeated lie... a vicious... vicious, dirty lie. It was not Gaelic. It was Church Slavonic... a sanctioned Greek Catholic Uniate rite... recognized... under the Church of Rome. He got a special dispensation... from the bishop."

Daisy:

"Oh, was that the bishop, his bosom buddy, who used to go hunting young boys with him? I'm not religious but that <u>was</u> a sacrilege; he <u>is</u> a sacrilege. Did he get a dispensation from the bishop or did he have to go directly to the pope...? Then, when out of it drunk, he was hearing confessions and granting mass absolutions at ten dollars a pop... a small donation for the poor and the lepers. Boy, he loved those lepers. What is it with you Papists and the fucking lepers?

"The last time he was booted... no carried out by Gatsby's heavies... they dropped him like a hot potato... at the postern of his favorite seminary in the wilds of Westchester... and then skedaddled.

"You're a panderer, coming and going... your own special little niche in life.

"You lived through Gatsby. You were hopeless.

"'Her voice compelled me forward breathlessly as I listened.' You love-sick putz. 'Give me a break' as they say in Brooklyn.

"You have a mind made for the Saturday Evening Post and Colliers. How did you ever manage to rise above the incredible shit you wrote? By what miracle did you not drown in it? When you told your writer friend, the bullfighter wanabee... how you tailored, cheapened your stories for the slicks, the unfreeest of all forms of writing... writing by the numbers... to rake in the money, he called you a whore, swearing such whoring would ruin your talent.

"And on the priest who you whored yourself to... you got your revenge... on your mentor, your best friend... the man who loved you... who you loved... revenge but good.

"When the priest showed up at your door, like an abandoned, beaten, old hound, drunk, demoralized, and delirious that night, you turned him away and said he disgusted you... made you sick. That was the night he was beaten to death.

"Didn't you say that his death was like an awakening and made you nearly sure that you would become a priest just like him, just like him... how very touching... that his mantle had fallen upon you from on high... to recreate the atmosphere of him? What mantle would that be? And when he died it was as if the evil spell was broken... the wicked witch was dead and his power usurped by Mencken's violent hostility to Papism."

Nick:

"He was not beaten to death... that is totally untrue... totally untrue, a false rumor... Who told you that? He went to a place he shouldn't have gone to... He was roughed up a little... that's all, just roughed up. He was in the hospital... just for a while... He's fine now. I visit him in the home."

Daisy:

"What? What home would that be? The home for old pederast priests... they must have a grand old time all together... sending out for little boys to share?... or is it... the lost home locked in your own warped little brain?

"Besides, in your pilfered tome you describe, in what is no doubt your personal contribution, being alone in the bedroom of the pale, feminine McKee sitting up between his sheets clad in his underwear... you and McKee, a match made in whatever passes for hell these days.

"It's very expedient to use a narrator as a cover, a shield and when the readers, the critics, discover how banal, how stupid, how immoral that narrator really is, another fool critic sallies forth to reveal the true author's brilliance ingeniously hidden beneath this unreliable, fatuous narrator. There is no confusion like the confusion of a simple mind.

"And you associate your two main female characters... by name, for the sake of almighty god... with that depraved debauchee... that disgusting, degenerate old semi-albino.

"Are you... serious? How sick is that?"

Nick:

"Oh, you like to appear so innocent, so innocent... but you're the malevolent manipulator, the prime perpetrator of that old first slaughter... on the dump road, at the marble pool. I'm a piker next to you.

"Gatsby may have stage-managed you, but you worked Gatsby back when you realized he might be using you. You instigated the confrontation between Tom and Gatsby. Gatsby called me at your request 'would I come to lunch at your house.' Tomorrow? Jordan would be there. You yourself called and seemed relieved to find I was coming. Something was up. You planned the whole bloody debacle and wanted an audience for the spectacle, your own production.

"You flaunt your relationship with Gatsby right under Tom's eyes. 'You look so cool. You always look so cool.'

"It is you who choreographed the macabre dance of death.

"It is you who suggested that we all go to New York.

"'But it's so hot,' you whined like a peevish little girl … 'Let's all go to town. … Who wants to go to town?' you practically demanded.

"It is you who determined who went with whom and in what car,

"'Tom, You take Nick and Jordan. We'll follow in the coup', remember.

"In New York, you tell Tom to break out the whiskey which brings things to a drunken boil. That's what you wanted, a tournament between dark knights for the love of the dark queen... You orchestrated the whole black catastrophe like a maniac impresario.

"The joust, with you as prize, ends with you choosing Tom when Tom vows to treat you better which is what you had been maneuvering for. But the whole thing is a sham because Gatsby doesn't want you, well, at least not the way you want him to want you, which Tom doesn't have a clue to.

"Gatsby played his part... to ease you out.

"'I want to speak to Daisy alone,' He wanted to know what the hell was going on.

"Do you remember your words? 'Even alone I can't say I never loved Tom... It wouldn't be true.' 'Of course, it wouldn't,' Tom stupidly agreed. Shades of those cello chords. 'As if it mattered to you,'

"This is where you act out your so called 'choice' although there is no choice to be made. This is all kabuki, a puppet show, charade, cheap melodrama with Tom forever the dupe. 'Of course, it matters to me. I'm going to treat you better, take care of you from now on.'

"You made it... just what you wanted. You couldn't have Gatsby but you got Tom or at least extracted a new treaty... new rules of engagement.

"You choreographed the entire death scene. You wanted Miranda to see Tom with Jordan so she'd go crazy with jealousy, over his new 'girlfriend'. Miranda knew what you looked like; you were in the papers, all the time, that wouldn't drive her nuts. I think you might even have murdered her in that instantaneous moment of decision, which way to swerve... run her down like a dog, purposely... to lock up the whole package nice and neat. Wasn't it you who in mocking me said we have-to beat down the lower orders? Or was that Tom? Wasn't Miranda one of the lower orders, out of control, literally at the gates, intruding aggressively with her phone calls at the most intimate 'family' moments?

"Go and run off with your darkie grease-ball, your Flamenco adoring greaser spick. Did you know that high class Spaniards hate the Flamenco and how it reflects upon their nation... call it a whorehouse Gypsy dance? It's the flacks for the great unwashed who call it a masterpiece of the oral and intangible heritage of humanity. There is an anarchist society that demands that clog dancing be declared the cultural equal of the classic ballet? They want an official proclamation... equal time with the Bolshoi or they'll blow it up. Next it will be that asinine Irish jigging where they are paralyzed from the waist up... dreamt up by some jokester who wanted to perfectly imitate wooden marionettes strung-up, spastic below the waist.

"You think we don't know. Everybody knows. Tom knows. He doesn't understand. Tom's the one who said: 'Africa begins at the Pyrenees'. Or was that me."

No Respect

From the papers of Thomas Buchanan, written in pencil in a strange hand; without explanation:

> Fitzgerald was never accorded the respect he deserved. In his mind's eye he was a great writer and as such a great man. We are social beings even the most self-reliant and self-sufficient of us. It is inevitable that we see ourselves as reflected in the eyes of others. In his photographs there is not the slightest air of greatness. He appears wimp-like, weak and beaten.
>
> There is a story of him going to a Hollywood party thrown by Norma Shearer and Irving Thalberg and performing some skit as the other guests were doing, and being drowned out with boos by some pompous silent film star, John Gilbert or some such clown; one of the finest writers of the twentieth century booed by an arrogant fool. That's a potent image for Fitzgerald's entire life.

Suitable Behavior in Hollywood

From the papers of Thomas Buchanan, uncatalogued, unnumbered, undated:

> The Fitzgeralds didn't comprehend correctly what was suitable behavior in Hollywood. These were not the decadent lazy rich Fitzgerald and

Zelda were accustomed to back home, but
rather a kind of self-made aristocracy,
industrious and self-disciplined professionals
steeling themselves for the long hours on the
movie set.

> "Hollywood is not gay like the magazines
> say but very quiet. The stars never go out
> in public and everyplace closes at
> midnight." Zelda

Yeh. They have-to get up in the morning to work.

An Old Dodge from Winslow

After his first visit to the Buchanans Nick was
eventually able to pull himself together enough to buy
himself an old Dodge, from Winslow, of all people, at
an inflated price. Nick kept making outrageous passes
at the woman at the garage and was absolutely
thrilled, if somewhat taken aback, that they
reciprocated. They misinterpreted his signals and he
theirs. He didn't seem to understand that a trip
upstairs was part of the deal, part of what he
bargained for.

Actually, driving the Dodge was another matter; it was
back in the "shop" for body work on a weekly basis.
Winslow proffered a poor man's transport service; he
would drive whatever repaired or purchased car to the
customer and then walk back to his own pintsized
Main Street; he knew all the shortcuts and where he
could trespass with impunity. He looked forward to the

walks, an excuse to take hours off from the wasteland of soot and cinders and walk in the providential shadow of millionaires. He could have had one of the women follow him and drive him back; Miranda knew how to drive, haltingly. He claimed he didn't want to leave the place alone; that he couldn't afford to sacrifice the business; but that wasn't the reason. At first, he had been stopped by police cars who would invariably enquire:

> "May we help you? Have you broken down?"

which really meant:

> "What the hell are you doing here, you dumb fuck? Don't you know you don't belong out here? We got our eye on you."

The first few times they would deliver him back to his down-scale Main Street to confirm his story. But after a while they knew him by sight, made an exception and would shrug: "It's only Winslow." Only Winslow. It became an ironic mantra before and after the bloody murders with a different twist:

> "It's only Winslow."

On the fateful day he had been seen by a motorcycle cop and calls of complaint had tumbled in about a crazed man trekking the roads and trespassing the wide lawns and entangling hedges. "It's only Winslow." It was repeated so often it was no longer vaguely funny, if it ever was.

Winslow was a practiced, wary walker attuning himself to the particular sounds of approaching cars which he learned to recognize, even as they were gaining ground on him from his rear. On that future inauspicious day, he would blaze his own path chopping with his body through the meticulously pruned ornamental bushes like a shark gone berserk on fresh surfer chum served up bloody and raw.

One cop who recognized him from his solitary treks called him, lying there "deader-an-a-mackerel", blood simple, "poor blood-simple fool", which was misinterpreted and misquoted by the press which blared the headline: Cop Calls Assassin BLOOD THIRSTY. But blood-simple is not blood-thirsty. He went blood simple in Poisonville, not from The War but from the aftermath; the befuddled, frightened mentality after a long-drawn-out entanglement in ferocious conditions; so steeped in violence or the violence of intolerable circumstances of one kind or another that sensitivity to it has evaporated. His neighbor in purgatory, Mike Elias said of him:

> "He used to tell me that God forsook America, skipped out... ditched... left it to its own devices... sat back and laughed, dropping matches to watch us... scurry like ants. He was so close... so... so close. He just about made it atta here alive... against all the odds. But the empty ghost of god, Doctor T. J. Mecklenburger... him with the dead vacant eyes... wouldn't let him go... took him close, held him tight and whispered in his ear the way to hell."

This was back in the day when a host thought nothing of letting his drunken guests drive off with a friendly wave-off at the door, the kiss-off as an accessory to negligent homicide, to play a life and death variation of bumper cars, a blood sport, while divining their way home aimlessly, targeting the ambulatory locals for their delectation, to see how quick they can jump, like scared rabbits, into the roadside bushes.

Dodge Under the Shed Roof

By celestial navigation a thoroughly well-oiled Nick managed to inch back to his Great Neck Manse after another night of drunken revelry, or what passed for revelry, at the Buchanans; Jordan failed to show; again.

He pulled the old Dodge under the shed roof, shrouding it from the rain and dark and took off his shoe gingerly, almost indecently, lewdly peeling off the moist, sticky sock with a peculiar delicacy, nauseated by the festering stink, as if undressing a wound that declined to heal; he rubbed and stroked the small, repulsive, bone tired foot, a foot which he dared never expose to anyone, staring sneakily, with embarrassed covetousness, at Gatsby's colossal mansion, glowing like Coney Island in the night, looming over him like a hulking giant, massively erect, a portent, a tethered balloon, outlandish in captivity, meant only to travel in, a balloon which when you weren't looking would float high into the sky and disappear; only the never-ending rope remained visible, an astonishing rope which only the trickster could cut without losing it irretrievably; levitating, a big yellow Chinese lantern with the pole knocked out from under it.

It was the devil that stalked him in his dreams clomping around with monstrous feet; in answer to his demonical prayers his own ugly little feet ballooning to gargantuan size, lifted him off the ground, just high enough to make him lose his balance and hit the hard ground.

Whip Out Like a Magician

From the archives of J. Gatsby, date obscured by water damage, number 11,588

Only a Fitzgerald, the wizard, the creator, could whip out like a magician from his old bag of tricks the intoxicating metaphor from the spilt blood of his ink; could find the dizzying image on the point of his pen, a way of expelling the Roman Catholic demons howling inside of him. His images are hallucinogenic and press up against, cozy-up to the boundaries of terrifying irrationality.

He paid an extravagant price for everything. He courted, no he made love to failure; personal humiliation was his private catastrophe; reality could climb the ladder but never touch the dream; illusion itself was the climbing rope from which he hanged himself in an Irish style suicide by whiskey dragged out pitilessly over a sinking lifetime. How many decent writers drove themselves to distraction and exhaustion to cover their debts of one kind or another: Walter

Scott, Dumas, Dostoevsky, Balzac, Lamartine and countless others?

Let us blame no writer that drowns himself in a whiskey death; in a one hundred proof goblet of fake dreams; or are dreams fake by their very definition or are they the only "reality" that matters?

Bernard Shaw, (an Anglo-Irishman who went native and pretended otherwise) has said of the Irish:

> "An Irishman's imagination never lets him alone, never convinces him, never satisfies him; but it makes him that he can't face reality nor deal with it nor handle it nor conquer it: he can only sneer at them that do ... and imagination's such a torture that you can't bear it without whisky... And all the while there goes on a horrible, senseless, mischievous laughter."

An accurate perception of reality may spur the imagination which should ideally serve as wings to escape from that unacceptable reality. But an escape to whiskey is not the exclusive refuge of the Irish. Of America's Nobel Prize winners for Literature five were drunks including Sinclair Lewis, Eugene O'Neill, William Faulkner, Ernest Hemingway, *F. Scott Fitzgerald*, John Steinbeck and then there was: Dashiell Hammett, Thomas Wolfe, James Thurber, John O'Hara, Jack London, Tennessee Williams, Raymond Chandler; and from across the sea: Dylan Thomas, Kingsley Amis, Malcolm Lowry and Philip Larkin.

There are those who have proposed an existential explanation for Fitzgerald's drunken debauchery, which even Edmund Wilson alludes to with the typical pompous airs of the prissy disapproving schoolmarm that he remained steadfastly to the very end of his fat, bloated life.

If society's most revered institutions are in fact ridiculous, the deserving object of the merciless scorn which Fitzgerald subjcctcd them to, then the sanest and even most honorable course may be to escape the absurdity through the exhilaration and thrill of a descent into the immediate. If these inescapable structures of society are absurd and irremediable, why not... why not drown in whiskey?

But if institutions, the structures of society, at least in theory, <u>can</u> be redeemed, reformed, this leads to anarchism, bloody revolution and endless class war not necessarily to death by alcohol.

But even if beyond its corrupt institutions the world itself is utterly absurd, inevitably and necessarily corrupting those institutions, it does not mean we have to succumb to its absurdity. There is the power of the mind to create meaning where there is none; call this delusion if you will, but an empowering delusion it can be. To wallow hopelessly in the absurdity of the world is useless if often wildly entertaining, preciously trendy, puerile, and prurient, pornographic even, an ignoble, obscene capitulation, abject prostration. This kind of pessimism or rather realism leads to weakness, is weakness; optimism, no matter how insubstantially founded more likely leads to power even if that optimism is a mind trick, the power is real, an exercise of will, an assertion of identity, an end-in-itself.

It is better to be an optimist and a fool than a pessimist and right.

Life has-to be given a meaning because of the obvious fact that it has absolutely no meaning. Henry Miller said something like this.

Tell the truth, and they'll accuse you of writing black humor.

> "We are fabulists, all of us; we reconstruct with handicapped brains what we half-knowingly fantasize as the factual truth and vehemently deny that we lie through rotten teeth."

Abject failure was the proximate cause of Fitzgerald's personal calamity; also, the breakdown of that vulnerable, susceptible manner of self-confidence which is founded on illusion, on this dream, this imagination of self. Like Nick's Gatsby he grudgingly came to realize that experience could never measure up to the dream; increasingly he learned how pathetic his efforts were, to be the man he struggled in his own way to be. He knew, too, that only the imagination can bridge the gap; but only with a suspension bridge of hanging rope weathering ominously in the sun.

To be possessed of ideals is to be self-deceived, because of the very nature of ideals, but to attempt to endure bereft of them is to live vacantly and vainly, thwarting an innate, ingrained, human craving. A commitment to a grand ideal by those rare men, while by the evidence of the world is dubious at best, it is none-the-less worthy of our conscientious scrutiny; more properly it should be observed with a reverential, if dumbfounding wonder.

Cast Their 'Characters' in Concrete

From the archives of Jordan Gatsby "recording" Thomas Buchanan in the middle of one of his perorations:

> "Writers too often cast their 'characters' in concrete; they craft a type, a caricature, consistent, cohesive, and predictable while people in the world are unpredictable, complex, contradictory, ambiguous. Such a writer's characters may develop but they develop in highly predictable ways.

> "This Joyce fellow does a decent job creating or recreating a world but it is a nauseating world of small, mean, stupid, insular people that makes you want to slam down the book so that you catch it before it invades, poisons your consciousness, sickens your soul.

> "And he's not the first to create this 'stream of consciousness' crap which is too often a cover for muddle and a deficiency of discipline.

> "This Norwegian fellow does it better, making instability of character his core. What does he say? I will make my hero laugh when sensible

people think he ought to cry. The disconnected... the outcast.... They are his heroes... alienation, existentialism, surrealism... his subject."

Daisy:

Tom. Would you please, please be quiet? You're making my brain hurt.

Tom:

I'm so very sorry Daisy. I had no idea you had a brain.

Jordan:

Come now children, play nice.

Daisy:

I just can't stand it anymore. Nobody knows what he's talking about or cares.

Jordan:

That's not fair. I care. Where did you get a translation from the Norwegian?

Daisy:

Stop it. Stop it... both of you. You're ganging up on me. I can't stand it. You both planned this little farce between you... this charade. There is nobody with that ridiculous name. Tom does that, he makes things up. He doesn't like the way the world is, so he makes things up, invents his own world. He tells me stories, false facts that I'm not well-informed enough to know are phony, then he laughs up his sleeve at me. He tried to reinvent himself but it didn't stick. Nobody believed him. So, he's stuck, stuck with the same old self which he doesn't like very much.

Tom, paying absolutely no attention to Daisy:

"Actually, I had a tutor who happened to be Norwegian... University graduate who used to sing to me in Nor..."

At this point, Daisy screamed as if mortally wounded. Everyone ran to Daisy's aid. But Tom accustomed to Daisy's violent theatrics, as if oblivious, held forth in a tongue only he, of those in the room, understood. If it were French or Spanish, I think Daisy's reaction would have been less hysterical. But the fact that it was to her mind such an exotic tongue, whether it was Norwegian or old Anglo-Saxon, or Old High German or the opening stanza of Beowulf, really didn't matter; it burned through Daisy like some magic incantation accusing her of what she was. Tom later told Jordan it was the opening passage of a book he had read. But Tom was known to lie, was famous for his ironic lies, like an old timey newspaperman concocting hoaxes and watching to see who gets the joke. The incantation might have been no more than skillfully harmonious Germanic sounding gibberish.

Tom:

Den lange, lange Sti over Myrene og ind I Skogene, hvem har trakket op den? Manden,

Mennesket, den forste som var her. Det var ingen Sti for ham. Siden fulgte et og andet Dyr de svake Spor over Moer og Myrer og gjorde dem tydeligere og siden igjen begyndte rawi anden Lap at snuse Stien op og gaa den naar han skulde fra Fjaeld til Fjaeld og se til sin Ren.

The chant was melodic in a Gregorian way, each word searing, a red-hot rivet and still they poured forth unstoppable, scalding water from a broken volcanic spigot.

The Mysterious Stranger

It was only years later that I heard the story that helped explain Tom's seeming mastery of what turned out to be the Norwegian tongue. The story of the Norwegian tutor who sang Norwegian songs to him was patently absurd. And yet not so absurd.

When his mother was a young woman there was an assistant to Mister Thomas Buchanan Senior who originally showed up for a gardener's job but so impressed the Senior Buchanan that he made him his personal driver and in short order promoted him to secretary and personal assistant. The Senior Buchanan was usually a stickler for flawless references carefully verified, but in this case, inexplicably, he threw all caution to the wind for a man who may well have descended from the clouds or risen out of the primordial swamps of Louisiana. The mysterious stranger was possessed of no formal education or at least no evidence of any in the form of credentials or degrees; he was self-made, such as he was, and self-educated with a voluminous knowledge much of it in error, a learning with vast gaping holes in it typical of the supremely arrogant autodidact and he was gripped by a passion, a compulsion, to get it all down, to write. Although he stepped or washed upon these very foreign shores penniless, an itinerant wanderer with an uncanny knack to insinuate himself; devoid of outside connections; he had the natural air of a born aristocrat or rather of a stage actor one imagines would play an aristocrat; tall with striking good looks he made most of the reigning grandees resident to the place look genetically degenerate.

Mrs. Buchanan resented her husband's new man, begrudging him the obvious dispensations which to her mind he was unworthy of. There are rumors that she too fell sway to the power of his charms but she in no way ever openly acknowledged this fact.

She had been barren her seven years with Thomas Buchanan and yearned desperately for a child. Buchanan longed equally for an heir. Buchanan never suspected a thing and Mrs. Buchanan projected the image of the ever-proper lady. Mr. and Mrs. Buchanan linked together, joyously, proclaimed it a miracle. He would fulfill his responsibility and continue his line; his house would stand.

And if the Senior didn't believe in the basic decency of mankind, then at least he himself would be decent, regardless. Buchanan was staunch in his conservative principles, believing in noblesse oblige with an emphasis on the oblige. And if he believed in the born superiority of the ruling-class he also believed that any one demonstrating superior talent should be welcomed to become part of that ruling class, with an appropriate initiation, of course. The aspirer had a responsibility to take pains to prove himself. Willing! Intelligent! Quiet! Honest! Grateful! Modest! These were the essential characteristics required from the new man. The fact that Knut possessed only one of these traits seems to have escaped Master Tom entirely. The fact that the "Norwegian fellow", as the staff called him, although he spoke far better English than they did, might have no inclination whatever to prove anything to anybody was simply beyond his frame of reference.

Buchanan had been astounded to learn that his charge, (as he condescendingly thought of him), in his few free hours, had become a valued assistant to a local Lutheran minister, wrote incendiary editorials for a local temperance magazine and preached sparsely attended lectures on Balzac, Flaubert, Zola, Ibsen, Strindberg; and other Scandinavian writers. The problem was his tendency to give impromptu orations to whoever would listen and often to those who wouldn't and resisted.

The new man was not let go for cause, quite the contrary; he bolted as soon as he had the chance. Buchanan obligingly provided the excuse.

Buchanan came from a long line of self-righteous abolitionists; the kind that burned and pillaged the South with a kind of priggish bravado and sanctimonious manic glee, exacting god's revenge as they saw fit. His kind had always adopted the Negro with a paternalistic, condescending, untouching embrace.

When Buchanan took on the new Black driver with impeccable credentials it was too much for Knut; it chased him straight off the continent in a rage. Before departing he held forth with an Old Testament fury venting his hatred not for the Black Man, not in the least, but for stupid America:

> "The Negroes are and will remain Negroes, an emergent human form forcibly extracted from the jungle, rudimentary appendages on the corpus of white society. Instead of founding an intellectual elite, America has established a mulatto stud farm."

If it was any consolation, he also hated the British, viscerally, who he regarded as a pest to all their neighboring countries, where they spread their tourism, gawking at the native folk like an inferior species, props for their amusement; and more despicable still, their vile sports enthusiasm.

He loathed the American baseball more than Wolf ever did. He found it juvenile, silly, unmanly, "sisterish", beyond ridiculous. He lacked the meticulous elegance, contacts and clout to rig the World Series, which he would have done if he could, simply for the fun of it. He yearned instead to blow it sky high along with all its harebrained fans: "overgrown idiot kinder folk", he called them; with the help of well-placed high explosives and the cooperation of the anarchists whose intimate company he liked to keep. Sports represented to him an area of American customs where democratic inclination, which he loathed in any event, inevitably surrendered to:

> "...atavistic impulses, reversion to the mad howling of a backward savage tribe: the worship of authority, the celebration of discipline and conformity, the absorption of the individual's voice drowned in the mindless roar of the crowd:

> "They unembarrassedly cavort like big sissies in funny clothes and make believe it is an easy substitute for the manliness they obviously lack."

He did not consider fisticuffs a sport in any way related to these infantile ball games; rather it was the manly art of self-defense. He had been a formidable bare-knuckle boxer in his youth and a lethal streetfighter.

I Rigged the Stupid World Series

Wolf knew Comiskey, dealt with him personally, knew him to be a crook, although a "secret crook" and carefully connived his scrupulous revenge:

> "Comiskey comes from the world of the established, deep-rooted wealth, which, though straitlaced and sneering at barefaced kinds of illegality... goes in for bribery, blackmail, and scheming to keep and amalgamate its dirty criminal power."

Everybody hated Comiskey, especially his own players, who he repeatedly cheated out of promised bonuses. They were called the Black Sox long before the fix. Comiskey made them pay to launder their own uniforms and they protested by coming out on the field covered in filth. But Wolf seemed to hate everybody connected to this "amusement" as he called it.

Wolf:

> "This was a game played by ignorant thugs and bigots, who hated Jews and Negroes... with disgusting habits, barflies incapable of an honest day's work... even my guys, not exactly the crème de la crème, didn't like delivering bags of payola to this lowlife scum. Ty Cobb beat up his teammate, Ed Siever, continuing to pummel him as he lay unconscious on the ground, kicking him mercilessly in the head. Cobb stormed into the stands viciously attacking a heckler who was missing most of one hand, and part of the other, having been wounded in a workplace accident, with spectators screaming for Cobb to stop:
>
>> 'He has no hands. He has no hands!'
>
> "I knew this one guy, and he was not a totally stupid guy... talked about this inane game as if it were really important... this professor, this putz... some professor. How did he put it:
>
>> 'I am not one of those who can live without illusion or without the hope of illusion; I am not that grown-up or up-to-date. I am

a simpler creature, tied to more primitive patterns and cycles. I need to think something lasts forever, and it might as well be that state of being that is a game.'

"Or some such shit... Would you believe this is baseball he's talking about? This is from a professor... in a genuine university, which has students that pay good money, which gives out degrees... What kind of a university would have such a professor? This is a child... stuck in his crib with shit in his diaper and probably shit smeared all over his face because he doesn't know any better. This is a professor? This is a putz.

"This is the kind of clown who inspired me. For him and his ilk, but especially with him in mind, I rigged the stupid World Series. And I'd do it again, every year... and I did, I did. But after the first they never found out it was rigged... that's the incredible beauty of it. The bets were placed more carefully. Fixing is easy... the bums practically fall all over themselves scuffling for the payoff. It's them that came to me. Like cheap whores come begging at my door for their fix:

'Please fuck me Wolfie. Please fuck me more.'

It's putting down the bets without showing your hand... that's the trick. The real art is screwing the chumps good, but them never finding out they got fucked. Kind of like rape after being slipped a mickey. They wake up with this strange feeling but no precise recollection.

"This Lardner character had it all wrong. The crooks didn't corrupt baseball... baseball was always corrupt to its rotten core from the start. We only cashed in on the corruption and made them eat their own shit with gusto while they sent compliments to the chef and left a big tip."

"Kenesaw Mountain Landis, who tried to clean out the city sewers with a box of wet Kleenex:

> 'Baseball is something more than a game to an American boy; it is his training field for life work. Destroy his faith in its squareness and honesty and you have destroyed something more; you have planted suspicion of all things in his heart.'

"America has been brought low... down into the gutter, from the Puritans... tight assed bastards though they were... they had their real dream and their New Eden... to the New Republic of the men who started this county like Jefferson, Washington, Madison, Franklyn and Hamilton and my personal hero Thomas Paine... and like that racketeer Carnegie... who though he crushed his competitors like bugs talked a good... a very good line. His God-chosen rich men would lead us out of the wilderness and make all America rich... from this to a dopey children's game played by hooligans who you wouldn't let your sisters go anywhere near, never mind your mother."

Wolf thought it was a fraud and maybe he got some perverse joy in methodically bursting balloons, a hopping mad trickster armed with pins. It wasn't enough to expose the feet of their (by "their" he meant the idiot goyim, who make an athletic performance the repository of all their pathetic hopes; though he never says as much) gods as unfired clay; he had to pulverize the feet to fine dust with a ballpeen hammer wielded with an intoxicated glee, watching the feetless gods lose their balance, teeter, totter, shake violently then tip over; rotten trees in an empty wood, fall and shatter; all the while laughing hilariously.

Wolf had been a superb athlete, a "real athlete", which he was careful to distinguish from the little boys playing with their balls or the beer gut couch potatoes, semi-comatose, reminiscing vicariously of a glory that was never theirs. He was a warrior, a boxer in his youth; set a state record for the 100-yard dash while in high school and could swim like a fish. But most of all he loved boxing, "the purity, the cleanness of it", pitting one man directly against another, "mano a mano". He also loved the ponies, which he rigged; taking some of the enthusiasm out of it.

He would if he could, bring back gladiatorial combat, fighting to the death for the honor of the good fight which brought into serious question the soundness of his judgment on the entire issue.

Wolf:

"This is what we've degenerated into... that some queer coach can stand up and pontificate in front of these poor boys... that sports represented the most direct and secure passage into the world of men.

"This is no initiation into real manhood... it's a way to sidestep manhood... to substitute a phony rite of passage because you could never reach the standards to pass any real test. And you don't even have to play sports... all you have to do is watch, pick up the patter like you're interested... pure voyeurism. This whole thing is for very sick fucks who can't get it up. I'd like to shove a spear into the little hand of one of these armchair jocks and launch them with a boot in the ass into the jungle... to kill a lion... a fucking lion with a spear and their bare hands... then and only then would they have earned their manhood... then and only then would they be allowed to fuck women."

Norwegian Cook

Young Tom Buchanan was taken under the wing of the Norwegian cook who was a second nanny to him. It was rumored that the cook was Knut's mother and that it was she who was the stalking horse who insinuated her son into the household with the subversive idea of cuckolding the master and initiating a new race of supermen; but this was ludicrous since she had never laid eyes on Knut before that first-day he materialized like a strayed dog coming home. The cook suspected what the others couldn't see. She adopted Tom in her own mind long after Knut deserted them; in her heart she considered his abrupt departure an abandonment; he didn't even so much as say goodbye.

By the time Tom grew into the image of his father there were conveniently few left who remembered that father, the staff rotated, new blood brought in. The cook having formed a bond with the young Tom was one of the few who could in no way be induced to leave even by way of bribery. Although she was never given formal notice it would have taken a forcible eviction by burly men to drag her howling from her stove with the young Tom clinging to her apron. The Senior Buchanan, who saw only Tom's Nordic good looks and amazingly quick intelligence, was either blind or chose not to see.

But there were those like the holdout cook who suspected that taking-on the black driver so long ago was no coincidence. The Senior Buchanan was well-aware of Knut's tenacious judgments. The driver stayed less than a year and exploited his position to step up in the world. Though a professed ardent believer in Negro rights this was the first Black person Senior had ever hired and strangely or not so strangely, it would be his last.

Exactly what Knut knew is the unanswered question. There was never a question of whether Mrs. Buchanan would run off with him or whether he wanted her to. The fact that he was impoverished was entirely beside the point, at least as far as Knut was concerned; it was irrelevant. Knut thought too highly of himself to let a mere lack of money stand in the way of his exalted self-regard. He was no egalitarian, nor even a democrat. "Egalitarianism was the enemy of excellence" he pontificated. He believed that social harmony existed only where each person knew his place which place would be based on talent, intelligence and hard work; his own place was naturally at the very top and he resolutely believed that he would rise inevitably to that pinnacle.

The Senior Buchanan was the better man, by his own dim lights, an ethical man, although one could say the same of Knut, by his own lights; kinder, more understanding, a better husband than Knut could even conceive of being.

Mrs. Buchanan was mesmerized or dumb-founded by Knut's speeches and they were speeches:

> "I take life as it comes, as it is. Who am I to change it? If I don't like it, I will enumerate that which is unacceptable (not I will tell you what I don't like). It is absurd and to the best of my ability I will tell you why it is absurd or will tell you in my own way I don't care that it is absurd. I may laugh at it, but as far as changing it; the fight would be futile. I would be crashing my head into a brick wall."

This was his idea of intimate, compelling conversation, wooing the womenfolk, and it worked. Knut spoke English with a studied precise excellence which just missed being ridiculous. He was very much missed by all, except, of course, the Black driver who marveled at his own unaccustomed position and the new power at his fingertips; there was an added triumphalism in his step which the Master found disconcerting, if not positively ludicrous. He wrote him sterling references and aided him in his move up in the world and out of his house.

Modern Man

Found in the archives of Thomas Buchanan, untitled, undated, uncatalogued:

> Does not the artist, especially the writer, create his own world while existing exclusively in his imagination; does he not achieve a reality through his creations more beautiful and transcendent than the humdrum, stale, grubby "real" world in which we are doomed to drag our leaden feet?
>
> Nick's Gatsby's quest is not for an external treasure or the object of his desire but rather for himself; not by looking within to discover it but by creation and recreation, to give birth to it. This is a greater burden, a higher task than seeking a grail or rescuing a damsel in deadly distress.
>
> He is modern man, which is man as artist; existence precedes essence; he defines his own; he does not search outside of himself for the

meaning of existence, for some holy grail, for some secret that if discovered will explain everything; nor does he look within himself, as if contemplation will reveal that same secret.

He is the man of action; for the conception cannot live alone in his head but must be fulfilled, proved and proofed in the world outside of him. This essence exists not in the mind of some God but in the mind of modern man the self-creator.

The artist like the self-made man, who is the artist-creator of himself, is god-like; he creates an existence limited only by that which he can envisage, alive in his own world only, in which his dreams materialize, ghosts incarnated in vulnerable flesh and red blood.

And if he comes crashing down, blown out of the sky by the iron cannon balls of actuality shot high, to the hard unyielding concrete earth beneath, he can be sustained by the memory of that flight, for his moment of transcendent glory, broken, bleeding, beating wings singed but glorified by the flames of an imaginary sun that dwarfs our own with a blinding light.

The Ghost

The following is a verbatim transcript from the files of James Gatsby based presumably on a voice recording.

It is also possible that Buchanan is one of the speakers and transcribed the conversation from memory; which, however, doesn't explain how it came into the possession of Gatsby. It is not based on one of Gatsby's recordings because it would have been designated as such and the speakers would have been identified. It is dated 1929 and specifies that three or perhaps four people are speaking but does not name the speakers nor does it distinguish between them in the transcript. I originally separated the words among four speakers titled speakers one, two, three and four; but since this is conjecture on my part, I thought it would be better to let the reader make up his own mind since he has before him the same transcript that I have. The transcript:

Did you notice that Nick's ghost seems to understand Gatsby better than Nick?

What ghost? What are you talking about?

Oh, I'm sorry. The writer... the writer.

What writer? Do you mean Fitzgerald?

He means the one who helped Nick polish the work: the ghost writer.

Well, call him that instead of being cute and calling him the ghost.

But it seems so appropriate, like a magic muse taking corporeal form. Who else but a supernatural spirit called forth by a magician, a wizard could produce such a work.

Some people think Nick doesn't even exist... that he's a construct of the ghost or of Fitzgerald.

That's ridiculous.

Did you read Nick's original?

I didn't but a friend of mine at Scribner's did. He says the ghost is the real writer. He didn't believe in Nick... in Fitzgerald either.

But the ghost was a drunk, a fool... he exposed himself at dinner parties.

No... that was Fitzgerald... because he didn't think he was big enough.

You're making excuses. I didn't know you knew him.

Not well.

Does the fact that you're a drunk and ineffectual buffoon who exposes himself mean you can't be a fine writer?

I grant you, he was a boob, a real buffoon.

The question stands: can you write wisely without being wise?

How did the ghost know Gatsby?

I didn't know he knew him.

Did he know him?

I saw him at one of the parties.

Saw who? Which party?

Gatsby's.

No, I mean which one.

I don't know which one.

But the ghost wrote nothing but mostly trash before and after.

You're confusing him with Fitzgerald... but the same can be said of Nick.

Who said Nick doesn't exist... in reality?

Lots.

That's absurd. You might as well say Gatsby doesn't exist.

Whose Gatsby?

Do you mean who is Gatsby or whose Gatsby?

Both, I guess.

You can't mean both; it's either one or the other.

No, I mean whose Gatsby. If you answer the one it answers the other, well, to some extent.

No, it doesn't.

Didn't you say, they say Gatsby didn't exist? You might as well say you don't exist or I don't exist... that we are all creations of some hack.

The question stands. You can't question whether he exists unless you know which one you are questioning. The question stands. Whose Gatsby?

Nick's Gatsby, Gatsby, is pure fantasy... the wishful conjurings of an overwrought adolescent mind... exaggerated, unstable. He himself admits his incredulity was submerged in fascination. Because of his impressionability, Nick clutches an image; he's an old lady with a holy picture, a persona; and clothes it with his wishes... fascination generates credulity. The Gatsby or Gatsby, if you prefer, that he foists upon us is a cliché and on insubstantial bona fides he becomes a supernatural wonder.

Who said fascination generates credulity, wonder makes us need to believe?

You just did.

The ghost comes closer but he's necessarily lashed to Nick... can only manage to get the word out through Nick.

That's not true. There are other devises. Fitzgerald undermines Nick repeatedly and by calling him into question we manage to get the picture.

What? We have Nick, who even the ghost regards as a fool but who is a fool himself and maybe even a greater fool than Nick. And from this mishmash we expect to get at the truth

Who says?

What do you mean who says?

I mean who says we have to unearth the truth?

What's the point of reading it if we can't find the truth?

The truth. The truth, you say. Whose truth? You can't stand the truth. The truth is impossible. You, excuse me, <u>we</u> can't stand the truth. We will wither at its touch; shrivel up at its sight. It will make us miserable. It will destroy us.... How about just the glory of the experience... confused, misled, delusional as we are, the imaginative experience itself... transcendental... the mind experience, an end in itself, the only meaningful end.

If you're going to live in or for this magical imaginational experience you might as well trip out on drugs; if the reality of it is irrelevant.... if truth doesn't matter.

And what megalomaniac has the unmitigated gall to shove the truth, his version of the truth in our face, with the idea of rousing us from our supposed stupor, like a dog's face smeared with his own shit to house break him, not to make him free? Truth? The truth will set you free only after it's eaten you alive and spit you out. I get back to the question: whose truth?

Fuck the truth.

I am not talking about some big truth; I'm just talking about the truth of the story, the facts.

But that's the point; maybe the truth of the story is tied up with some big truth. You can't discover one without the other.

That's bullshit. And for Christ's sake stop calling him the ghost... it's a little bit too clever by half for me. Call him what he is... a ghostwriter or collaborator or alter ego or living muse or whatever.

A dim-witted person can make only certain, limited kinds of blunders, limited as they are by the size of his mind; but the mistakes open to a really intelligent fellow are far greater. But to the one who knows how terribly smart he is compared to the rest of the stupid world, the possibilities for true idiocy are breathtaking.

Who are you talking about? Are you trying to start a fight?

If the shoe...? (long pause) No not at all.

Besides I don't think it makes any sense. It's too clever by...

I think it does make sense.

You would... you said it.

Besides... I don't think the idea is original.

So few ideas are. But why would somebody repeat such a lame idea.

People are always repeating lame ideas. If they really thought about it themselves, they probably wouldn't repeat it. They'd realize how stupid it was.

Nick or the ghost, or whoever, seriously misleads us. He tells us Gatsby turned out all right. Is he serious? He's murdered, at least so far as the story is concerned. Everybody thinks he's murdered. Nick is a full-blown narcissist. He is directly complicit in three murders and he thinks Gatsby, or the creative fantasy which replaces him, turned out all right. He's fucking dead.

But the point is he's not dead.

Nick doesn't know that. Nick thinks he's dead. Besides, three people are dead, one of them very close to Gatsby.

Besides one was a prostitute the other her pimp.

You make it sound so black and white... a little money on the side... trying to make ends meet... to put together a nest egg... get away from it all. It was so much more complex. Winslow loved her and she was run down like a dog. He went crazy... he couldn't make her happy himself. She didn't walk the streets. She picked her lovers, clients, or whatever... from Manhasset and Great Neck... those who didn't want to make the trip in... all the way to the City.

It's as clear as day that Tom's affair with Miranda is a financial transaction. She was carefully attuned to price and market place values... she prudently chooses Tom, picks him up impressed by his shoes and suit. He's a commodity as much as she is. It was like a family business. Her sister came in on it... to share the overflow... to watch her back.

You keep confusing Nick's book with reality.

Winslow was so proud of the place. He was like a little kid who just built a palace with an erector set... giving his friends the grand tour. The interior apartments rivalled any penthouse on Park Avenue or so he bragged... though he had never been anywhere near a penthouse on Park Avenue. I think he honestly forgot that it was a whorehouse. If you called it that he would have been dumbstruck for a moment... his feelings wounded. He was a skilled carpenter and furniture maker... he missed his calling... he was a miserable motor car mechanic... good but miserable... he hated cars. The men he served with came by on Sundays to do the plumbing, electrical and marble work. They all asked him why he didn't fix up the outside... he said he liked it that way. He liked the surprise, the shock when they walked inside and up the magic steps ascending into another kingdom.

I thought it was business... he lost his money maker... that why he killed himself.

He didn't kill himself... that was the story they concocted for press consumption... less questions asked. He had six bullets in him. How do you shoot yourself six times? He took six bullets before he fired the one final fatal shot that went straight through the heart. He was a pistol marksman in the Marines, also a sniper in The War... 4th Marine Brigade... he picked off twenty-one Germans from on top of a church bell tower. They blew the tower out from under him with a howitzer, but he managed to survive... spread-eagle on top of a pile of rubble like he was claiming it or embracing it... it collapsed from under him... making him loose his footing. They say it was a sight to behold as the blasted rock tower descended ahead of him as if in a slow-motion movie... as if he was somehow the cause of the collapse and orchestrating it from above as a spectacular deception: the disappearing tower.

I remember him saying almost as if he had memorized it, repeating it like a holy incantation, a mantra:

> '...a Marine who is proficient in pistol marksmanship handles any challenge without escalating the level of violence or causing unnecessary collateral damage.'

And he was a Marine, a committed warrior conjured out of the mists of the past... like a Samurai on the streets of New York City... just like Gatsby. With six clumsily aimed bullets in him, he just had time to take out the three soldiers who were methodically, if inaccurately, filling him full of lead... he chose not to... he had hit his only chosen target dead on. In that sense he did kill himself. I don't think he ever signed the Armistice... he never declared peace... he didn't want to live... not without Miranda... she was his love and she loved him too in her own way... she did it all for him, for the both of them. Nick got the wrong love story... he missed the real one... he was too stupid to see it. He was too stupid to see anything. And she was not plump... she was voluptuous, curvaceous, and quite beautiful... stunningly athletic. She had been a dancer in her youth and stayed fit until the death car reduced her firm dancer's body to butcher cuts. Nick liked them anorexic with boy-like builds, wraiths, unsexed gamines minus the mesmerizing effervescence often erroneously associated with the term... devoid of flesh, unthreatening disembodied voices jingling only with the chinks.

But weren't they rolling in dough with Tom's deep pockets.

You don't understand. Tom didn't pay in so much hard cash money.

But he must have known that she was a prostitute.

He did.... but he didn't. I don't think he ever quite admitted it, to himself. He was such a pompous fool in so many ways that he thought she loved him for his undeniable charms.

But everyone knew. It was a kind of landmark... the whorehouse in the dump by the gas pumps... Mrs. Winslow and her sister displaying themselves incongruously, shoving in the nozzle suggestively with a wink, intoxicated by the rich organic smell emanating from the gas nozzle... making them breathless: Fuck under the ever-watchful eyes of Doctor Mecklenburger... he knows what you've done or more accurately couldn't care less... even if you do it again and again. The deus absconditus or more precisely deus otiosus, the idle god, the irresponsible creator retiring from the tired world... set the whole shebang in motion, didn't like what he started... then slipped out through a trap door like a third-rate conjuror to let in all run down like a racing automobile with a full tank of gas and no one at the wheel. His sightless, empty gaze, though without judgement, is without sense or reason. This creation was a Frankenstein horror; maybe he just ran from it; or stepped on it, a broken fiasco abandoned on the floor.

There were always motor cars out front.

But that was his legitimate business... he actually repaired and bought and sold motor cars. Tom paid without exactly admitting to himself that he paid... he supplied Winslow with a steady stream of customers, for the motor cars... he sold him his own cars at less than market value. That's why Winslow became so agitated... the accustomed car from Tom wasn't coming, not on schedule. He was in a panic. He didn't know how to go about collecting what was owed them without spoiling the show. Tom was descending into some kind of fantasy... some imaginative recreation of reality... breaking down... in a way. Winslow was saving to make their getaway. He had unearthed a buyer for his little Main Street, his diminutive version of the American Dream... living smack dab in the middle of New York City's garbage... and he almost had enough. He was going to start a medicinal herb farm in Hunterdon County New Jersey just west of Clinton... he loved it out there... he said it was like something out of a picture postcard that you tack on to the kitchen door, like those towns in Vermont that seem lost in time... some pre-industrial pastoral paradise... like America used to be or what we think it used to be. He wanted to go back. He wanted to find something he had lost... to get back to something he started with but hadn't been able to find again. He had lived there as a child. His father had owned a large and prosperous farm but had somehow been cheated out of it by means Winslow could never understand. The magic memory of that farm, that time, that place, was the only happiness Winslow had ever known; but it was a happiness after the fact in memory only.

But Tom was hogging too much of Miranda's time... expecting exclusive rights. The apartment in the city created a bigger problem... it took her away from her steady cash paying clientele and it was dangerous without Winslow's ever watchful eyes protecting the women and there is no doubt that he would protect them... that was his purpose... with his life if the occasion came up.

No Outside Commanding Authority

From the papers of Thomas Buchanan, uncatalogued, unnumbered, undated:

In Nick's book we are given no outside commanding authority against which to judge Nick's unreliable testimony.

Everything is filtered, distorted through the inept ignorant narrator, Nick. Even if he stumbled on the truth, he wouldn't recognize it. The pursuit of some accurate authority, the truth, is undercut repeatedly by the process of his searching. The more he searches the more he mucks things up; the muddier the water gets.

Like some film noir gumshoe, he never sees the whole picture clearly; he isn't part of the solution he's part of the problem. He makes things worse. He is an ignorant bit player but equally complicit with the leading actors.

He's like the reporter in *Citizen Kane*; the more he investigates the less he really knows. He never figures it out; he's as lost in the end as in the beginning; more so.

Two Unidentified Speakers

Transcript from the F.B.I. records, two unidentified speakers, date and circumstances unreadable, cover water and mold damaged:

"See, the problem is these guys all write. They may not consider themselves writers... may not publish what passes for the slicks these days... but they are all intoxicated with words... they love them... they all leave their testimony... their record... you just have-to dig for it. The best record is Jordan's but it's locked in a vault and her executor has the key... or the combination and nobody can even look at it until 2018.

Why that date?

I have no idea.

Maybe she wants to have the last word. I always had the feeling she was smarter than all of them... the real power behind the throne.

But Gatsby was very rich before he met her.

Only in money.

But she's dead. Why would it matter?

With this crowd you never know. She was so strong willed I wouldn't be surprised if she lived forever. She might be writing the definitive book right now under an assumed name, taking on the guise of a stumbling narrator to set the record straight once and for all."

Thoroughgoing Vulgarian

From the files of J. Gatsby, dated Oct 4, 1924. Number 5,240

It has been observed that jazz in Fitzgerald's *The Great Gatsby* exemplifies the debasement of the era. Jazz is seen as the consequence of the Anglo-Saxon upper crust surrendering its belief in itself, of losing its sustaining cultural myths, of voluntarily relinquishing the high culture for the low and pretending the low is just as good and tweaking it to make it more palatable to save face. According to this view they have lost the war and declared victory by adopting as their own the uniform and weapons of their enemies.

But Fitzgerald was not that perceptive, not consciously. He was himself a thoroughgoing vulgarian. He had no love of great art or music or even great literature; his reading list of chosen authors appalled his more culturally sophisticated friends.

One of the surest signs of the Philistine is his reverence for the superior tastes of those who put him down, who humiliate him. Somebody else said this first, particularly in-regard-to Fitzgerald; while cute it's worth repeating. It may not be true but it certainly applies to Fitzgerald who invited humiliation.

Edmund Wilson contrasts their reading at Princeton:

> "I had been reading Plato and Dante. Scott had been reading Booth Tarkington, Compton Mackenzie, H. G. Wells and Swinburne".

What a reading list. By what miracle did he escape the permanent taint of his early influences?

Like O'Hara, the "taint of his personality seeped into the way his books were received." We dislike Fitzgerald and his harebrained attitudes so much, consider him such an ignorant, self-indulgent, self-destructive fool that it does irreparable harm to our judgment of his work. As Edna St. Vincent Millay, who loathed the man, is famous for observing:

> Fitzgerald was a stupid old woman with whom someone has left a diamond; she is extremely proud of the diamond and shows it to everyone who comes by, and everyone is surprised that such an ignorant old woman should possess so valuable a jewel; for in nothing does she appear so inept as in the remarks she makes about the diamond.

The image itself is dead on, right down to the "old woman".

Fitzgerald had no desire to emulate the high culture of the previous generation of the select rich; he wished to mimic, instead, their most degenerate issue, with their compulsive and indeed perverse socializing, their unquenchable need to satiate their own vacuity with a daily carnival.

Zelda was perfectly literal and not entirely crazy and quite consistent when she expressed the wisdom to

Hemingway that Al Jolson was greater than Jesus Christ. Fitzgerald practically wets himself in venting his ridiculous, misplaced enthusiasm for Charlie Chaplin. He was heard to gush girlishly that Chaplin was:

> "…one of the greatest men in the world… and that his pictures are sophisticated and hilarious and will make him immortal".

Chaplin, a man who took himself very seriously and when off the screen carried himself like an aristocrat, significantly, was never heard to return the compliment. And though Chaplin may have been more than simply a slapstick clown, we are astounded when we steel ourselves to suffer through his admittedly skillful, if dated, shtick today, as an exercise in cultural anthropology, and sit slack-jawed in utter amazement at the level of mass hypnosis, the enormity of the infectious big lie that elevated him to the rank of a semi-deity. Chaplin's two-reelers are often coarse and vulgar, with the equivalent of adolescent fart jokes and a declared class warfare aversion to work and simple decent manners.

Both Fitzgerald and Zelda were thrilled by popular entertainment, Fitzgerald emasculated by it, always eager to play the fool, humiliating himself with his idiot opinions, ever the schoolboy juvenile panting breathlessly, the stage door Johnnie coming too soon. We are mortally embarrassed to disinter his facile gibberish:

> "We trembled in the presence of the familiar face of *The Birth of a Nation…*"

He wallowed in low culture and was besotted with junk writers. Fitzgerald wrote more tripe than any author of equal talent. And for those inept, incoherent fools who wish to redeem his whoredom by positing some supposed symbiotic relationship between his garbage and his masterpiece we have Fitzgerald's own words.

He wrote to Mencken in May 1925: "My trash for the Post grows worse". In a letter to Hemingway of September 9, 1929: "The Post now pays the old whore $4,000 a screw." But he'd been tramping those mean streets so long they were rote. He'd been a whore for so long that only the price fluctuated. In 1921, T. A. Boyd wrote in the St. Paul Daily News:

> "His short stories, almost without exception, show that there was one thing uppermost in his mind when he was writing them and that was no more nor less than $350."

In a letter to Maxwell Perkins concerning *The Great Gatsby* Fitzgerald acknowledges the "trashy imaginings as in my stories."

As for *This Side of Paradise* the consensus of informed critical judgment found it sophomoric, a novelty, pretentious, utterly puerile, coming along at the perfect time when the public had an insatiable appetite for this kind of twaddle. His good friend hit the target:

> "*This Side of Paradise* ... is really not about anything: its intellectual and moral content amounts to little more than a gesture... a gesture of indefinite revolt. The story itself, furthermore, is very immaturely imagined: it is

always just verging on the ludicrous. And, finally, [it] is one of the most illiterate books of any merit ever published (a fault which the publisher's proofreader seems to have made no effort to remedy). Not only is it ornamented with bogus ideas and faked literary references, but it is full of literary words tossed about with the most reckless inaccuracy ... full of malapropisms of the most disconcerting kind."

Although he lamented himself a prostitute and flagellated himself accordingly, he, nonetheless, gloried in the big bucks he reaped, rolled hilariously drunk in its muck and the interminable, incessant festival it bankrolled. And if his Gatsby's money was perceived as ill-gotten how much more so was Fitzgerald's own, who degraded and shilled a magnificent talent for a cheap, tawdry thrill. He was a fine bred race horse who harnessed himself to the plow, to bury potatoes in rocky dirt which spit out money. Whores only sell their bodies. Fitzgerald mutilated the best of his own soul, its pieces thrown to unworthy swine for filthy lucre. Gatsby, Nick's alter ego, his ideal self, was the most honest man of the bunch. I would rather be a gangster than a whore, any day; streetwalkers had a jump on him; better to sell your body than to sell your soul.

Baudelaire lamented to himself: "What is art? Prostitution." Perhaps he was having a bad day or having trouble figuring out what art was. Whether we write for the dollar or for the public taste or for the perceived taste of some imagined elevated intelligentsia who will pat us on the back like good dogs but pay us nothing, like the deadbeats that they are, or some future nebulous posterity which we naively presume will be wiser. Who is to say we who write are not all in danger of falling into prostitution.

Since the late nineteenth century artists have been obsessed with prostitutes. The conman, the shapeshifter, the self-made man, the man on the make, the man without a rock-solid inviolable core, if there is such a thing, became the new man. The new world, the city, was oily and slick, shifty, racing without a printed roadmap, ambiguous, an empty spectacle. Who the hell was who? With the passing of arranged marriages, without the careful knitting of family connections and the compulsive examination of roots, of provenance, how could we be certain? Was anyone what they pretended to be?

Sheila Graham

Sheila Graham, Fitzgerald's last lover, whose proclaimed background was nothing but a carefully constructed sham, a fabricated past as a British society lady, was branded by Fitzgerald, who had been taken in, as a prostitute. He wrote it in his own hand in big letters on her picture, on its back, while displaying its front.

Graham's parents were in fact Ukrainian Jews. Her father, a tailor, fled the pogroms, died of tuberculosis in Berlin. Her mother took the eight children to

England and lived in a basement in a Stepney Green slum. She provided for her children as best she could by cleaning public toilets. In 1914, her mother in desperation was forced to give Sheila up to the Jews' Hospital and Orphanage at Norwood. Graham's daughter Wendy Fairey tells us:

> "Entering this institution at age six, my mother had her golden hair shaved to the scalp as a precaution against lice. To the end of her life, she was haunted by the degradation of this experience. Eight years later when she 'graduated,' she had established herself as Norwood's 'head girl': captain of the cricket team and recipient of many prizes, including both the Hebrew prize and a prize for reciting a poem by Elizabeth Barrett Browning."

At eighteen, she married John Graham Gillam, whom her daughter Wendy Fairey describes as:

> "...a kindly older man who proved impotent, went bankrupt, and looked the other way when she went out with other men."

This husband became her Professor Henry Higgins, educating her in speech and manners and bankrolling her further social climb. She enrolled herself in the Royal Academy of Dramatic Arts and became a music hall dancer, one of the 'Cochran Girls.'

Graham had the uncanny ability to advance herself by latching on to a succession of older, powerful, wealthy men. How is this different than Fitzgerald's imagined Horatio Alger sycophant attaching himself to a Kodi or a Wolf? She shamelessly, if justifiably, advanced her career by concocting a self-serving fiction, *Beloved Infidel*, exploiting her relationship with Fitzgerald after he was dead. There is ample evidence that Fitzgerald not only despised her but despised himself for having been so totally taken in. He took his vicious revenge by broadcasting the secrets of her origins to her enemies; revealed by her in their most intimate revelatory moments together. The irony is that she is a product of self-creation every bit as astounding as that of the fictive Gatsby and is infinitely more admirable than Fitzgerald's undying, institutionalized love, Zelda. There is no snobbery quite so extreme as the snobbery of the "failed snob", the exposed bounder, the single-minded snobbery of the viciously snubbed. Fitzgerald remained a prisoner of his corrosive bigotry and racism right to the bitter end, poisoning even his final years.

Letters to his Daughter

Jordan preserved the bulk of her writing in her own papers, which are still "under seal", as my father mockingly referred to their safe-keeping. I think he was offended that their guardian, more properly their trustee is a literary agent acting on behalf of all of her children and grandchildren. This doesn't sound like a transcript of a voice recording; more like a short essay. It has no heading and is undated.

> "There are those who love his work, who love to imagine a wisdom gained by Fitzgerald as he

aged; there is none. Some cite the letters to his daughter as evidence of a ripening. Unfortunately, they are nothing more than the pathetic, vapid, weary reveries of an unregenerate sophomore romantic in a beaten and bloodied man of forty, a callow, fatuous, misguided, gifted little boy who got old, crumbled, and fell apart without ever growing up; he rotted without ever ripening. He was not 'young to the bitter end' but merely juvenile and puerile to his very bitterest end.

"And if he regretted his vicious bigotry as he neared his demise it was voiced more out of defeat than enlightenment; the pathetic pleadings of a pounded man bleeding on the ground in utter rout. It is always too convenient when people get religion and sing Halleluiah as they are about to fall into the grave, they've been digging assiduously for themselves their entire lives. Finally, his abhorrence was properly directed:

> 'I hated Italians once. Jews too. Most foreigners. Mostly my fault like everything else. Now I only hate myself.'

"This from the most despised of 'foreigners'. These words should be carved on his gravestone along with 'No Irish Need Apply'.

"There is no arrogance like the arrogated arrogance of the inferior, the excluded, who lay down a barrage of blinding smoke to hide what they are or what people think they are and are inadvertently poisoned by it.

"Fitzgerald loathed himself, loathed what he came from. He was morbidly, self-eviseratingly conscious of being Irish. As John O'Hara's alter ego in BUtterfield 8, Jimmy Malloy explains to the old money debutante Isabel Stannard: 'I am a Mick. I wear Brooks Brothers clothes and I don't eat salad with a spoon and I could probably play five-goal polo in two years, but I am a Mick. Still a Mick … The people who think I am a Yale man aren't very observing about people.' O'Hara himself had the further disadvantage of looking the part he so despised; fat, big ears and dopey face, a caricature of a drunken bartender. Fran Lebowitz, *The Paris Review*, 1993: "To me, O'Hara is the real Fitzgerald." Well, maybe not, but both were hounded by identical demons and both succumbed. O'Hara could be an embarrassingly bad writer, wallowing in it, while Fitzgerald could rise through his art, above the tacky, self-indulgent melodrama that was his own life.

"O'Hara, at least, had the moral superiority to empathize and identify with the others, who were also excluded by the old-money Anglo Saxons, while Fitzgerald, pathetically deluded as he was, fancied himself in league with this old-moneyed elite, who wanted no part of him; to look down upon the Jews, the Italians, the French, the Armenians, the Poles, or anyone else he could find to kick around.

"But a man who learned absolutely nothing, took away nothing."

Incorruptible Man in a Thoroughly Unscrupulous World

Discovered in the archives of Thomas Buchanan, untitled, undated and uncatalogued; author uncertain:

And if Fitzgerald's personal life was tawdry, chaotic, pathetic and absurd, tumbling clownishly down a drunken path of dissolution, sickness, failure and rejection, it is Fitzgerald the great writer standing over the ruin who never lost his majesty, the great man, wise and knowing, deep in his subconscious, manifesting himself through the sweat of endless rewrites, like the godly spirit that he was himself, exacting hard labor to be set free, to come to life on the flimsy paper page and live forever.

This may all seem bleak, even nihilistic, but it's not, not necessarily. It suggests that we are all delusional, in it all together cooperatively, reinforcing each other's delusions. It is not the "reality" of what happened that so much matters but the way we remember it, creatively through a godlike imagining. It is that blissful memory which exists timelessly, which supersedes time, time, which is, after all but a construct of our conscious workaday mind. Gatsby gives testimony to this truth.

And if you tell me he was a gangster, a racketeer, I say what of it. He helped me when I was in desperate need of it. He was better than all the lot of us; better than the perpetually campaigning politician always with his hand out, the judges on the take and the predator priest who rape the young sons of the criminally credulous, unembarrassedly, as if by divine right.

No Gatsby was all right; it was the small corrupt, mean world, unfit to encompass his godly dreams that finally broke his heart.

Gatsby, Nick and the ghost, who is not holy; they are all in this together. And they are each other in many ways. Gatsby may not have died that night and may have been as tough as Damascus steel, but Fitzgerald in his almost infinite ineptitude got just a part of him fundamentally right. He lived on, an incorruptible man in a thoroughly unscrupulous world.

Zerobbabel

The following is a purported conversation between Thomas Buchanan and an unknown person as found in the archives of J. Gatsby. The cover of the transcript is missing; the date and circumstances unknown:

In the 1920s Halbwachs and Durkheim argued that societal groups determine what is memorable and also how it will be remembered. Zerobbabel argues that we need to recognize society's ubiquitous cognitive role as mediator between individuals and their own experiences. Some fool preferred to refer to it as a remembrance environment, as the harmless sounding defanged mechanism through which ideas and concepts of a culture, culture mind you, culture without culture, gain access to individual brains.

Excuse me, I forgot who Zerobbabel was.

Fuck you.

What kind of way is that to talk? I'm just trying to learn. Talking to you is like going to school. Did I say talking? I meant listening. Do I get course credit for this? Is there going to be a test?

Fuck you, again.... No wait... I'm sorry... I like to bounce ideas off of you... they coalesce this way.

Bounce... did you say bounce? How about hitting me in the head with them and having them fall with a dead thud.

No... No... you're a good audience.

That's because I don't say anything.

That's not true... You're an incisive critic.

Would you just let me finish this thought? And then let me know what you think.

Societal groups determine not only how reality is remembered but how reality is perceived in the first place. We are suborned by our social environment, society's pervasive cognitive role as intermediary, intercessor between persons and what they only perceive as their own experiences. Reality is a mass hallucination into which we are coerced with all the magic guile of an underground secret police state. We are bombarded incessantly with the drumbeat of its relentless, insidious propaganda. How else to explain societal structures which are corrupt to their core; these structures would disintegrate, fly apart into social chaos without the illusion of justice, fairness, and order.

We elevate mountebanks and buffoons to lead us, applauding these nincompoops as deities because they reinforce our convenient and meticulously crafted lies. There is in fact no such thing as normal human memory; we have only culturally contrived memory molded to serve distinct objectives corresponding to diverse structural stratagems of society. Our minds are structured to manipulate and deceive us so that we can function efficiently in a corrupt society.

Wow. Do you expect me to comment on that?

Daisy's Granddaughter

I got a phone call from someone claiming to be Daisy's granddaughter. She revealed that her mother, Daisy's daughter, her only child, never died in that car wreck; that it was a hoax engineered by her loving father, Tom Buchanan with the help of Gatsby. She just wanted out; she couldn't stand the burden of the history, the interminable cars cruising by the house on a summer night like an endless funeral caravan. Everybody knew the story or thought they did thanks to the book. She was sick to death of gawkers. She hated the book.

Daisy's daughter, escaped to California, became a movie actress though not a big star; she worked for Gatsby for a while; retired at her height, modest though it was, to write the genuine true story which she claimed "no one dared to publish". She promised to send me the manuscript convinced it was a potential blockbuster. She refused to give me her real name, or address and I never did receive the book. Maybe she had second thoughts.

I started watching all of Gatsby's movies into the middle of the night seeing if I could get a glimpse of a familial look; I had seen many photographs of Daisy and of her daughter. I looked for Thomas Buchanan and James Gatsby. I unearthed a promising lead and hired a private investigator who filed encouraging reports weekly for six months and then stopped returning my phone calls. I guess he milked it for all it was worth or maybe there were secrets powerful people didn't want uncovered. Finally, his phone was disconnected; he seemed to have closed-up shop. I discovered that his license wasn't renewed. A neighbor told me he had gone to Tahiti but for some reason I didn't believe him. Tahiti? That's preposterous. I don't think he was murdered; that would have been plain stupid. He struck me as the type of man who could be bought off at a very reasonable price.

Then there was the priceless nitrate film footage turning up, ready to explode at the softest touch, purporting to show everyone, including Gatsby playing the impresario with the exaggerated hokey panache of a silent film star. For a time, I believed it was my grandfather but one old timer watching the film said it wasn't Gatsby at all but a look-a-like, an actor playing Gatsby in a film at a later date than that depicted. It was produced by Gatsby himself, when he owned the studio, but for some reason never released, or more likely released and subsequently lost. He might have had second thoughts, not wishing to dredge up painful memories or throwing it in their face; besides by this time he was already quite dead, technically.

And then there was the film from a lost Edison archive showing an acrobat magician on the high wire doing a double summersault backward flip and then disappearing in a puff of smoke; it could have been The Great Gatsby; it might have been him; but the film was of such questionable quality and from such a distance that it was impossible to tell for sure; it could also have been an early example of trick photography; however the audience would have had to have been professional actors because they looked genuinely awe-struck.

Then there was what seemed like an early documentary or "how-to" film, explicating in detail what was represented as an engineering feat; hauling this huge floating house out of the Sound like a gigantic whale fighting them the whole way, with hundreds of roustabouts choreographed in a precision caper; demonic June Taylor dancers hoofing to the rapid-fire beat; or Volga boatmen trudging with a lightning step tripping the light fantastic. How many must have marveled at the ghostly apparitions floating from the fog of some inland waterway, lagoon, inlet, fjord, firth or sound, ultimately rejecting it as some transitory hallucination, trick of the mind or eye. The nameless man with the "how to" film wanted a sizable sum for it, seeming to think it answered some essential riddle. But you have-to know the question and how to pose that question in precise language before the answer does you any good. I half suspected that he believed that I would use its trade secrets as the basis of a lucrative future business, hauling the homes of the rich like monstrous waterborne Winnebagos. What he didn't seem to realize is that they would sink like a stone if launched in the open stormy sea; but these tranquil waterways, cast upon, lead nowhere or to the uttermost ends of the earth, flowing ever into a hollow immense darkness dismal under a graying sky.

Graciousness of Buchanan's Grandson

Through the generosity and graciousness of Tom Buchanan's grandson I was allowed to spend extensive time studying the wide-ranging records that he left;

none have been catalogued but they have been carefully preserved, waiting anxiously on the shelf for some driven and determined descendant looking for the secret of how such a vast immeasurable treasure could possibly have been so depleted in one single generation. He seems to have written manically, maniacally, and continually without stop, as if keeping the wolf at bay; as if as long as he could write he could substantiate his existence and continue to live.

There are three finished novels; all having been submitted anonymously and summarily rejected by publishers; the rejection slips are markers in the books as if to prove to posterity what fools these publishers had been. He was too proud to purchase the publishing house, although a few well-placed phone calls would have done the trick; too proud to even underwrite the cost of publication which was a big mistake, considering what a crap shoot getting published is. As far as I could tell they would be eminently publishable today and would probably sell given the unique provenance. The press would have a field-day loving the corny chronicle of resurrected ruined "aristocracy": The Suspected Murderer of Gatsby Resurgent. What an irony if Gatsby's descendant should be the instrument of Thomas Buchanan's posthumous fame and reconstructed riches.

However, there was enough money left so that none of his issue were absolutely obliged to grunt and toil by their own sweat. His descendants have reentered the workforce with a vengeance. Most have graduated from his alma mater, no doubt helped by the formidable buildings which bear the family name squat down in the middle of campus ready to stand against Armageddon; but his descendants were too collectively embarrassed to apply for the scholarships which his endowment underwrote. It was a kind of code that they kept, though not without rancor. They would remain in ferocious competition with poor men's sons and daughters, the descendants of the huddled masses, the wretched refuse seeking solace on these shores and need to claw their way back up and trot hat in hand, mere supplicants, to lay out their heart and soul, their germinal schemes for scrutiny before venture capitalists who they regarded as vultures. Even the Silicon Valley little boys club, was doomed, at least initially, to perfect the subtleties of the kowtow, the dance of abject submission, to lure the magic seminal seed from angel investors, although enriching demons they may be. The days of raising working capital, like Benjamin Franklin, by going on a strict diet of hasty pudding (gruel) and potatoes is long gone.

Deep-rooted Spanish Family

Tom's daughter with Daisy died in a car crash when she was seventeen, or so it was told. There was no funeral service, at her dying request; cremated and relegated to her beloved Sound, scattered at the end of the dock, the famous one, her favorite spot. Fact follows fiction, fiction fact. It was said that Daisy had abandoned her when she was young and broke her heart; ran off with a bullfighter. Although appropriately histrionic this was too melodramatic to be true. In fact, she married into a deep-rooted Spanish family in a fungus encrusted, crumbling Madrid cathedral, very old world, which mirrored perfectly the Spanish family's straitened condition.

Jordan attempted to attend the wedding but was given the bum's rush out the door of the cathedral by a group of ominous black draped nuns who moved in upon her in a dense wave like a single organism, a devouring giant amoebic macrophage flapping their vulturous bat habits like bloodsucking brides of Dracula. Jordan, it seems, was "disrespectfully dressed" to enter "God's holy house", although decked in the height of fashion, straight out of a magazine cover, for an early summer wedding in Newport.

Daisy's marriage to Thomas Buchanan of the renowned Chicago Buchanans did not exist according to the Spanish family's church, which was especially adept at ignoring cold hard facts. The family treated her no better than a whore, a "non-Catholic fornicatress", in spite of her coerced conversion to the one true faith; a pagan, nouveau riche trash, "low-born gutter slut", who their none-too-intelligent son, "blinded by the glitz", had picked up on one of his boozy sojourns, strike that, "mining" trips to America.

She did not bear children to the Spaniard, thanks to one too many clandestine abortions of Thomas Buchanan's posterity. Tom had given her a solid platinum watch, trying to persuade her to have another child; she grabbed the watch and had the abortion anyway, behind his back.

But it was the Spaniard's merest touch that had come to give her the heebee-jeebees, to use her infantile locution as she shivered in pantomime. In an imaginary movie the Spaniard might be played by Marc Anthony as he projected himself from the screen in *Man on Fire.* Coincidently the Spaniard also kept an elaborate shrine to the Blessed Virgin Mary Immaculate Mother of God (with the name tacked on to one of her numerous special appearances.)

It wasn't the Lady of Guadalupe, I don't think. There she appeared to an Indian peasant, Juan Diego, in the appropriated body of a Mestizo and magically spoke to him in his native Nahuatl language, the language of the Aztec empire, thus establishing Mexican legitimacy against Spain at least in the eyes of God. The lady came out firmly against human sacrifice which was a very good thing and much appreciated by the potential sacrificees.

Trying to establish that not all Catholics were complete idiots, a level headed abbot of the "Lady's" basilica for thirty years, Monsignor Guillermo Schulenburg, openly doubted even the existence of this Juan Diego, a symbol, not a reality, of course opposing this nonentity's canonization, which would entail the recognition of a stupid cult. Politically insensitive to the danger of killing off a tourist attraction that drew a million people a month he was forced to resign his position.

To the Lady of Whatever, the Spaniard worshipped on his knees, continually and lit up enough candles to make it look like the room was on fire. It's a miracle he didn't burn the house down.

They whispered behind Daisy's back of her barrenness and snickered. She fell out of a church tower while making plans for its restoration. The police chief, surrounded by his epauleted underlings, insisted she was inebriated and laughed hilariously up his dirty sleeve, immune to the earnest pleas of the foreign inquisitors newly arrived; but Daisy did not drink.

Tom, for old times' sake, for the mother of his beloved daughter, sent over a contingent of Pinkertons and family retainers and spoke to the American Ambassador, a family friend. Stonewalled by the corrupt officials in the pocket of the husband's family, Tom's people were all rounded up, arrested, and beaten savagely, one to death, for good measure, as a warning; carrying firearms without permission; and deported.

The Spanish paterfamilias screamed uproariously in broken but unaccented English:

"I don't give shit for Ambassador American."

He was having such a grand old time; it was almost a shame to disillusion him. He had no clue as to what a mountain of shit was about to descend upon him.

It was Tom who sought out Gatsby, implored him, although he only had a vague idea of who Gatsby was, exactly, or what price would be exacted of him. He pleaded for his help, "for justice". How perfect, Gatsby the instrument of justice, commander-in-chief of the celestial dominions, Saint Michael the Archangel,

Prince of the Heavenly Host who would cast into the perpetual fires of hell all the evil spirits who prowl through the Earth seeking the ruination of souls.

> "Where there is no law, where the law is corrupt, a man is required to take the law into his own hands."

Gatsby:

> "If you're going to assume the role of avenging angel you damn well better get your facts straight."

Who's to doom when the judge himself is dragged to the bar.

The Gangster Who Fucked his Wife

I'm not certain that Buchanan ever connected Gatsby with the gangster who fucked his wife, got shot to death in his own marble swimming pool and had lived across the bay in the great big house; or that he himself may have had the pivotal role in engineering this Gatsby's purported murder. Tom's memory grew increasingly forgiving both of himself and others; age does that, or is it early onset dementia?

But it was Daisy's young daughter whose appeal persuaded. She liked to imagine herself as Gatsby's secret daughter, his "love child", an antiquated idiom seldom used even at the time; gifted as she was at quirky self-dramatization.

Gatsby, more formidable than Buchanan, procured indigenous help, greased with sacks full of greenbacks and newly minted coin; and himself disembarked with a small army, all speaking colloquial Spanish, including a leathery Mexican with well-honed Indian gifts who did not speak at all. They smoked out the murderers, the lowly henchman, quickly, who gratefully confessed, naming all the names for the mercy of a swifter death.

They came clean to a gratuitous bevy of gruesome bloodbaths. This family was a Machiavellian version, Old World, of Murder Incorporated, about to be subjected to unanticipated Yankee know-how from a very un-Yankee. This, after being exposed to medieval implements which through unfamiliarity had to be improvised clumsily with much superfluous blood; looted from the local church, a proud Inquisition collection celebrated for miles which the faithful trooped in droves to marvel at in nostalgia; the just old tools to deal with Infidels and secret Jews.

They were hunted down systematically, with alacrity. It seems there had been a family conclave with a unanimous vote taken, presided over by the family priest, a "saintly man", a distant cousin, revered locally, who granted his own ecclesiastical sanction; who got it first, twice in the head and once in the heart another in the private parts for the unrevealed privileged reasons of the particular hired assassin locally recruited who reveled ecstatically in his mission, settling his own special family score; (it is he who personally delivered the rotting precious piece of the priest now housed in a venerated reliquary, to which pious old ladies and stupid young girls light candles and pretend there is no stench while gagging unperceptively as they mumble their mindless singsong prayers by rote). The police chief was slaughtered next, with all his minions, every damned one of them.

They died unanimously, the utter extinction of an ancient rotted name; obliteration; their Renaissance family mausoleum fashioned by an unrecognized apprentice of Bernini vaporized as if by enchantment, swallowed up by a yawning maw cracking open the earth; blown sky-high with an over-indulgence in high explosives, showering the countryside for miles around with dirty marble dust and incinerated corpse debris.

Some ran, chased like panicky little beasts tripping over each other; one uncle tracked down like prey in the guise of a poor goat herder into the foothills of the Pyrenees. Locally they called it a mystery, a "holocaust of the disappeared"; without a vestige; no corpses were recovered except for, "mercifully, by a miracle of God", bits of the pious priest, which were parceled-out like sliced lunch meat to local churches; now on proud exhibition in his own parish in the diabolical monstrance. Some said the family was assumed directly into heaven to sit with their peculiar god in conclave forever, planning murders; this was before the craze of alien abductions.

This little incident gave rise to a purely local expression translated loosely as: "Don't fuck with the Americans." Only the common people connected it all to the murder of the innocent foreign lady, (and they all knew it was murder), who smiled at them, contrary to stiff-necked family protocol which decreed that they stare right through them like smelly air; a reckless unforgiveable breach on her part, not knowing her proper place, her family stature and the behavior associated with it. Without enthusiastic indigenous cooperation, collaboration really, Gatsby's task would have been infinitely more difficult.

Gatsby was a romantic after all; his gift; everyone heard of it. He wept bitterly:

> "There was no reason in the world to kill her. That was unnecessary... gratuitous.

> "A token settlement would have packed her peacefully on her way back home to America... where she belonged. The world she lived in hadn't reached this Old-World family yet and never would. She was caught in a time disconnect."

Too slippery, too sloppy; a church annulment would have proved expensive, enticements all the way up to the unholy "see". The local bishop frowned on such things and lined his pocket most generously in compensation; he would take the bribe but remember and always resent it. This would heap dishonor down upon the family with every crooked look of the bishop.

Does Life Imitate Art?

From the archives of Thomas Buchanan, number 6,402, date illegible

We are in a media saturated urbanized world where the precise demarcations between life and art, broadcast stereotypes and strictly private individualities, has lost its definiteness and in which the question of when someone is being truly themselves is problematical or meaningless at best and perhaps absurd.

Does art imitate life or does life imitate art? Fitzgerald metamorphosed everything that moved him into fiction, and the backfire transformed fiction into reality or what passed for reality. The legerdemain left him bewildered at times about whether he was in the audience or on the stage; he questioned whether Zelda might be a character of his own fabrication; that he needed a Zelda to wield the whip he craved. Zelda was his destroyer, brandishing the shears to castrate, demean and ultimately ruin. But she was his ruthless, hallucinogenic muse plying the sweet lash, setting his imagination on frenzied fire. He is a savage islander, suddenly touched with Grace, transcending in his prayers and aspirations the grotesque little fetish he clutches in which he imagines he discovers the object of his longing.

Getting back to the primary question, which question is, none-the-less, hackneyed and clichéd. Are the media "arts" so commanding that the movies and advertising can present a prototype or model so powerful that it becomes an archetype to imitate? We admire, we even worship these powerful images so that life and artifice become blurred, indistinguishable.

Advertising's subtle realization into a consumer responsive system of cunning persuasion in the early twentieth century was hypnotically successful in conscripting the worker-consumers (workers who worked to consume) as obsessive accomplices in their self-enslavement.

But advertising inadvertently taught the poor to brush their teeth, shower every day, groom themselves and clean their houses, if somewhat compulsively, as no government public health campaign or educational system could ever hope to accomplish.

In the near past when a man looked for guidance for the person he wished to become, he had his father, his teachers, his clergyman, the great personages of history who he could read about. These models are enfeebled in comparison to the overpowering media circus which inevitably marches forth to infect the imagination of even the most careful and meticulous decrier of mindless popular culture banalities.

Nick repeats his father's stale and trivial clichés as if they were the wisdom of the ages and yet we are thereby made glaringly aware that the rootless Gatsby has no parents, at least none that he acknowledges or would quote, certainly not his birth parents, who he does not rightly recognize as his forebears, his kin. Orphaned he becomes unmoored but also liberated, set free to create himself, adopt his own fathers floating in the heavens like disembodied intelligences. Ye Gads... Judas Priest... Gadsboy.

Nick claims that he witnessed his own version of Gatsby, Gatsby that is, praying one night to the stars when he thought he was utterly alone and safe:

> "I have no mother. I have no father. I take the sun and the moon to be my only father and my only mother."

It sounds like an old Cherokee chant to me; but for the life of me I couldn't find an old Cherokee who remembered it; they laughed when I repeated it.

Orphan

Although many said that Gatsby was an orphan, he wasn't, though he often said he was. He was speaking metaphorically.... He didn't feel connected with his own people, his family. He seriously believed that these relations could not possibly be his blood, his biological kin.

He was always spinning his own yarns, like cotton candy floating in the mist, the warm updrafts from the heat of the candy making machine, conceiving myths. He was intrigued by the idea of the foundling, the king's secret son, the golden boy, given over to the care of devotedly loyal common people, salt of the earth, who are entirely ignorant of his regal origins; this for the royal heir's own protection and the threads tying him to the king broken by multiple murder and betrayal; the king's secret emissaries slaughtered by marauders and thus the king's son irretrievably lost to the care of these idiots who not knowing who he was, regularly beat him for his own good, to whip him into shape, their shape.

But if Gatsby felt disconnected from his own family it does not follow that he felt some other family here on earth might fit the bill. "What am I doing in Akron, Ohio?" "Utah is not my middle-name." he cryptically mumbled. Gatsby was convinced that he had landed on the wrong planet. Or was he the ultimate immigrant, a superior being, the last survivor of a vastly advanced alien world, stranded without the hope of ever mastering their language, a mean patois, a step above gibberish.

As a self-proclaimed orphan he turned out to be mysterious in his roots, unlocking himself to boundless potential. As an orphan he was liberated, could do, be, or mean anything, become one of those singular beings that belongs only to himself, no inextricable alliances; the ultimate survivor, abandoned, or set free, let loose in the woods, alone, alienated, eating his way back on a subsistence of breadcrumb tracks and magic mushrooms, leaving his own bloody trail and a holocaust of crows.

The orphan is the elemental metaphor for the dispossessed, the isolated self, a self we all exemplify as involuntary participants in a disconnected existence devoid of genuine history. We are orphans all, those who think.

Although Gatsby dragged his baggage behind him in his widening wake, there was no readable label or return address.

Casuistry

The Right Reverend Monsignor Sigourney Fey was shadowed whenever he attended one of Gatsby's parties. Why he was admitted in the first place is still something of a mystery, although Nick imagined that all doors swung open as if by magic because of a wave of his hand. Perhaps Fey was the intended target and Nick the useful tool. Fey was a fund of information, rumor, and innuendo; he gossiped like a fishwife and dished the dirt on the entire Roman Catholic hierarchy. The secrets of the confessional were fair game without naming names thus maintaining the technical sanctity of the sacrament, at least in his own mind. But it didn't take a genius to fill in the missing pieces and the names easily fell into place helped by a staff of stenographers, researchers and private eyes. Gatsby's mansion was wired, with an attendant staff in the basement, to record any useful tidbits of information that might come in handy. It's amazing the things people will say when a little drunk and off their guard. This is, presumably a transcript of a recording of Fey, holding-forth, made in the late summer of 1922, shortly before the murders, culled from the archives of J. Gatsby, number 11,502.

Monsignor Sigourney Fey:

"The Jesuits were men before their time.... with this wonderful liberating idea. Jesuit theologians, trying to buttress personal responsibility and because of their reverence for freedom of conscience, emphasized the value of the 'case by case' methodology to personal moral evaluation and developed what would come to be called casuistry (the study of cases of conscience case by case) where at the time of choice, individual judgements were more important than any perceived absolute moral law in itself. It is in this way that we may achieve holy ends by unholy means. And thus, the means become sanctified because of the ends they produce.

"The infinite, all knowing, all powerful, all merciful God couldn't care less what I do with my silly sexual appendage; and this infinite God loves me for loving these boys in the most intimate physical way. It is essential that the boys are very young and innocent so that they can be educated about God's way, before they have been corrupted by an evil world which would turn them against the perfect love that I have for them and the sacred way I consummate that love. God knows that it is for their greater good and for the glory of God Himself; that I love these boys, selflessly, with pure Christian love, agape, the same love Jesus Christ gave to humanity; I love them more than myself; I would give my life for them. I love these boys more than anyone else could possibly love them, more than anyone will ever love them, more even than their own mothers and fathers. I teach them; I nurture them, guide them, council them to succeed at their dreams. I show them the possibilities of life; open new broader horizons, introduce them to the finest people, people who share values with me and with them, who will help them make their way in the world. I could put together a small army of my boys who would go to battle for me, die for me.

"And they come to me willingly, enthusiastically; seek me out even, because they have heard of my perfect love from the other boys and the boys together are like brothers to each other; we are a tight knit family. And the other boys love each other just as I love them and they love me and I watch over them and teach them to perfect their love for each other and they are like apostles who go forth and spread the good word and bring other boys to share our love and make it perfect in the eyes of God. I have brought scores of boys to the holy priesthood of Christ by the power of my love and they each in turn have brought scores of others; we are a powerful union of perfect love.

"I warn them always that they must be ever vigilant of those that are envious of our love and would seek, out of spite, to destroy that perfect love that God and His Beloved Son gives us. These are the agents of Satan that are made angry by love and will sow the seeds of disunion among our family. There are those who do not understand the details of our great love so we therefore must be secretive about the physical bonds of our love. I have explained to these boys that as a result of the sacred vows of my vocation and the holy canon law I am bound to lie even under oath to protect the Holy Mother Church from scandal and that I am bound to do anything at all to protect our Holy Mother Church. Therefore, they must all take a sacred vow sworn directly to God and Our Savior never to speak of the nature of our powerful love under pain of mortal sin and eternal damnation in the fires of hell; that to break such an oath to God and Jesus Christ is the one unforgivable sin and that no priest has the power to grant absolution from this most heinous sin and that God himself never forgives it because they would have broken their direct pledge to Him.

"I have explained to them that I have a vocation, which means that I have been singled out, chosen personally by God, that this is his greatest gift, to be his servant, that what I do is good and right because I am chosen, that what I do I do as a servant of God to spread his infinite love. I am but a vessel to channel God's love to them and it is through me that they can love God.

"And the parents knowing my goodness and my power to nurture love in their boys bring them to me and beg me to help and cultivate their boys. They implore me: 'Please help my Johnny, teach him your goodness.' And they bathe him and dress him and prepare him for me, like a sacrament, a virgin to be presented to a king, through me, the King of Heaven, whose appointed surrogate I am and deep down they know the secrets of my love and are honored that I have blessed and chosen their sons, that God and Our Lord Jesus Christ has chosen their sons through me. And that God has chosen them also, because of their sons and that the doors of heaven shall swing open for them and that they shall be ushered before God by a trumpeting host of angels.

"And if ever I am accused by the forces of Satan they will stand as one by my side, all the mothers, even if they have-to die for me. They will barricade the way, lay down their bodies when the legions of Satan come for me; they will stand vigil through the night with lighted candles in procession loudly reciting the rosary to the Madonna, Holy Virgin Mother of God, Mary the Immaculate who also gave Her Son as they have given theirs and she will be their strength and their courage and stand beside them, Mother to mother, as they march for me."

Monsignor Sigourney Fey

Nick's desperate unhappiness at the Papist school opened him up, made him vulnerable to the attention, encouragement and flattery of this bizarre, ridiculous priest.

Monsignor Sigourney Fey unabashedly and mawkishly flattered his fledgling disciple, continually burying him with saccharin sweet-talk, snowing him in an avalanche of blarney:

> "I have ten thousand things to say that I cannot write. There are intimacies that cannot be put upon paper. . . . Really the whole thing is most startling; I am keen beyond words to read the rest of that book. I may be frightfully prejudiced but I have never read anything more interesting than that book. . . . The more I see of it the more amazingly good I think it is."

This about writing, long before *The Great Gatsby*, that was no more than run of the mill pulp; the besoted padre was hootin and hollerin over trash; anything to get in his charge's pants.

> "We are many other things— we're extraordinary, we're clever, we could be said I suppose to be brilliant. We can attract people, we can make atmosphere, we can almost always have our own way..."

Monsignor Fey sucked him in, an old technique of practiced pederasts, escorting his protégé by the hand to the mountain-top, into his purported sphere, embellishing his own associations with celebrated figures of the greater world of religion and politics, by joining Fitzgerald with himself and by stuffing his seductive missives, love notes really, with shameless adulation.

Mentorship

Nick is always foisting mentors on his imaginary Gatsby; Kodi then Wolf. Gatsby, himself, considered it un-American. If America was anything it was a place where a man could rise high on his own lone efforts. There was something old world, corrupt, decadent, European, effete, a whiff of indentured servitude about it. Ben Franklin gleefully escaped the prison-like obligations of his own apprenticeship, the beatings from his brother, scuttled to Philadelphia, a new world in a new world. Mentorship: there was something girly about it, weak, like being procured, an alacritous child bride; or pressed into coy service, a willing prison bitch for the perks.

It was Wolf, the real Wolf, who said that any man who subjects himself to mentorship should have his manhood checked; what was left would be wrung out of him by the subservience. Wolf, the quintessential American, not Nick's pale fiction; who counseled in his best colloquial verbiage, advice dispensed to his own young sons like a throwaway line, which they knew better than to ever quote:

> "If you ever hear the words mentorship or protégé grab your dick and run like hell."

It was the obscene Monsignor who had prepped and primed Carraway for this un-American bondage. As a result, Nick was always demeaning, disgracing himself to more self-possessed men who had markedly less talent; midgets in comparison; they assumed the position of ordained noblesse, condescended, and thus emasculated what little was left of him, meticulously, ritualistically. It was Wilson, his purported friend, who reinforced any way he could Carraway-Fitzgerald's sense of inferiority. Even when it became obvious that Wilson had no literary talent, whatsoever, Fitzgerald continued to acquiesce and humble himself to Wilson's superior posturing and, also assumed an obsequiousness to a host of others who held themselves high above him. Even Fitzgerald grudgingly confesses in superb understatement: "... I had let myself be snubbed by people who had not been my betters in character or ability." He groveled, debased himself in front of his inferiors.

His acute sense of insufficiency was exaggerated by his "old world", very Roman Catholic guilt and an unacknowledged desire for humiliation and punishment, his secret love of the strong hand, of the priest's whip even after his supposed abandonment of Catholicism.

Hemingway exploited and manipulated his many mentors and when he had used them up and wrung them out, he discarded them with a bitter even vicious resentment that he ever needed them in the first place. No more than an amanuensis and minion shamelessly currying favor to the condescending Gertrude Stein, it is Hemingway who got the last word in and his revenge by rewriting the reality, his reality, from the grave, as writers often do, posthumously. By biting off and feeding on the many hands that had fed him Hemingway kept his balls somewhat intact and paid obeisance to no man; paid not even simple gratitude.

Edmund Wilson was viciously jealous of Fitzgerald and could never acknowledge, at least not while Fitzgerald was alive, that it was Fitzgerald who was the infinitely superior talent:

> "He has been given imagination without intellectual control of it; ... a gift of expression without very many ideas to express."

> "...a rather childlike fellow extraordinarily little occupied with the general affairs of the world... he is not much given to abstract or impersonal thought".

His "imagination suffers badly from...poverty of aesthetic ideas"; and he suffers from a Midwestern "sensitivity and eagerness for life without a sound base of culture and taste"; his values are those of the nouveau riche: a "preoccupation with display, the appetite for visible magnificence and audible jamboree" As so many did, Wilson confused the art with the artist. He had read too much of Fitzgerald's trash and couldn't recognize the magnitude of the masterpiece when it presented itself rising in glory out of the stinking shit. More than anyone he would have been astounded by Fitzgerald's posthumous triumph, which ironically Wilson helped engineer.

But it was not only Wilson who harbored a deep hatred and resentment of Fitzgerald. He had a knack for offending a myriad with his gross behavior and his mean, childish pranks. He was at a party in Hollywood where he gathered-together everyone's jewelry and watches for a trick, but the so-called trick was nothing more than boiling their personal possessions, some valuable family heirlooms in a vat of canned tomato sauce. There are people who carried an enduring hatred for him like a sacred ember in their heart. He mortally wounded people and thought nothing of it like a spoiled child inured or indifferent to all consequences.

Champions of High Culture

The old robber barons for all their gangster ways were champions of high culture. They raided Europe armed to the teeth with new money; buccaneers buying the greatest art that mankind had ever produced; they founded and funded parks and gardens, libraries, museums, and orchestras. And if they brought the same hard-nosed acquisitiveness to their purchases of high culture, at least there was collateral merit in their ruthless culture climbing. And if some of their acquisitions were formless and without taste and perhaps desecrated the conceivable canons of style, in most instances, this was certainly not the case. They endowed the museums of America with incomparable treasures, the best art which enriched every one of us. It was much more than just "statuary, paintings, pottery, and rugs"; more than just "jewels, fabrics, wines, and metals".

Their descendants in stark contrast used their inherited unearned treasure to debauch themselves and degrade and cheapen the surrounding civilization by their gross acquiescence, surrender even, to an emerging popular culture at war with the culture their fathers campaigned so ruthlessly for. They pissed hilariously on their patrimony and self-declared it youth culture although the phrase was not in use at the time; the eruption of perpetual adolescence, a self-propelled pustule shooting into the sky.

Rootless as Gatsby

The Buchanans and their bunch were a product of the "media", of advertising, magazines and movies, of the then current social milieu. For all their talk of privilege and family they were as rootless, more rootless than Gatsby, who sank his own roots where he chose to stand. They are faithful to no past; they have inherited nothing, but money. They might as well have stepped out of a movie screen. There are no adults in evidence anywhere; no old patriarch or matriarchs exemplifying and demanding a standard of values. The children have inherited the house, seized control in a dark night's palace coup; snuffed out the grownups, figuratively; the great die-off of the finest. Like Nick's fictitious Jordan they are unmoored, have no real family, only an old senile aunt, irrelevant, easily placated.

Buchanan's father, an old-style paterfamilias, of biblical proportions, his uncle and older brother, all the adults, died in the Spanish Flu. The 1918 Pandemic killed the most robust through a "cytokine storm"; the best and fittest having their perfectly primed immune systems turned against them, to self-destruct; like something out of a fifties sci-fi movie;

which left this unholy vacuity of the inept orphaned dregs; survival of the feeblest.

Upwards of 100 million, among them the strongest, the richest and the most powerful, were dead.

Both Dodge Brothers, of automotive fame; Guillaume Apollinaire, French poet, son of Poland; Felix Arndt, American pianist, his mother was the Countess Fevrier, related to Napoleon III, composer of novelty ragtime and "Nola", composed songs for the vaudeville team of Jack Norworth and Nora Bayes, and recorded over 3000 piano rolls; Sophie Halberstadt, Freud's daughter; Phoebe Hearst, mother of William Randolph Hearst; Harold Gilman, British painter who painted "Halifax Harbour" which hangs in the Tate; Henry G. Ginaca, American engineer who invented a machine that could peel and core pineapples which exponentially increased production and revolutionized the fruit canning industry and made Dole fabulously rich; Alan Arnett McLeod, described as "the finest flower of chivalry", destroyed an enemy triplane and was immediately attacked by eight more, three of which he brought down, crash landed in No Man's Land, dragged his comrade from the burning wreckage to safety, under heavy fire, for which he received the Victoria Cross; Sir Hubert Parry, British composer, radical in his politics who shunned his own moneyed class, a free thinker who refused to go to his daughters christening and was widely described as an ascetic who spent little of his vast inherited fortune on himself; William Leefe Robinson, British flying ace, first to shoot down a German Zeppelin over Britain during The Great War; Edmond Rostand, author of

Cyrano de Bergerac; Egon Schiele, Austrian painter, protégé of Klimt, he and his lover, seventeen year-old Walburga Neuzil were driven out of the small Bohemian town by the enraged townspeople, alleged by some to be carrying torches, who condemned his employment of the town's teenage girls as models; Yakov Sverdlov, whose parents were Jews, his father, an engraver, was a forger and arms smuggler for the Bolsheviks; rumors persist that Sverdlov was beaten to death with axes and clubs by workers in Oryol, because he was a Jew, who sought to destroy Orthodox Christian Russia, Bolshevik party leader, murderer of Tsar Nicholas II; Colonel Sir Mark Sykes, 6th Baronet, British politician, promoter of Arab Nationalism to counter the Turks, wrote to Faisal I of Iraq, warning of the Jews: "... this race, despised and weak, is universal and all powerful and cannot be put down"; Max Weber, German political economist, whose primary preoccupation was understanding the processes that he associated with the rise of capitalism and modernity. In The Protestant Ethic and the Spirit of Capitalism, he proposed that ascetic Protestantism was one of the major "elective affinities" associated with the rise in the Western world of market-driven capitalism and the "rational-legal nation-state". He condemned the migration of Poles into "German Lands" blaming the Junker class for promoting Slavic entry to serve their selfish interests; Prince Erik Gustav Ludwig Albert Bernadotte, Prince of Sweden and Norway, Duke of Västmanland with not enough names and titles to protect him from The Plague.

The Sudden Extinction of a Clan

For the Buchanans the Plague was a personal family holocaust, the sudden extinction of a clan, the kind of mass death that Nick invents or rather has his Gatsby invent for Gatsby's own fictitious people. Buchanan's father had advised Tom against his "entanglement" with Daisy Fey, but died before he could complete the meticulous details of his son's honorable extrication.

The paterfamilias was above all a man of honor. He was accustomed to quote the Reverend William Lawrence:

> "To seek for and earn wealth is a sign of a natural, vigorous, and strong character,"

The rich man is obligated by his very wealth to perform works of charity and is the chosen instrument of God; he, the generous rich man:

> "...is Christ's as much as was St. Paul, he is consecrated as was St. Francis of Assisi. ... If ever Christ's words have been obeyed to the letter, they are obeyed today by those who are living out His precepts of the stewardship of wealth."

He would thunder forth like an Old Testament prophet:

> "The wealth is not mine; it is given to me by God for safe keeping. I am only the trustee with the obligation to distribute it among the just and worthy.

"I am but the agent for my poorer brethren, their servant, bringing to them my superior wisdom, experience, and ability to administer, doing for them better than they would or could for themselves."

"It were better for the human race that the rich were thrown into the sea rather than fail in this sacred obligation and become slothful, drunken, and dissipated. It is better to give than to spend.

"I am not interested in ending poverty but rather I want to create the conditions for worthy men of excellence to rise in America. Like Carnegie I will give to institutions that will enable the ascent of the next generation of self-made men. I will endow libraries, colleges, museums, and concert halls where men might cultivate an appreciation of the arts, just as I have learned to appreciate those arts."

By his high standards, by his own hand Nick's Tom and his ilk would have been thrown in and drowned in that very sea.

What the children begot was a carnival, or more nearly a circus, a lewd festival of derision of what once was sacrosanct, of crazy prodigality instead of the old spirit of prudence, charity, and thrift. The "youth" rebelled against their elders' American Way of Life with the same spirit of the so-called "counter culture" of the 1960s.

There is a lot of empty talk about birth in Nick's book with the concept used in its traditional sense of inherited class privilege. But they have obliterated that tradition and can invoke it only with biting irony. It's like Nick's Tom lamenting the loss of family values when he is in fact its prime destroyer.

If Tom and Daisy's "entertaining" is staider than Gatsby's lewd imitation of it, it is still mindless socializing. This generation of the Twenties fancied themselves radicals and iconoclasts but were only mindless destroyers and never found anything to supplant the old virtues of work and courage and the old graces of courtesy and politeness.

And it is this affluent decadence of incessant celebration that becomes an added means of exclusion. An upper class that practices and exemplifies the old virtues... not only thrift and diligence but chastity and sobriety... will be more penetrable, less self-protected and self-perpetuating, than an upper class that tells the aspirationally ambitious that they can't climb the ladder unless they strip down and join them in the mud, join the party first; the initiation is debauchery; dissipation the ticket in.

The perpetual jamboree, the unceasing fiesta becomes a means of rejection; if you practice the old virtues or any virtue at all you are labelled a pariah, a stick in the mud, not with it. That life must be a unending party is ingrained in the corrupt culture of the country; the cocktail parties of the fifties, the ceaseless intoxicated bull sessions of the Sixties fueled by pot, all critical capacity guttered and thus to partake of a communal intellectual love-in or more properly a know-nothing orgy, union of the dumbed-down; in which people carried on upon subjects about which they knew absolutely nothing, into the middle of interminable nights; the infantile need to constantly hang out. In party colleges today unless you have well-off parents to fund your party life you are marginalized, left to the side-lines, which is probably a blessing.

Tom comes to dinner in his riding clothes; Nick's fabricated Tom does; carrying with him the stink of the stables. Fitzgerald got into an altercation in Hollywood with an influential actor over just such an outrageous social breach; asking him with feigned humor: "where's your horse?" What he may not have understood completely was that the actor may not have been anywhere near a horse and was just play acting in costume; polo outfits are very pretty.

For the Buchanans and their ilk there is this infantile need to smear their shit on the walls now that mommy and daddy are not here to reprimand and send them to their room; to break the rules of simple decorum and common-sense manners; to mock all etiquette as so square, to use a square word.

Self-made Man

The new man, the self-made man was up and coming, shrewd, practical, full of compulsive energy, his eye on the ball rolling toward the future, manic in his enterprise, indomitable in his optimistic idealism, natural openness and relentless will to succeed.

Henry Clay is erroneously reputed to have coined the expression "self-made man" on February 2, 1832 while arguing on the Senate floor for a protective tariff:

> "In Kentucky, almost every manufactory known to me, is in the hands of enterprising and self-made men, who have acquired whatever wealth they possess by patient and diligent labor."

No silver spoons in these mouths, no-siree, Bob. This is Amurica, by gosh.

In a letter signed by a Prof Newman published October 9, 1828 in the Delaware Advertiser and Farmer's Journal the self-proclaimed professor extolled the virtues of Roger Sherman (1721–1793), the Connecticut politician who rose from humble beginnings to serve on the Committee of Five that drafted the Declaration of Independence and who later served as Connecticut's Senator in the new U.S. Congress. He was the only person to sign all four great state papers of the United States: the Continental Association, the Declaration of Independence, the Articles of Confederation and the Constitution. He had no formal education and his early years were spent as a shoe-maker. With no formal legal training he passed the exam and was admitted to the Bar of Litchfield, Connecticut in 1754.

The self-made man as the embodiment of the American Dream come true became an industry in itself, part and parcel of the dream machine; a self-satisfied America inviting itself to its own party. Charles C.B. Seymour's book *Self-Made Men* (1858) related 60 such paragons; Harriet Beecher Stowe recounted 19 American idols among them her brother, Henry Ward Beecher, who preached the American virtues of self-creation from his pulpit at Brooklyn's Plymouth Church.

We Honor the Self-made Man

We have sabotaged the meaning of the term. We honor the self-made man but destructively calculate his success, as he himself is subverted into calculating his own success, by the money he has amassed. It is that idealism itself which is sabotaged and supplanted, channeled into evaluating that idealism through the quantity of material wealth accumulated. We measure the man not for who he has become but rather for the things he has, the stuff he has acquired; money becomes the corrupted gauge of the realization of the ideal, and thereby a substitute for it and a demolisher of that very paradigm.

In the late nineteenth century, a man established his worth by working diligently at his chosen vocation; he lived carefully and frugally within the confines of his class and thus achieved a certain moral wellbeing.

The debauched new dream of success is seen in terms of limitless opportunity, sudden enormous riches achieved almost instantaneously without the plodding work previously associated with the accumulation of wealth. And there seems to be no commensurate obligation by way of morals or even simple manners attached to it.

The Confidence-Man

Herman Melville's satirical, very modern novel *The Confidence-Man* (1857), dealing with problems of identity, sincerity, nihilism, existentialism, and absurdity but decorated incongruously with festoons of exuberant fancy, is attempting to instruct us in philosophical truths through the vehicle of nonsensical people talking absolute nonsense at length for the fun of it. The eponymous character, the stranger in the extreme, pushes fraudulent stock deals and solicits donations to fictitious charities on a Mississippi steamboat as it descends the magic river, a protean shape-shifter, he repeatedly reappears chameleon-like, separating the passengers from their money, reinforcing the author's belief that all that happens to a man in this life is only by way of joke and the confidence man is the jokester and joked upon, Shakespearian jester, delivering serious truths hidden in a likeness antic and ludicrous or merely absurd.

Confidence is seen not just as a method of deception, but as a needed and inevitable duplicity, a mutual surrender, a social necessity, which holds the corrupt world together. The refusal to suspend disbelief is a failure of imagination, which imagination allows surrender to the mass hallucination that affords us entrée to the social group. If we see things clearly, we will be shut out or more precisely we will shut ourselves out, never able, because of our clear vision, to join the pack and violently excluded from it.

American social activity, perhaps all social activity, is a confidence game. Melville presents an hallucinatory mirror image of the self-made man's success story, the promise of America's free-spirited economic engine into a menace, walking evidence of a ruined Eden.

That which makes Americans open, fluid and mobile also makes us an easy mark, exposing the naïve gullibility of the Yankee Republic. We, the down to earth Americans, don't demand impeccable references or rock-solid personal recommendations. We pride ourselves on judging a man by what he is or what we see or what we think he is. The confidence man exploits this; he recreates himself, is born again and again only to dupe or to test his fellow man.

The writer's narrator is yet another form of the confidence man and comes to represent fiction itself; a mask from behind which a besieged Melville reaches out from his armed camp, fugitive and cloistered, as he sallies forth to meet the enemy, his audience. This is the confidence man as the perfectly accomplished artist. Thomas Mann's unfinished novel, *The Confessions of Felix Krull, Confidence Trickster,* portrays the criminal as just such a consummate artist.

He is different from Benjamin Franklin but not so absolutely different; Franklin absconds from his indentured apprenticeship, the prison of his old identity, shamelessly hypes his success to further prime his business, reinventing himself as a printer, scientist, inventor and founding father of a new country, a new world.

Typical Horatio Alger Story

Fitzgerald's own story was a typical Horatio Alger story: an older, seemingly homosexual man, Monsignor Sigourney Fey, taking a much younger male under his wing, mentoring him, paving his way, praising him extravagantly, buying him the inevitable new suit of clothes (oh, this is the only part that may be missing.)

Horatio Alger served for a very brief period as a minister in Brewster, Massachusetts but was soon accused of practicing "evil deeds" on a young boy. A parish committee turned up further evidence of offences "too revolting to relate". Confronted by the evidence Alger "neither denied nor attempted to extenuate" the evidence "but received it with the apparent calmness of an old offender". Alger's father begged the committee not to prosecute legally. The committee decided that the scandal would do even more harm and cause "a serious injury to the church… the injury is greater the wider it is known." Alger took the next train to New York where he started a new beginning with young boys less likely to complain.

Alger cultivated New York's "street Arabs", those hawking newspapers, blacking boots, living in the streets or decrepit flop houses; he haunted the docks, wherever "friendless urchins" could be picked up; he bought them cheap with candy and small sums of money. Alger's lodgings, first in St. Mark's Place and after 1875 at boarding houses, became a "salon for street boys."

These young boys had a loyalty to Horatio Alger that rivalled the devotion of any whore to her fancy-man-pimp, or the prey of the pederast priests, revered by their game, their sycophants, not as good men but as saints on the fast track to early canonization. Alger's suck-ups felt an astonishing bond to their "patron and benefactor". "Mr. Alger could raise a regiment of boys in New York alone, who would fight to the death for him," gushed one of the minions shamelessly, shifting in his seat, suffering a sore ass, to a reporter in 1885. It is a symbiosis bred in hell: Alger mined them for their sordid stories which he sanitized or sterilized rather, in return for new clothes and safe-haven from the mean streets; like a streetwalker elevated to the comparatively cushy life of the uptown brothel and a cleaner more limited clientele.

Wear One Face to Himself

> "No man, for any considerable period, can wear one face to himself, and another to the multitude, without finally getting bewildered as to which may be the true."

This quote is actually carved in stone which attests to the durability of silliness. It's naïve. The human's skill at duplicity is myriad and enormously complex and didn't begin with the American confidence man. The practiced manipulator has a deep grab-bag of masks that he is constantly remolding as circumstances dictate. Whether simple actor, politician, salesman, promoter, entrepreneur or confidence man, any adept social being dexterously modulates his persona as circumstances and the people that he meets dictate. As for true? None of them are true or all of them are, or true in this context means nothing. The perfected pretense is the means by which we create who we are.

Through the ability to act convincingly we beget ourselves, become our own fathers. The trick is to pull off the act, to be a great actor. If others believe what we project and if we come to believe it ourselves, who is to say that is not who we are. If we pretend to be courageous, repeatedly act courageously, and are willing to die to prove it, we are courageous. If the mask doesn't slip and the wearer doesn't trip and falter, the mask becomes flesh and fuses fast to the bone, drills down arteries in blood like an enchanted plant, Jack's plant sinking roots which will catapult us to the heavens.

The more intelligent and cultivated a man is, the more multifaceted his mind, the more subtly and successfully he can deceive himself and conscript others to join in an enthusiastic chorus of his own personal subterfuge. An essential part of the performance is to believe utterly and completely in the show, which necessitates dyed-in-the-wool accomplices. It has been said that man has as many social selves as there are individuals who recognize him.

But it is celebrity, the loose little fanged sister of fame, which will devour us with its third-rate play. Celebrity sinks poison roots into flesh, poisoning it, grows a mask that eats into the face like slow acting lye. Celebrity will destroy the good man. If he is stupid enough to tell the truth, they, who have granted him his moment in the scorching sun, will not take it away, rather they will turn it against him; mock him with it. But if he plays along, his elaborate lies will humiliate him. If he perfects too intricate a cover he risks self-annihilation.

The American Dream

The American Dream moves in time from a dream of perfect order and harmony to an anti-dream of total disorder and chaos; the American Dream transmutes into the America nightmare even as our eyes are glued to it. It represents a titanic theme of the shrinking and sleazing of American idealism. The idealism of the colonists and the Founding Fathers has metamorphosed into a consumerist ideology. An ethic of work and striving has degenerated into an empty-headed puzzled contemplation of "what shall we do, what do people do", of the nagging problem of filling empty meaningless time with worthless, mind-numbing activity, sports: golf and polo; travel: moving aimlessly from place to place, rootlessly taking up space, driven by leisure and consumption; a degenerate society that measures itself not by what it produces or what it creates but rather by what and how much it consumes and acquires.

The predatory cannibalism of American capitalism walks hand in hand with the Dream, which it has kidnapped, compelling it into becoming the prototype for all human relationships in America; the Beast walking down the aisle with Beauty is no secret prince.

This degenerate offspring, the American Success Ethos, mercilessly tramples under foot all who are incapable of or unwilling to enter the ring.

But it is popular culture most of all that has turned the America Dream on its ear, made a mockery of it. The icons of mass culture are worshipped for the very reason that they are not worthy or deserving of their success; these personages are idolized because they are indistinguishable from the people who idealize them, with one big difference: money; they are poor people with ready cash, money to blow; big children with their pockets stuffed with big bucks; they have stepped in shit, won the lottery through a freak of fate, a cosmic disconnect: the inglorious empowerment of the talentless, of stupidity and bad taste run amuck. An American comedian hit-the-nail-on-the-head by describing herself and her husband:

> "We are America's worst nightmare: white trash with money."

Plunges Herself into Gatsby's Shirts

The closest we come to witnessing a personal sexual encounter between Daisy and Nick's Gatsby is Daisy's first visit to Gatsby's house with Nick tagging along, the uninvited voyeur. Daisy is overcome with powerful emotion only when she plunges herself into Gatsby's shirts, his clothing, his cloaking, encompassing the wardrobe, coming into it at the same time ruining her meticulously applied maquillage in a rainstorm of seminal tears. This is the high point of the relationship as it is revealed to us in Nick's book; Daisy's love for Gatsby, consumerism joined inextricably with fetishism, things standing in and replacing genuine relationships, the power to purchase replacing the power to engage and control events and people. Cargo worship. Commodity fetishism.

Daisy swoons when Gatsby presents himself as a big man self-aggrandizing through his largess, securing prestige through the accumulation of goods and providing lavish entertainments. The more wealth a man could distribute, the more people subject to his obligation, the greater his prominence. Those unable to reciprocate in kind are reduced to mere "rubbish men". Consumerism becomes empty totemism, making sacred the goods in themselves which, rather that representing the sacred, supplants it and destroys any possibility of the sacrosanct. If you want to make a sworn enemy, relegate him to a rubbish man, entertain him beyond his capacity to entertain you in return. Even Samuel Johnson knew this.

The Melted Snows of Yesteryear

From the archives of Thomas Buchanan, Number 2450, date illegible.

Someone said that Fitzgerald and his heroes do not yearn for the melted snows of yesteryear, they mourn for their lost capacity to respond to those snows.

Fitzgerald himself lamented the loss of those illusions that give such color to the world that you don't care whether things are true or false as long as they partake of the magical lost glory?

At the end of "Winter Dreams" Green, the main character is told that the beauty of his dream girl has faded:

> "For the first time in years the tears were streaming down his face. But they were for himself now. He did not care about mouth and eyes and moving hands. He wanted to care but could not. For he had gone away and he could never come back any more. The gates were closed, the sun was gone down, and there was no beauty but the gay beauty of steel that withstands all time. Even the grief he could have borne was left behind in the country of illusion, of youth of the richness of life, when his winter dreams had flourished....

> "Long ago... long ago there was something in me, but now that thing is gone. Now that thing is gone, that thing is gone. I cannot cry. I cannot care. That thing will come back no more."

A portrayal not just of first love, but how a writer exploited the uncorrupted memories of the idealistic naiveté of his imagined youth and its bittersweet emotion to shamelessly feed not only his profession, as a writer, but his very existence.

In a Forty-Second Street Cellar

In the middle of the summer of 1922 Gatsby drove in with his persistent trespasser Carraway, to the City, booming traffic and the deafening blare of horns. In a Forty-Second Street cellar full of smoke, heat and din pushed uselessly around by wobbly ceiling fans seeming to work their way loose by stirring the thick air, creating the illusion of ventilation, they met for lunch. Batting away the haze of the suffocating cigarette smoke burning his eyes, squinting away the brilliance of noon outside, yielding to blindness in the comparatively black interior his eyes sensed shadows shifting in the distance and the figure of what might have been a man began to enlarge and clarify itself, rising out of the smoke, assuming a familiar countenance.

Gatsby:

'Mr. Carraway, this is my friend Mr. Wolf.'

Carraway had been pestering Gatsby for a "head-to-head" with Mr. Wolf, hoping to gain a "connection", a stock deal to "line his pockets". Gatsby excused himself after a hurried lunch leaving the table for an "urgent telephone call". Gatsby didn't want to hear any of this. He wanted deniability. He wanted to be able to deny that he had ever had this meeting with Mr. Carraway.

Gatsby:

"Enjoy your coffee... I'll be right back... gentlemen."

Lazarus Wolf was a large, powerful man with the deep bass voice, the trained, picked voice of a radio man announcing the morning news or a stage actor who had toured the provinces in the high heat of summer. He played King Lear when he was young. He looked like Lee J. Cobb when Cobb played in the movie "Anna and the King", but leaner and hungrier and without the make-up. If you did a movie in your mind Cobb might do him justice combined with a Chaim Topol or a Walter Mathau, but fit enough to run the hundred-yard dash or go the distance, ten rounds in the ring. Wolf fought professionally in his youth. Sam Jaffe as he portrayed Erwin "Doc" Riedenschneider in *The Asphalt Jungle* would be a good third choice. Jerry Orbach would be fine.

Wolf would indulge himself in a very slight Yiddish-German lilt and Yiddish locutions, self-consciously, to amuse himself, like he was play acting. This was a highly educated man, graduated from City College and NYU law school. He spoke in a strange mix of rich ironic street slang interspersed with a seeding from his prodigious vocabulary which he was unafraid to broadcast liberally. He had no tolerance for ignorance. This was back in the day when they gave elocution lessons in the public schools and students labored, hunched over long vocabulary lists in the public library; when even the city school teachers, proper spinsters, spoke in unembarrassed Mid-Atlantic accents and cracked your knuckles with an oak ruler if you didn't imitate them correctly.

Wolf's Flunky:

> "Mr. Wolf, I'm sorry... half the time I don't know
> what you're talking about. I don't know these big
> words."

Wolf gave him a book. From that day on all his flunkies studied vocabulary like dutiful schoolboys.

Wolf sometimes spoke quickly with a machine gun rapidity, rattling non-stop, which some took for browbeating, which it definitely was, not giving them time to breathe, much less to think; that it was purposely hard to follow, to trip them up; their guilty conscience filling in the missed words and as a result saying the wrong thing; what Wolf wanted to hear.

Wolf did not relish this meeting with Nick, feeling put upon, looking for trouble. I don't think he fully understood the implied quid pro quo, payment for services to be rendered but rendered more to Gatsby than to Wolf. They were unequal partners and Wolf didn't like the risk, hanging himself out like this, to dry, for an unknown quantity, for a foreign loose cannon rolling around the deck of his own personal ship.

Wolf extended his broad, flat hand like a weapon, for examination, with not very well-concealed contempt.

Wolf:

> "I understand you're a college man."

Nick:

> "Yes, New Haven."

Wolf:

"Yeh... I went to New Haven too... never liked the fucking place.

"Me and Mr. Gatsby opened a play there... it bombed. We took it to New York anyway... ran 480 performances there... just goes to show you New Haven don't count for shit."

Nick:

"Yes... Jay told me you invest together in shows. But New Haven..."

Wolf, insulted, purposefully interrupting, stepping on Nick's lines, every chance he got, squashing them like quick little bugs trying to run out from under a rug:

"I never invested in a fucking 'show' in my entire life. You mean that musical shit. I would die a slow painful death first. They make me sick... in the pit of my stomach sick... so I want to throw-up... vomit all over the place. I get sick just thinking about it. I invest only in serious drama... promising young writers or the classical theater... Chekhov.... Ibsen... Shakespeare."

Abruptly, as if coming to his senses, waking from a momentary lapse of consciousness, realizing what was said:

"Who is this 'Jay' character you're talking about?"

Nick, hesitating, beginning to realize he has said something wrong:

"Jay Gatsby."

Wolf:

"You mean Mr. Gatsby... James to his very... very close friends.

"This nickname shit always rubbed me the wrong way... got under my skin.

"This Bubba, Chuck... Curley... Billy Joe, BooBoo, Doolittle, Billy Bob, Billy Rae, JohnBoy, Cooter, Clyde, Clitus, Woody, Mooney. It's for retarded hillbillies... or is that a redundancy... retarded hillbillies.

"Jay...? You call him this? You have his permission?

"He told you to call him this?

Nick:

"No... but Daisy sometimes called him...."

Wolf:

"'Daisy'! What the... that's a fucking cow's name for chrissake.

"These crazy rich sons-a-bitches are as bad as the inbred slack-jawed cracker yokels, their Anglo-Saxon brethren, with their asinine monikers already. Cookie, Cece, Paige, Piper, Peachy, Pippa, Polly, Posie, Buffy, Bunny, Bitsy, Booboo, Bambi, Heide, Happy, Sneezy, Kiki, Dede, Mimi, Missy, Muffy, Mindy, Maisie, Delsey, Sissy, Tibby, Topsy, Turvey. What an abomination... enough to make me want to toss my lunch. These people deserve to be separated from their money... cavorting like buffoons... they lack dignity, all sense of propriety. They give money a bad name."

Nick:

"Well... you see... her grandfather had a farm... a kind of gentleman's farm... where she spent the summer... as a child... over a thousand of the most beautiful acres and she had this favorite cow... the prettiest cow you ever did see... like out of an advertisement for milk at the A&P... and she loved this cow more than anything on earth...

Wolf, raising his voice:

"Stop... enough... enough already about the cow. I don't want to hear anything about any cows... goats or pigs either for that matter.

"Are we talking about this same twat he fucked down in Louisville... who's setting up the...?

Nick:

"Yes... but... but. (long, frightened pause) Don't you mean Charleston?"

Wolf:

"What the fuck... again you're at it. Does it really matter Mr. Carraway? Think about it. Who fucking cares where she comes from? This Annabel... or whatever.

"Are you a girl Mr. Carraway?

Nick:

"What...?

Wolf:

"I said... are you a girl?

Nick:

"What...?

Wolf:

"You say 'what' one more fucking time and I will blow your fucking brains out... I guaruntee. (the run and tee accentuated like a Cajun.)

"Are you a girl, Mr. Carraway?

Nick:

"No... but... but..."

Wolf:

"First the 'whats' now the 'buts'. You are trying my patience, mightily. Maybe we should have you examined... by a doctor, maybe, a proctologist psychiatrist... to get your head out from up your ass.

"There are three men in this restaurant watching us very closely... three more belong to Mr. Gatsby but they're busy watching him. I want you to look around at them. They are not as inconspicuous as they would like to believe...

actually they stick out like a sore thumb... it's really comical when you think about it... they've got big heaters bulging out of their pockets... they might as well stick a sign around their neck... but that's okay... it's the deterrence factor. Like big dogs they scare people... just to look at them. What particular persons that don't last never figure out is that there is always a fourth man... that even the three others don't know about... he's tougher, quicker and smarter than the other three put together... you'd never be able to pick him out... and it is this fourth man that always saves the day. The three men, in fact, very often serve only as a distraction... like a decoy. Don't ever tell them I said that... it would hurt their feelings.

But you see... right now they all see that I am getting agitated and as a result they are getting very agitated... they don't like when I get agitated. It is their job to see that I don't get agitated.

"If you continue in this vein... I will give them a sign... two of them... it will only take two... will drag you out of here so I can personally shoot you in the nearest alley. I will shoot you in the head twice until your brains come out... so there is no mistake. If you resist, they will shoot you down right on the spot... right here... in front of all these people. Then they will leave town... for the West Coast... I have interests on the West Coast. They will be gone for years until the whole thing blows over... it will blow over... it always does. But they will most likely decide to stay on the West Coast... it's nice out there... the weather... the ocean... palm trees... that's if you like palm trees... I, myself, can take them or leave them... these men will sink roots... it's inevitable. I will miss them a great deal... good men are hard to find... but I will manage.

"Now... once again... one more time... so there's no question... are you a girl Mr. Carraway and is Mr. Gatsby fucking you?"

Nick:

"No... no... absolutely not."

Wolf:

"So... if you're not a girl and not being fucked by Mr. Gatsby then please do not call him Jay... not ever... not in my presence, or anywhere I might hear about it from someone else. People are always carrying tales to me... like they're doing me some sort of big favor, like I want nothing better than to hear.

"If a little twat wants to call him Jay that's a personal matter between the twat and Mr. Gatsby... twats do and say very silly things... it can't be helped. Mr. Gatsby understands this... one could say he's an expert on twats. There are certain dispensations that accrue to the station... being a recognized twat, that is. Do we understand each other, Mr. Carraway?"

Nick, shaking visibly, not knowing what to say:

"Yes.

Wolf:

"Say it one more time so there's no misunderstanding. Say: 'Yes I understand'".

Nick:

"Yes, I understand."

Changing the subject clumsily in something of a panic, never knowing when to shut up, digging himself deeper:

"Mr. Gatsby tells me you're a man of culture, that you're a patron of the arts... sit on the board of the Metr..."

Wolf, interupting:

"What? Man of culture? What the hell does that mean? 'Man of culture.' Everybody wants to pigeon-hole everybody else, put 'em in a box... so they can make simple sense of something that's not so simple.

For instance... here, in this country, the detective mystery book is looked down on as not literature. But a writer who writes of loftier subjects, of 'social significancc' cvcn if he's a stinking writer is taken seriously. This is the 'parvenu's insecurity', if I can borrow that fancy phrase.

"But the man who can take the humble murder mystery and turn it into art... this is a magician… this is the man I respect, that I can sit down and talk to. Who was it that called the fictional private detective: the new mythic hero, investigating a cultural response to universal unconscious fantasy and plunging into it without understanding society's narcissistic fixations? Boy… what a crock-a-shit. Do these bums even listen to themselves? But he's on to something… No? These writers also got murder out of the vicar's stupid rose garden and gave it back to people who are really good at it… murderers.

But it may take a real wizard to write shit one day and literature the next and not to carry the stink of the shit into the area where he lives. What serious writer dares to stray to write popular fiction in the optimistic hope of coming back by underground tunnels and devious ways into the light again, dripping with darkness? Mostly they dig down, accidently break into sewers and drown from the darkness or are asphyxiated by sewer gas.

As far as what is literature…? I know it when I see it. As for what it is, this I leave to the fat fucks… like Edmund Wilson who has the distinction in his own self-described 'serious literature' of making fornication as dull as a railway timetable… so dull that you would want no part of it… this is not an easy trick… take my word for it.

"I got side-tracked... I was off on a tangent... the tangents always get me. Getting back to the subject at hand... what the fuck do you know about culture?

Nick:

"No... I just...

Wolf, interrupting, more calmly now, getting control of himself:

"'No... I just...' You know you're a very annoying person... very annoying... What are we going to do with you? You don't learn. You don't listen.

"Whenever I hear the term culture... careful, so nobody notices, I chamber a round in my old Luger... from the war... a souvenir... pried from the cold, stiff fingers of a dead Heinie... his handsome face and blond hair pressed down in the mud... like he was nothing... and I finger it like a talisman... and laugh loud to myself.

"People who prattle on about culture are hard to stomach and don't know their ass from their elbow. These are the crumb bums that ruin it, walking around with their noses high in the air like the ground stinks... the ground does stink, sometimes... especially with people pissing on it... but not always. They have the attitude that I'm better than you because I appreciate real art. Fuck 'em... that's what I say.

"You see these cuff buttons...? Take a good close look... Do you know what they are?"

Nick, leaning hesitantly in to look, but not too close, afraid it was a trap, afraid he would have his head bitten off:

"Molars?"

Wolf:

"Molars? Molars... yes... very good... (like Nick had just passed an important quiz and won a contest) human molars... molars pulled from a screaming man without any anesthesia. I used to practice dentistry. I like to keep my hand in... my finger in the pie, so to speak... to keep in practice... so I don't lose the touch.

"I dream that overnight people won't want to buy pearls anymore (Nick at this point knew nothing of Wolf's pearl business)... that they'll come to their senses... that they'll regard them as silly or they'll only buy them in little cheap cloth bags for pennies like glass marbles. I worry about such things. I have a nest egg of course... what man in my position does not... but a man must keep gainfully employed... for his peace of mind and to keep himself sharp... to keep his edge. You never know... if everything goes to shit, I have something to fall back on... a cushion... to catch me if I fall... my dentistry... my safety net... my first profession.

"I worked hard to be a good dentist... my parents scrimped and saved to send me to school. I wanted to be a writer but my father told me this is not a career for a real man... this is a hobby... something to do on the side. When you make a living as a dentist... when you're comfortable... independent... then you can write all you like. But until then... you can write on Sundays... evenings... on vacation... during lunchtime... early in the morning instead of reading the newspaper. This way you can write literature... by your own standards without having to please anyone but yourself. Chekhov was a medical doctor first... the greatest writer there ever was besides Shakespeare. It is Anton Chekhov, not Dostoevsky or Tolstoy who is the greatest of the Russian writers... the grandson of a freed serf, son of a ruined owner of a humble general store... Chekhov supported his family from the age of sixteen and put himself through medical school... started writing junk... pulp... made good money at it... but once he graduated to literature, he never turned to writing garbage again. And the garbage didn't suck his soul out. He could probably jump from one to the other without compromising his integrity; like it was a game... and he was on top of it. He was independent... his own man. He liked to live well... yes... I grant you... but not a slave to the dollar or the ruble... never having to demean and disgrace himself... to grovel in front of rich men... always able to hold his head high. I know there was that rich publisher, Savorin or whatever... the money bags. But he seems to have held his own.

"It is possible to write trash without selling your soul especially if it pays well… but it ain't easy… it ain't easy… Maybe it beats teaching writing in Podunk U. But you have to keep your wits about you… leave plenty of time to write the good stuff… be able to change gears and you need a big nest egg so you never feel forced to write the shit. It's too easy to drown in it.

"My uncle… my father's brother… who I never liked very much… told me I should be a college teacher… a professor of literature and language… as training to be a writer… if that's really what I wanted to be. I told him this was no good… that they were not 'analogous' fields as he said but instead were mutually exclusive … had nothing whatever to do with each other. The college world of literature is a totally different industry like meat packing or car tires… only they don't make anything… not anything that you can use. The papers they churn out on fiction have nothing to do at all with writing fiction… they're not only useless they're probably harmful to a writer. It's a recycling business, a boondoggle to keep otherwise intelligent people uselessly employed and taking money for it… trying to capture precious chemicals from smoke. I can say categorically that if you want to be a great writer or even a decent one, stay the hell out of the universities… they wouldn't know great literature if it came up and bit them in the ass.

"Good writing is the highest form of human endeavor with the exception of the love for another human being. I have promised myself to write one good book before I die. And if I fail... so, be it... at least I will have given it my best shot. What more can you ask of a man? Good writing is magic... you stare into a sheet, blank white, slice open an artery, figuratively, and bleed into the bottomless inkwell until there is nothing left to give and you become rapturous... probably from loss of blood.

"Life is funny that way... it pays to think ahead... to be prepared for any eventuality. I was especially good at difficult extractions... they would call me in for special, tricky cases... impacted wisdom teeth. I was a master at extracting impacted, infected wisdom teeth. It's not as easy as it looks. It's a matter of technique.

"This screaming man called me by a nickname... he owed me money too... very sad... a debauched gambler... a disgusting, immoral person... robbed food out of his children's mouths to play the ponies... to bet on the future... stole from the present to give everything to wager on a future that is problematic at best.

I think deep down all-of these gambling degenerates want to lose or don't care one way or another. They ache for the fix... the high... that adrenalin jolt... like electrocution... they hunger for that brush with death... no... they want to dance the tango with a homicidal insane lady who wants only to eat them up or teach them crazy dance steps... hang on to her like a bucking bronco while she's working to sink her teeth into their flesh... lie in the mud with the hooves coming down on their head... wallow in their ruin. I got carried away. I don't know what comes over me.

"You live in the past... you live in the future... the here and now is what counts... the only real world... the present instant... the past is no good when we want to dwell in it... it robs us... we squander our time reliving all of our mistakes or fantasize about some magic moment that never was... we give up our lives for a dream of what we think happened... the future full of anxiety and anticipation... both rob us of the now... strangle us... stifle us... smother us in its soft down bed.

 "Grab tight hold... the here and now and live... live for God's sake...

"The past can never be recovered but truly it can never be escaped. We carry it with us forever like a sack on our back; it makes us who we are. Without memory we have no identity.... We carry it with us forever; it makes us who we are.

"I don't know. No... No... this only sounds good but I don't know if it's true. We are not the prisoners of our history... mostly but not absolutely.

"Besides, memory is just another fiction which we create.

"I got lost on a side track. Sometimes I think too loud to myself.

"Another thing... another thing is you have-to pay attention... pay close attention! Most people sleep fitfully through life like drowsing through a movie... a picture they never heard of... to be startled awake by people stepping on their toes getting out of the aisle. It's too late, when they finally realize it's over. They discover how little a light the sputtering, trembling glimmer of consciousness is and have no real clue as to what exactly the movie was about. They try to divine meaning from the closing credits while people are pushing and poking against them telling them the movie is over and they're holding up the line. You can't hide and stay for another showing... the ushers are uniformed alike... they look like doormen... or those stupid looking toy soldiers on display at Kensington Palace with those high furry hats and they keep close watch wielding old-fashioned batons... not those with the rubber cushions on both ends. Don't mistake it for the fancy stick either, that's passed from runner to runner in a relay race... make no mistake it's a cudgel or truncheon and it's deadly. You only get one ticket... that's it. They don't let you stay for another showing. Thems the rules. It's a real shame though... the second time around you'd maybe learn to stay awake and might actually discover what the movie was about. Life is like money... both act like spilt quicksilver in a nest of cracks. Try to chase after that.

"Who was it that said?

> 'It is death that makes a mockery of life. We struggle to a level of consciousness, claw our way up, as if for no other purpose than to inflict upon ourselves the excruciating pain of the awareness of its fleetingness.'

"This was a wise man who said this. This is a man who knew.

"This stock 'deal' I am told you are looking for is not what you think it is, not some pump and dump... not a swindle of any kind like you imagine... not counterfeit certificates or anything like that. With such things I would never get involved and certainly Mr. Gatsby, who is a very upright man, would never go near such a thing... not so much as touch such illegality. This is simply about information... nothing more nothing less... knowing what other people don't know. This is Mr. Gatsby's specialty, his genius... if you want to know the truth. Where he gets his information, I couldn't tell you even if I knew. This knowledge is invaluable... it's like money and must be kept scarce.... Otherwise, the stock moves suspiciously and the jig is up. The more people who know... the less valuable the information. Giving you this information is like handing you money but more than that it is giving you the power to make that very money less valuable so that the others who come after you suffer. We supply the information in a very particular order to a very select few. If you are near the top of the list, you have the power to ruin it for those further down on the list... if you speak out of class... shoot off your mouth. It's like giving you the keys to the bank and you set the money on fire instead of only taking a reasonable amount for yourself. If you are chosen you will be given this information in a way that can never be traced to Mr. Gatsby or myself. You must never speak directly to me or Mr. Gatsby about these matters in any way whatsoever... ever again. You may receive a telephone call from someone you don't know or have some strange person strike up a conversation with you totally from out of the blue. He'll say something very out of the ordinary with very exact words like: 'I understand you have an interest in Oklahoma oil stocks'... those words must not be different in any way... not so much as one word out of place. And you must answer 'Texas' so he knows you understand and you're the right man. But never answer with your special word unless the words you are given are exactly right.

"By your look you seem to hesitate. He who hesitates is lost.

"Jesus! I have the unquiet feeling this is the first time you've ever done anything like this? What a fine lollipop you are! What are you going to do next... get down on your knees and pray for heavenly guidance? Never trust a man who gets down on his knees for any reason. George Washington never got on his knees, especially not in church. God doesn't want you to grovel... it's unbecoming. Maybe you should talk it over with your grandmother or your old nanny. You did have a nanny didn't you Mr. Filtchcroft? Of course, you had a nanny; all you fellows had nannys.

"Nothing... but nothing... is without risk... nothing is one thousand percent. Rarely, but sometimes... just sometimes... the information is bogus. People lie, even in secret conversations, even to themselves... especially to themselves.

"I don't know Mr. Filtchcroft. Can you be trusted to keep a secret? Or do you like to play the big man... proving to people how smart you are... what a skillful picker of stocks you are... how you're in the know, privy to the inside scoop. I'm afraid, Mr. Filtchcroft, that you're going to throw a wild and unpredictable monkey wrench into the works. But what you don't understand, is that when the busted machinery comes flying apart it will take your head off first. It won't be a pretty sight... you standing there without your head. And these things that you contemplate: are they in fact wild or just downright stupid? No matter how orderly you think your existence is, no matter how well planned, death waits for you... lurking just around the corner... for you to cross the street... and you will cross the street.

"What are you going to do with all this money you're going to come into?

"You want to gamble on some stock deal...? put money in thy purse?

"If you're intent on going to hell... at least get there in a more pleasurable way.

"Chasing after money for its own sake is a kind of homicide ... more like self-slaughter, very often gory. Money must come to you by indirection without ever hunting it down... like a wild animal which you coax and which finally comes to you entirely on its own when you're not looking... and there it is, out of the blue... all of a sudden, this huge creature, scary to look at, licking your hand like a friendly dog. And if the big beast stays in the woods... sticking out its big nose for you to see between the leaves... coming teasingly close... but never close enough... That's alright too. You have a roof over your head... food on the table... clothes on your back... some good books you buy cheap from the secondhand store... maybe even a rare public library you discovered by accident... like a jewel in the forest... that's hidden away so the bums don't ferret it out... to piss on the chair cushions, blow their nose in the books and generously share with everyone some rare highly communicable disease which drops liberally from the scabs they're covered with.

What more do you really need? This is America... no one starves to death. Do your best and do what you love and the rest will follow or maybe not. I'm this way with my pearls.

To think always of money is to think the way America wants you to think... This is what the dream has become... what the country has become... This is the trap they lay... This is the way it grinds your face into the dirt... the mud... with the boot pressing on the back of your head... then you will never be your own master.

"Save your money and save your life.

"But remember what the great Roman, Seneca said: 'a great fortune is a great slavery.' Well... it doesn't have to be... not if you play your cards right. You have to learn to delegate... to find people you can trust.

"Never forget this. Money can make you free... so you never have to humble yourself to the boss man whether that boss man is an unreasonably demanding client or an overseer with a whip. Money gives you the freedom to be yourself... to create yourself... to recreate the world... With money you buy yourself out of slavery... ransom your soul, from the heavy oppression of the clock, lift it with your own hands, from off your back. With money you buy maybe a really nice house, in a good neighborhood, a strong, solid house made of brick or stone, with a full basement... the mortgage paid off, money in a protected account and you can say FUCK YOU to any man. You do a good job and they don't like it... you say FUCK YOU. You tell them honestly and reasonably what you think and they give you trouble... you say FUCK YOU. You open your heart and arms to them and they turn their back on you... you say FUCK YOU. FUCK YOU. FUCK YOU. FUCK YOU. This is the only way for a man to stay on his feet, to stay alive and breathe clean air. FUCK YOU. FUCK YOU. These two words are the free man's prayer. It is better to save your money, to live like a monk, if necessary, to pile up the greenbacks in tall stacks like armor for your soul in order to be able to say one thing and one thing only: FUCK YOU.

"I pity these poor ambitious young fellows who think they are so smart and that believe that the world is going to recognize just how smart they are and reward them... give them their due. This is bullshit. This is what the swindlers in power want you to believe. Make no mistake: it is the scum that rises to the top.

"In the classroom the most intelligent are beaten down and methodically broken by the idiot teachers who rein like despots; who deep down regard intelligence as a threat to their small brains and puny little egos. It's the ass-kissers with brown, shit-stinking noses, the shameless suck-ups who become the teacher's pet. By deciding to educate everyone we really educate no one. Where are the Shakespeares? Every single year, maybe twice a year, a Shakespeare is systematically squashed like a bug on the classroom floor. You can turn in the most keenly honed and magisterial prose and the drudge up front with terminal dandruff and the yellow teeth isn't going to give it an A... he's going to give it an F... he's going to flunk you out if he can because of the fact that you exist... can exist... and that existence threatens all that he stands for... his secure, mediocre, stupid, meaningless existence.

It's these morons on top who want to get rid of intelligence tests. They claim that the test is not predictive of either academic or worldly success. This is absolutely true. But this is an argument against the classroom and the world. I have never met a man who tested with a high IQ who wasn't extremely intelligent and worthy of better than he got. Many were ruined, shattered men... many criminals, some in jail. What intelligent man could live in this ridiculous world without striking out, without rebelling in some visceral, violent way?

"I have been asked why I have chosen this life for myself... but I'm not sure that I have chosen it... Perhaps it chose me. I am not sure that I am much different from the artist or the warrior... the hunter... the fanatic or the martyr for that matter... At all cost I wanted to avoid an everyday life.

I want uncertainty and doubt... I want turmoil and fight... I don't want to live in peace... How can any man make peace with this world the way it is...? And if the world makes war on me God help the world.

"But this is neither here nor there... I don't know why I carry on like this... it's entirely beside the point..."

Gatsby returned from his call, interrupting the never-ending narrative of Wolf, his particular one-man show, the well-worn, well-honed wise Mensch routine that Wolf loved to indulge so much.

There's a story of Wolf holding a gun on a man he was trying to decide whether or not to kill and speaking at very great length, not really to his target but more to himself, trying to plead the case one way then the other; the man had finally had enough and couldn't take it anymore, blurting out:

"Are ya gonna talk me to death or ya gonna shoot me?"

Without so much as another word Wolf shot him then and there, three times in the chest. If the man had only shut up and listened, he might have lived to an old age; it would have been worth the suffering. He was a wise guy; he liked the style of what he was saying, the quick, flippant backtalk... how it sounded in his head and he paid for his smartass quip with everything he had... his life.

Gatsby:

"I'm sorry I took so long. I hope you men have enjoyed your conversation."

Wolf:

> "Immensely... we have-to do this again... soon. It's so nice to make new and interesting friends... it's always a pleasure to meet cultured... high-toned people... people who understand what intelligent conversation is. But I must be leaving. I've stayed too long as it is. I don't wish to outstay my welcome. I have much business to attend to."

Wolf rose from the table with great ceremony, putting his hand on Gatsby's shoulder as if it were a sacramental ritual, a laying on, a benediction, leaning in close to his ear so only Gatsby could hear but looking at Carraway the whole time with a steely squint in his eye and a forced, crooked smile:

> "Where did you dig up this putz?"

When Wolf had left, Nick, visibly shaken, opined with a quaver in his voice:

> "I think the stock deal is off.

> "I don't think he likes me very much."

Gatsby:

> "No... not at all... what makes you say that?

> "You didn't call him Lazarus did you?

Nick:

> "No... no... of course not."

Gatsby:

"Good... good.

"He's very European, Continental... old school...
old world... proper manners are very important
to him. He's out of ... not of this time. He's a real
gentleman... a man of honor... very upright...
lives by a strict code. You must never offend
him. He's very sensitive... sentimental even...
maybe a little high strung."

Nick:

"How can you call him a man of honor? He
threatened to kill me... over nothing... nothing."

Gatsby:

"It couldn't have been nothing to him. You must
have said something that gave him offence...
some sort of insult. He wouldn't kill you without
a good reason. He never kills anybody without
good reason. People sometimes say things
without thinking. They have-to learn to think
before they speak. What exactly did you say?"

Nick:

"It was a misunderstanding... he took something
the wrong way."

Gatsby:

"The wrong way? A couple of hundred years ago
something said the wrong way, an insult, would
have been answered on a field of honor... by a
duel. How is this different? The point is he didn't

kill you... you're still alive? What are you complaining about?"

Nick:

"But I'm not even armed."

Gatsby:

"Well... as the man once said: If you're going to shoot off your mouth you better arm yourself."

Nick:

"I think if you looked at him funny, he might shoot you dead, then and there."

Gatsby:

"I don't understand. I don't understand at all. Why would someone in their right mind look at Lazarus Wolf "funny"? Maybe we all need to learn better manners. He's the kind of man who kills people for good reasons."

Nick:

"You say he's honest but I heard he fixed the World Series?"

Gatsby:

"Wow! No kidding? Is that what you heard? Boy... that's something... The World Series... shit.

You don't understand at all, do you...? Not at all...

That was a labor of love... a holy mission, a sacred quest even... his noblest act, for him a moment of moral grandeur. He considered it his duty to save America from itself...to win back the dream... to reestablish its purity... the purity of the dream... to rescue it from the racists, the jailbirds, the drunks and the goons, the barflies who infested it.

"Baseball to him represented everything that was wrong, what the Dream had degenerated into, a game for impoverished children played by big morons elevated to mythic status... this is what happened when the destitute had too much time on their hands and too much money... though still obstinately destitute.

But money had nothing to do with it... he wanted to show them the truth whether they wanted to see it or not, that the players were cheap, dirty racketeers always with their hand out. He risked everything by revealing that the World Series was rigged... he could have kept it hidden... it would have been better for him... He thought that the American people would come to their senses... that they'd wake up and see the light... But it was all a waste of time. Wolf wasted his time... the jury wouldn't even send the bums to jail."

Nick, as if tattling on an errant schoolboy to the headmaster:

"He asked me if I was a girl."

Gatsby, laughing:

"Oh... he's a real card... a great kibitzer. He likes to get a rise out of people. He was just playing with you. He has a great sense of humor... very dry.

"It means he likes you... when he kids you like that."

Nick:

"He told me his cufflinks were trophies, molars pulled from a screaming victim who called him Lazarus and owed him money."

Gatsby, laughing, forced, uneasily:

"Ha... ha... ha... now I know he was pulling your leg... they're cultured pearls... pearls for god sakes. Those cufflinks were his first failed efforts... that's why he keeps them... souvenirs... to remind him of what progress he's made... how far he's come... how humble his beginnings were. He's a scientist... a great genius... a marine biologist... a groundbreaker... he keeps his methods top secret. No one can tell his cultured pearls from the real thing.

"He goes to the South Pacific once a year and comes back with his treasure... so he wants everyone to believe. He comes through customs with nothing to declare but himself. He does this purposely to fuck with them. He's got them flummoxed. The customs people think he's a smuggler... they spent a whole week searching his ship, impounding his luggage... cutting open his clothes only to find marbles... marbles everywhere.

"He runs a small operation of native divers and diggers, mostly as a front... but they're always shoving the best of the pearls up their asses and won't subject themselves to a body search... they claim it's rape and dishonors their fathers and their mothers and all their ancestors right to the beginning of time. He forced them at gun point and found a treasure trove up their anuses, but all-out war broke loose. I guess shoving pearls up their ass is alright with their ancestors. He had to jump from island to island... one step ahead. It was called the "Pearls up the Ass War" by the islanders which only sounds particularly absurd when translated into English. They took it very serious.

"Finally, he was forced to smuggle pearls down to the South Seas and then declare them coming back in... just a very few to keep everybody happy.

"He's very secretive but he grows his pearls in the Bronx... in a factory... oysters in tanks tended by Chinese women who speak no English... in fact they don't speak at all. He made a deal with *The Sisters of Divine Mercy for the Deaf and Dumb*... a religious order in Shanghai... supervised by Chinese nuns who made the trip with them... they take a vow of silence... all one big quiet family... the nuns themselves are not deaf and dumb, they used to work with the deaf and dumb... he pays the nuns directly and sends money to the institution, the Shanghai nunnery. They lead a cloistered existence... work and prayer... work and prayer... never leave the property... he's got it decked out like a genuine nunnery... chapel and all... he's got it down to a science... a racket. He's got an arrangement with a defrocked Chinese priest friend who speaks Chinese... a little... an ex-con who comes in to hear confessions and say mass.

"Wolf says it shouldn't be illegal... to sell cultured pearls as real... who's to say what's real... which is more real. Isn't it better to farm... to cultivate wheat rather than trying to harvest the wild wheat grass? His pearls are better than what's dredged up from the bottom of the sea.

"If you tell anybody they wouldn't believe you and if he finds out you're blabbing he'll be very unhappy and act accordingly."

He knew this story went on too long and sounded ridiculous but felt it served its purpose. Wolf, meanwhile, couldn't seem to drag himself away, instead roaming from table-to-table reminiscing with old friends... interrupting everybody's lunch as if he were at a party... in his honor. He was like this at funerals too... he lived for funerals... the life of the party.

Gatsby, catching his eye, cut him off just as he was quickening his step, to slink out the door like a guilty little boy caught in the act of torturing the family cat.

Gatsby:

> "What the hell are you doing? You scared the bejesus out of him. Are you proud of yourself? Why must you fuck with people like that? The man has done you no harm... no harm whatsoever. There's something sadistic... I leave you alone for 60 minutes...

> "You know he's important to the operation... he's Daisy's cousin and Buchanan knew him at Yale. I got Outwater to get him to rent that cottage I was going to tear down. I thought we could throw him a bone. He doesn't have much money."

Wolf:

> "I'm sorry... I couldn't help myself. Someone like that... it does something to me. I don't know what comes over me. Why did you bring such a putz to meet me? Is this what you think of me? He wants a connection? I'll fucking connect him... I'll connect him good. I'll have him connected up the ass. Where do you find such people?

> What you don't understand... what he didn't understand at all... is that I was trying to teach the boy something. He carries away nothing.

"Buchanan I can understand, at least... he's got a set... and if I somehow offended him and he got the drop on me he would shoot me dead without blinking an eye... without so much as a hesitation... no ifs, ands or buts. I respect a man like that... I could sit down... do business... break bread even, with a man like that."

Obviously, Nick didn't measure up on a more down to earth, visceral level. I doubt that Wolf gave a hoot about family background or breeding... Patricians or Brahmans...or pondered much about Anglo-Saxons, Goths, Huns, Mongols or Magyars, except as a self-taught historian.

Put a bunch of twelve-year-olds who have never met into a room by themselves and a "natural" pecking order will assert itself. It takes all the king's men, all the power of society and the state to reassert a more orderly alignment.

Going off to college from a city public school isn't a rite of passage it is an ascent into a faraway galaxy. Who among the newly ascendant on return visit to the home planet hasn't been stunned to run into the homecoming king caked in layers of black grease pumping off-brand gas, the homecoming queen in a new contest to pack on weight, reeking the perfume of rancid cooking oil from bootleg, leaking, dented tins through her pores, waiting worn Formica tables at the local pizza joint for cheap tips and all she could eat and as part of her job being periodically goosed by the morbidly obese proprietor who gleefully applauds her alarming increase in girth and the reduced mobility it

implies, who slyly winks at his hanger-on cronies
draped on the greasy counter like the mildewed table
rags: "Her pussy ain't fat." Although there was
significant doubt as to whether he had touched or so
much as peeked at the object of his perfervid desire.

Gatsby:

> "I told him the pearl story… to calm him down…
> to distract… to confuse him. You're officially the
> Albert Einstein of pearls.

> You didn't tell him about the fourth man?

Wolf:

> "Tell him whatever you want. Right now, he's
> scared shitless. He won't so much as squeak.
> So, I told him about the fourth man… so what.
> Let me have my fun. He'll have dreams tonight
> and he will have learned absolutely nothing…
> taken away nothing."

Gatsby went back to his table, paid the bill and said
little further to Nick, extending his apologies. Once
again, he left Nick alone at table; he left as quickly as
he arrived, stopping to talk to only one table and then
seeming to disappear by way of a trap door in the
restaurant floor, just managing to sidestep Thomas
Buchanan with a mission, barrcling inexorably his
way.

Tom, jarred by the sudden, unexpected,
disappearance, thrown off balance, practically
stumbled into Nick's table.

Tom:

"Where'd he go? Wh... What happened?

"I thought I saw you with Pearl and Diamond. I didn't know you hung out with such rarified company... you best watch your step.... You're way out of your league... they'll eat you for breakfast and serve the leavings to the dogs. What's going on here... anyway...? I know about people... I have a sixth sense about things that tells me exactly what to do. Maybe you don't believe that, but...

Nick:

"You mean Gatsby and Wolf...?"

Tom:

"Excuse me? Were you sitting with someone else?

Nick:

"No... I mean...

Tom:

"No... I mean? What the... Yeh... Gatsby and Wolf.

"Wolf brokers the most beautiful pearls anyone has ever seen. I think they come from another planet. They slaughter the competition.

"I bought a string for Daisy... a buy... she fell in love with them... I've never seen her happier.

"He won't deal with just anybody. I needed an introduction... Gatsby was able to help me there... very select clientele... he deals with only the 500 richest families in America... he has a strict list... and in Europe and Asia only with shahs, sheiks, sultans, emperors, emirs, princes, tsars, pashas, rajas, maharajahs, Moghuls, Mikados, khans, Kaisers, caliphs, kings, and other assorted magnates, potentates, oligarchs and particularly powerful Counts, Dukes, generals, governors and samurai... otherwise you're out of luck."

Tom was always performing these verbal acrobatics, or tripping all over himself, thinking it clever or cute or maybe just entertaining. Some found it ridiculous, inept, or just plain lame, goofy and he suffered in other people's esteem as a result of it. But people will groan at even the most ingenious of word-play. Why is the "unsuccessful" exercise of wit resented to such a degree? The man who tries to make a joke without it being at anyone's expense, attempts in his own personal way to lighten the world, if that's what he really wants to do? I have a grudging admiration for anyone who will put themselves out in this way, on the line for judgment, when so many people's spiteful response is a stone face or an exaggerated rolling of the eyes, when a simple smile would be so gracious and welcomed. Because this is a highly social act; the response is critical; it is elicited and when it is not forthcoming, when there is a frown instead it is like a gift that's refused or worse still, snatched from your extended hand and stomped into the ground. In a way it made Buchanan more accessible, more vulnerable, more likeable in an inane way. Because here was a man who needed to please or amuse absolutely no one, who could, if he wished, sit down and break bread with the illustrious Lazarus Wolf.

Nick, puzzled, a not uncommon reaction for Nick, not knowing what to say:

"What?... wh... what about Mr. Diam... Gatsby?

Tom:

"Gatsby... Gatsby within a few short years had become the biggest diamond wholesaler in New York... bypassing the entire De Beers syndicate. First De Beers tried to get rid of him permanently... but they failed... they lost a small army chasing him. Then they spread the rumor that he was producing perfect diamonds 'artificially'... industrially... through some sort of process he developed. He studied physics in Berlin, after The War, after Oxford.

"Nobody could find his source... or his factory... he never revealed it... so the rumor gained traction. They say he amassed over a hundred million dollars before the De Beers campaign started crippling his sales. Then he threatened to flood the market... making diamonds worthless. Once Gatsby's diamonds were out there... in circulation... no one could tell the difference... well they could tell the difference... Gatsby's were better. So, provenance reared its ugly head as a root of value. Buyers wanted guaranteed genealogy before they would buy...

to know exactly what hole they were dug out of. De Beers tried to make certificates of origin mandatory... a birth certificate for rocks and a complete trail of records of purchase and sale... a certificate of title... like a passport. They tried to get laws passed. But some buyers just didn't care... they were perfect diamonds... what else mattered. If excellence or perfection is to be the ultimate criterion then Gatsby's were real and the De Beers were fake.

So, De Beers called for a truce and the story goes that they showed Gatsby hundreds of tons of diamonds that De Beers was withholding from the market... to prop it up... that diamonds were so plentiful they were virtually worthless if released into a free market... that it was De Beers... the magicians... that created value out of nothing... out of air... that it was all marketing, propaganda, and illusion... smoke and mirrors, mass hallucination. Gatsby was ruining it for everyone... cutting his own throat. And Gatsby strangely enough respected this... as a magician himself... the sheer wizardry and audacity of what De Beers was doing... had been able to do... and the story was out... it was no secret... and still people bought diamonds... at totally fabricated prices. They gave proof to the old saw that you don't hold up people with a gun you hold them up with a smile and a handshake and thereby avoid jail. So, they made him an offer... stop manufacturing ... close-down his operation... supposing this was his source... they never knew for sure... and come join them... come once a year and take your pick, first pickings, up to twenty million dollars of value each and every year... endlessly into the future. Why ruin it for everyone. He decided... reluctantly... to join them... I think he was demoralized that he had spent so much time and energy producing something that was so abundant and was so useless though beautiful... except as an industrial abrasive... the vision of those vaults overflowing with diamonds... it would take a bucket loader and a long line of dump trucks just to move the stuff. He stood fast... wrested agreement out of De Beers... keeping his operation going... but solely, exclusively for industrial abrasives... in fact, this has become his cash cow, industrial abrasives... he's the pioneer... and the last man standing... the lowest cost producer... he owns it... nobody can touch him. But it always breaks his heart a little to take those perfect gems... those perfect diamonds, bigger than ostrich eggs... far superior to anything in the De Beers's vault, picked out of the dirt... it's the only kind he knows how to make... and crush them for high grade abrasives. But I suspect that every year he takes the very best of the best and stashes them in his own private vault. Or at least so the rumor goes.

Nick:

"I don't know. It sounds like some story. I'm hearing a lot of stories today. If he's so rich, why would he hang out at that big pile he erected out on Long Island? He should rule his own country. How do you know so much?"

Tom:

"A friend... a business acquaintance really... was in the diamond business, an agent of De Beers, and he never knew what hit him. He sent a crew of private dicks chasing after Gatsby who morphed into Keystone Cops... chasing their tail... they couldn't nail him... couldn't get rid of him either. Gatsby seems to live a charmed life.

"They couldn't dig up anything on his family... he might have sprung full grown from the bayous of Louisiana. There's his military record... there's certainty that. His academic record... Oxford... all documented... his travels throughout Europe and Asia... some on his own passport... extensively in Germany... Russia... long stays in Monaco... the south of France...

"I'd be very careful if I were you. He's dangerous... very... The private dicks who took the contract never came back. Maybe they were bought off. There's no doubt... he has connections... high up... government...? Police? I just don't know. He gets information... lots of information. The stuff he knows... it's like he hears everything. The walls have ears."

Slocum

It's a miracle Carraway wasn't shot. He insisted on repeatedly crashing the Gatsby Estate, imagining that he had some special bond with the man, some vague dispensation that exempted him from the strict protocol, as if they were old army buddies, down in the trenches together. Gatsby's men regarded him with a certain pity, as a benign idiot, or the walking wounded, though fully aware of his combat record or lack thereof. They imagined that Gatsby had something in mind, some scheme in which Carraway would play his minuscule but critical part, which remained a secret to all but a chosen few, especially including Carraway who remained clueless.

Carraway, on his accustomed morning constitutional, shuffling through the neighborhood, had seen the horses, a party of three, granted entry through Gatsby's main gate and slid in on foot with the riders under the careful acquiescing eyes of Gatsby's retainers. Gatsby's servant followed with a bucket and scoop meticulously cleaning up the horse manure from the previously pristine crushed white marble drive which was carefully, mechanically raked every morning like a Japanese garden.

Buchanan was with them but didn't know exactly what was going on. A pretty woman in a brown riding-habit who had been to Gatsby's before had insisted that they stop to visit. Though he knew that he lived in the vicinity, Slocum, the third rider, had no suspicion this was Gatsby's home. The gates were locked shut behind them as soon as they entered and guards reassumed their post; as if a trap had been sprung. It is Tom that recounted that he felt as if some bizarre plot were unfolding, that Slocum had been lured and he himself was just window dressing, part of the cover. He knew Slocum vaguely, introduced to him by Outwater, a stock broker from the city, the pretty woman he knew hardly at all; her name long since forgotten if ever remembered that long hot summer ago which otherwise burned forever in his memory.

Gatsby stood on his porch, as if a welcoming host, carefully surveying the three, gleeful as a fat cat playing with a trapped mouse.

> "I'm delighted to see you. I'm delighted that you dropped in. Come right in. Sit right down. Have a cigarette or a cigar."

Dropped by? Shanghaied.

Slocum, his face drained of blood, grew increasingly petrified; would take nothing. A lemonade? No, thanks. A little champagne? Nothing at all, thanks. A breach of good manners? He was afraid of being poisoned; with good reason. In the course of the visit, through body language and furtive looks exchanged, it became increasingly obvious to the observant that the pretty woman had some intimate connection with Gatsby.

As if to assert that he had not in fact died, the color began to involuntarily flow back into Slocum's frozen face, turning him instead to an alarming beet red. He began to sweat profusely, drenching his brand-new prissy polo attire. He didn't enter into the conversation, but slumped back seated in a pool of his sweat, as if to disappear, in fear, shivering, too afraid to squeak.

Gatsby moved in close and said something to Slocum directly into his ear, that the others couldn't hear. A sewer smell filled the room and Slocum ran out through the front door; to his astonishment no one stopped him. Gatsby yelled out after him with mock good cheer:

> "I'll follow you by motor car. I'll catch up. Don't worry... I'll find you."

There was a large brown splotch on the back of Slocum's clean white jodhpurs, quite obvious but which Nick, oblivious, seems to have missed; Slocum had soiled himself. Gatsby's men opened the gates and Slocum trotted off, disconcerting his horse, squishing in his saddle, oozing shit, with Tom holding back, following him at a more leisurely pace, in his wake. Carraway, on foot, followed the other two men but couldn't catch up, a little boy chasing after a sold-out ice cream truck with a broken bell that wouldn't quit; the supernumerary appendage, tag along, vacant company, a foil to bounce empty words off, tolerated, never completely welcomed, out of breath, chasing unsuccessfully after shit. What a perfect picture summing up his existence.

The pretty woman in the brown riding-habit whose name has been forgotten stayed behind with Gatsby, as if overlooked in Slocum's panic, or just as if it had all been planned that way from the very beginning.

More about My Grandfather

I wish I knew more about my grandfather. He grew more like his old adversaries the Anglo-Saxons the older he got, until he was indistinguishable from them; that is the old Anglo Saxons, the ones he admired. Even when ensconced on the North Shore in the summer of '22 he retired to his own rather small modest apartment, like a monk's retreat; the resident keeper of a great cathedral to the greater glory of his achievement. The richer he grew the more ascetic, frugal, reserved, and laconic he became; he hated ostentatious displays of wealth. He rewarded his children, grandchildren and great-grandchildren according to the lives they lead as he measured them and he was not above making harsh judgments. He was a tough taskmaster; but the task, its choice and fulfillment he left up to the individual, within limits.

He gave no money to organized charity which he considered inefficient or an outright fraud. He chose deserving cases on an individual basis, those who seemed to have become the victim of a particularly cruel fate, from events entirely beyond their control. He had his own gum shoes scrutinize all cases that came to his attention. His help was given anonymously and a follow-up was always made.

He helped the victims of a crooked judicial system which task was Sisyphean; he couldn't fix the system; that was beyond even his power and wealth. He was especially supportive of victims of crimes and those who justly attempted to defend themselves. If you died fighting back, he came to the aid of your family and continued to support them as-long-as necessary often sending the children to college or trade school and finding them jobs, often within his own companies where he could look out for them. Very often they would win the lottery which Gatsby fixed. He called the lottery a perfect tax, a tax on stupidity and lazy desperation. He thought better of this remark and took it back as inappropriately cruel.

One reporter did a detailed study of over a thousand lottery winners, every one of whom was not only in need, but particularly deserving. Not one of them blew the money the way the typical old lottery winners did. No strip bars, no vacations to the islands. Only a few of them quit their job; some started businesses; miraculously, they all moved up in the world. They saved their money, bought a house or paid one off; a solid house made of brick or stone with a full basement; no flood plain or hurricane or tornado zone.

It was as if they had made a pact, a covenant, some secret deal; had met with John Beresford Tipton, who himself came personally to their door with documents to sign. The reporter, a devout atheist, concluded that this was irrefutable proof of some benevolent force in the universe, divine providence, the hand of God. However, he stubbornly remained true to his convictions. He believed in a myth, of a man whose name was unsayable, whose identity he never did discover, who held a few of the levers and helped level the field, just a very little.

Although the support was secret, one unscrupulous politician, a United States Senator, on the Senate floor, accused him, although he wasn't sure who <u>he</u> was, of encouraging vigilantism, claiming without any proof that individuals died fighting when they should have acquiesced, given in and saved their own skins, that they became too enthusiastic martyrs, knowing their families would be taken care of by the covert but famous, seeing but unseen, seemingly all-powerful Donor. Gatsby was railed against:

> "...driving men to heroism for the cash reward... battles were being won recklessly on the battlefield and in the streets".

Some crap about "impure motives". The Senator tried to have the FBI search for the secret donor's identity. But the assistant Director of the Bureau, born into a family without means, had been a recipient of more than one of Gatsby's scholarships and had been guided by an unknown helping hand all-of his life. He did not know for sure it was Gatsby; no letters or phone calls were ever exchanged. There was no communication whatsoever. The required court orders never came or weren't requested. Gatsby knew that any man or woman he had chosen, that's the word he used, "chosen", would do the right thing without any prodding, or so he hoped. This was naïve.

There was a case in New York in which a man came upon a young woman being gang raped by five men; when he screamed for them to stop, they opened fire on him; a crack shot, he returned fire and killed the five of them. Wounded and bleeding he was handcuffed and subsequently charged with possession of an unlicensed handgun, and murder. He lapsed into a coma and was shackled to his hospital bed. At 1:00 AM one morning, two weeks after the shootings, a team of Federal agents, FBI and US Marshals showed up with three doctors, two nurses and their attendant staff to effect a transfer to a "more secure facility, with a more specialized staff", the location of which they were "not at liberty to reveal." Phone calls were made to verify the transfer and the prisoner was loaded into what appeared to be an armored military ambulance. That was the last he was ever seen.

The prisoner's family had disappeared simultaneously leaving no trace behind. The press had a field day, claiming it was an inside job, without a shred of proof; heads rolled but no one was charged; those fired all seemed to find much better jobs and very strangely two of them won the lottery.

The rumor was that he was put into some super secure witness protection program; but who would he have testified against; the dead men were all cheap violent felons with arm-long records but no connections, at least none worth the trouble. There was another rumor, unsubstantiated, that the so-called Donor, as he was called in the tabloid press, (or is that an outdated term; the press is all tabloid these days) had arranged the whole thing; relocated them to the south of France with new passports, not forged but real and new genuine identities complete with histories which they had to study and learn; to a comfortable little house and a small "cultural liaison" team to ease their transition. The children learned French quickly and loved the adventure though they missed their old friends.

Having once headed the American Legion, Gatsby ran with his own idea of what a Veteran's Organization should be. Any man who died for his county had his family looked after by Gatsby. Anyone heroic in battle was rewarded when he came home; there were business loans, home mortgages at preferred interest rates that would never be foreclosed and jobs; his own predecessor and then adjunct to the GI Bill. There was always a welcoming committee at the train station, at the boat, girls with flowers (he had a fixation about girls bearing flowers) and a brass band no matter what time of the day or night. (One pencil pusher with an eye to counting beans found the brass band, although only a four-piece affair, a "ridiculous extravagance". He was helped to move on, to find employment more agreeable to his practical preoccupations and pencil pushing ways.)

One Good Soldier to Another

Gatsby never forgot the indignity of arriving back as if naked and unappreciated on the shores of America, so weighted down with medals that he could hardly stand up straight, but with empty pockets. He had stayed too long at Oxford, then Berlin. There were no brass bands, no cheering crowds, no pretty girls bearing flowers, not so much as a welcoming committee of one.

However, one old soldier from the United Confederate Veterans looked him up and bought him a hot dog at

Nedicks in a storefront of the Bartholdi Hotel, at 23rd Street and Broadway. He never forgot the day. Of all the lavish meals he'd eaten in the great houses, and in the finest restaurants throughout the world, this is the one he remembered. The old timer told him to meet him at the "Orange Room of the Hotel Nedicks"; he thought that was a riot; he was on a "tight budget", expressing his regrets.

He showed up in his Confederate officer's uniform; a sight to behold, an apparition, in a double-breasted captain's frockcoat of darker Richmond grey and sky-blue trim. He saluted the Colonel, long and slow, as if the Colonel were Robert E. Lee, returned. The uniform was still a perfect fit, custom tailored with a brand-new look; his best and only suit, saved for God knows what, for this very occasion, perhaps, and had the effect of rolling back the clock, a hand against the tide, like he stepped straight out of a time machine, come back especially by design so that at least one person, just one, would be there for the Colonel. The crowds gawked at him as if he just materialized from Mars and laughed like he was a buffoon; one fool asked if he was dressed for a movie part, or was he going to a masquerade. He apologized to Gatsby, the Colonel; he hadn't meant to create a spectacle; he wore the uniform as a sign of respect, one good soldier to another good soldier. The Colonel reassured him that no apology was needed; that he was indeed deeply honored.

His grandson had served under the command of the Colonel in The War, as it was then called; and had since died; run down by a car full of drunks on a warm summer Sunday evening while he was walking home exhausted from a long day at work.

He wanted to thank the Colonel; the Colonel couldn't understand for what. He said he was sick to death of living in Yankee territory, suffocating on Yankee sanctimony; that he wanted to return home to the South, which he knew was no more, if it ever was, where everything was civilized and rotted and polite. "Never ask the names of the villages, just remember them." He was afraid to break the spell. Perhaps he lived in an unusable past, sentimentalizing a way of life that had buckled under its own weight, folded like a geriatric circus absconded in the night. He lived on dreams of the Old South rising, unscathed, out of adversity, penury and abject defeat.

He spoke at length about his grandson who had graduated from West Point; he was exceedingly proud of him but didn't seem to entirely comprehend or want to comprehend the inherent contradiction or wicked irony in all of it. His wife, the boy's grandmother, knowing better, wept when she saw him in his dress blue uniform and embraced him tightly to stop from shaking uncontrollably, burying her eyes in the blue so she didn't have to see.

The old warrior called the Colonel a good Yankee, much as one would call a German a good German twenty-five years later, as an exception, an anomaly, against nature, but on good authority reputed to exist. The Colonel found the epithet jarring but held his peace. He was no Yankee; he was not taking on their sins; these were not his people, not by a long shot.

Kleinsinger

I don't remember the subterfuge that Nick employed to lure Gatsby to his rented cottage; whether it had something to do with the connection that Nick was yearning after or whether it fit into Gatsby's larger scheme, I never found out. Gatsby, being an old school gentleman never spoke of any of it. In any event he was trapped by his good manners; there was no easy way out. When, after years, he saw Daisy, his heart dropped out of his chest; his usually infectious convivial high spirits guttered. He was haunted by vivid memories of her crazy family, of her father the judge chasing her around the dinner table brandishing a knife. Gatsby was confident that this had not been some mock display, some empty posturing. He was convinced that if the judge had caught her, he would have killed her, slashed her to her bloody death. Daisy depended on the fact that her father was slow of foot and a bit sloshed and therefore felt free to taunt him mercilessly to her heart's content. And Gatsby knew that if he had continued with this woman, she would have similarly taunted him, but he, being quick of foot, and stone cold sober would have caught her, to no good end for either of them.

When exiting Nick's little cottage Daisy couldn't help but be overwhelmed by Gatsby's huge abode overshadowing them, seeming to grow as Daisy stared at it transfixed in immodest wonderment:

> "It's all yours… that huge thing there…? It's so… so big… my god"

she cried pointing.

Gatsby:

> "I'm glad you like it."

Daisy:

> "I love it, I just love it. It's so big. Can I see it? Will you show it to me?"

When Gatsby somewhat reluctantly gave Daisy the grand tour of the establishment after having reluctantly fucked her in Nick's thatched cottage, with Nick in unwelcomed tow, they startled Kleinsinger who hadn't been given his usual heads-up; he was caught off guard, in the act, practicing the piano.

Kleinsinger was the resident property manager, responsible for keeping the house and grounds in tiptop shape but really-much more than that. He coordinated the real work while the imported English butler was mostly for the entertainment and the show. Don't get me wrong; the butler was kept hopping and more than earned his keep as a performer; perfected a stiff-upper-lip obsequiousness and was re-christened Jeeves for the run of the show.

He was like the show captain on those latter-day behemoth cruise ships, which, dangerously top-heavy, look like they're ready to sink or tip over; where the over-fed hoi-polloi waddle to the trough, pretend they are just like the old-money rich folk; and are actually, positively, having fun swilling contaminated food served up by help with unclean hands and third world hygiene. The real captain steering the ship, sight unseen wouldn't be caught dead in the show captain's Hollywood costume and finds his employment cloying and embarrassing; finding it necessary to lie to his family telling them that he captains a swine boat on a slow run to China. Meanwhile the show captain has infinite time to socialize with guests, who pay extra. He maintains a captain's table in three separate dining rooms which he ferries between in shifts, pushing his food around the plate, smart enough not to eat it; which prompted one cheeky young lad "honored" to sit at one of his tables with him to enquire:

> "Shouldn't you be steering the ship or something?"

which led to nervous laughs all around the table.

Kleinsinger occupied an incongruously luxurious apartment over the garages and an office off the big house's main kitchen, but had the run of the place with Gatsby's blessing. If guests were expected he was given fair warning in advance.

He was a gifted concert pianist and practiced on the Steinway grand when time and opportunity permitted; managing the estate was 24 hour seven days a week commitment. But he was much more than manager; he was Gatsby's CFO, he had become overseer of all his earthly financial affairs.

They became partners in the drugstore business with over a hundred branches in New York alone and the manufacture and distribution of alternative medicinals. He also ran the casinos.

He had played Rachmaninoff at Carnegie Hall and practiced religiously for a return.

It was with a certain, almost familial pride that Gatsby persuaded a very reluctant Kleinsinger to play his Rachmaninoff, although Gatsby sensed intuitively that this wasn't the right crowd.

Half-way through the performance Daisy had had enough:

> "No… No… No… something cheerful and fun.

> "How about *Ain't We Got Fun?*"

Daisy broke into an impromptu Charleston, tripped precipitously, and landed dangerously on her ass with knees spread wide revealing just momentarily for all to admire); she quickly composed herself duly blushing and embarrassed like the modest school girl she incongruously pretended to be. It was only later that Nick observed that Daisy was just "showing off". This from Nick, a man who was accustomed to expose himself; but more in order to humiliate, degrade and self-flagellate. After reestablishing what passed for self-possession, as if nothing at all had happened or she could care less, Daisy resumed her ingenuous demeanor, giddily urging Kleinsinger to play *The Love Nest*; Kleinsinger, turning around and searching unhappily for Gatsby in the gloom with the look of:

> "How could you do this to me"?

Gatsby, mortified, dumbstruck, though he had been a fool not to expect it.

Kleinsinger protested courteously to each request:

"I've heard it but never played it before."

He plunked out the ridiculous ditties for the delectation of the mindless interlopers.

It sounds awful and even sexist but the last thing Gatsby had wanted, was to have sex again with Daisy. She chased him down when he set up shop in Great Neck; she was obsessed; of all the places to open a gin joint. She kept showing up at his parties, the uninvited guest, usually mixed in with invited groups and he didn't have the heart to throw her out or bar her at the door.   He tried to keep his distance, which was difficult. He was the host after all and needed to work the room.

What passes for charm in an eighteen-year-old can turn sickly sweet, nauseating even, in a woman in her twenties. She grew older without maturing, already beginning her slow, relentless descent into rot without any prospect of ripening. What passed as youthful rebelliousness revealed itself with age as the vicious, vacuous selfishness of the unregenerate vandal. One can see her, as in a bad dream, rising out of the mists, swinging a hammer against Roman marble. She dripped genuine blood.

He did it as an act of kindness, to keep from wounding her. It was his good deed, his mitzveh. I wonder how the priests and ministers, the self-appointed, pompous ethicists would feel about that; having sex, adultery technically, as an act of genuine kindness, and as such a highly moral act.

Gatsby had met Kleinsinger in an unusual way. One day he simply showed up at Gatsby's door without warning or introduction. For obvious reasons Gatsby was summoned immediately by an agitated staff. He took one look at him and said simply:

"You look like blood....

"That doesn't sound right, does it? What I meant to say is you have a familial look. We look related."

That was an understatement. Kleinsinger stood there speechless for a moment:

"I saw your picture in the newspaper and was struck by it."

He wasn't like a poor country cousin showing up unannounced with baggage at his feet. He was accomplished, better educated than Gatsby in many ways. He had money, substantial money, but seemed to be unaffected by it, not to care about it, certainly not about spending it, which is all very convenient for those who have plenty of it.

He was just profoundly curious. Early one warm summer Sunday morning when feeling restless, with the newspaper firmly in hand, as if to serve as proof, of whatever, he simply decided to impose upon his driver and travel to the wilds of Long Island to discover, God knows what, on its sandy shores. He had no idea if Gatsby was even in or really existed. Photographs prove nothing. It was a shot in the dark.

Searching for common roots he told Gatsby the story of his family. Kleinsinger's father and grandfather had been medicine men. His grandfather traveled with an entourage of wagons that looked more like a traveling fair or circus than a purveyor of healing potions. He called himself Doctor Good and had a cure for every ailment. He mixed his magic potions in New York City in his own factory which worked a double shift even when he was travelling. He traversed the rural areas of the Northeast by wagon, and the river cities by his own riverboat which was ocean worthy, materializing from the fog like an apparition with its calliope drowning out the fog horns; what a sound. It travelled up all the navigable rivers of the East coast, the Gulf and then the Mississippi. He had a crew of advance men who would travel ahead of him on land, booking the best accommodations, plastering the towns with posters, and taking full page advertisements in the newspapers. He would line up local endorsers, prominent, respected citizens who would give enthusiastic testimonials either written or as introductory speeches, all in return for complementary product. He tried to win the support of the local physicians, usually unsuccessfully; they saw him as the competition; who they slandered as a snake oil salesman.

He may have sold snake oil but mostly he kept the ingredients of his potions a deep dark secret. Actually, he sold black currant seed oil, grapeseed oil, extra virgin olive oil, coconut oil and the oil from octopus and tiny little shrimp called krill. He sold fermented milk whose recipe and culture came from Russia called Kefir and special aged cheeses and whey and his own special sauerkraut. He sold dried blueberries, sour cherries, strawberries, and blackberries; and nuts: almonds, walnuts, cashews, hazel nuts, pistachios, brazil nuts, macadamias and pine nuts and peanuts which aren't nuts at all; apple cider vinegar and wild raw honey. He sold miso from Japan and natto and his own green tea and black tea from Ceylon and strong Arabica coffee from the Columbian hills and unsweetened chocolate. He sold seaweed from off the coast of Korea and blue green algae from pure inland fresh water lakes. He grew his own mushrooms: Maitake, Chaga, Reishi, Cordyceps, Royal Sun Blaze, Enokitake, Mesima, Turkey Tail, Zhu Ling, Lion's Mane, Maitake, Artist's Conk, Agarikon, Amadou, Shiitake and another parasitic growth from the dessert called Cistanche known in China as Rou Congrong. He sold a host of different spices and herbs in a myriad of secret concoctions: Curcumin, Kava, Cat's Claw, Horney Goat Weed, Maca from South America, Kalmegh, Siberian Ginseng, Chinese Ginseng, Ashwagandha, Fenugreek, Echinacea, Rhodiola, Schisandra, Milk Thistle, Tribulus Terrestris, Muira Puama, Bacopa, Cinnamon, Holy Basil, Boswellian, an extract from white willow bark and French maritime pine bark; a sleep potion made with Valerian Root, Chamomile Flower, Passionflower, Lemon Balm, Hops and just a faint touch of opium tincture; and dozens of varieties of garlic. He sold fresh onions, cabbage and broccoli. For colds he had a mix of Guaifenesin, Ephedra and Codeine. The list went on and on and on, all learned by heart and sealed securely in memory. Kleinsinger shared these secrets with Gatsby as the basis for their evolving partnership in the patent medicine business; locked fast in a safe now; hundreds of ingredients based on folk remedies, Ayurveda, Chinese traditional medicine and Native America potions. Kleinsinger recalled nostalgically how his own father recited the lists to him to learn by heart like an incantation, a fairytale which lulled him to sleep at night.

The grandfather hired his own gunman as protection, who far outmatched the local thugs sent by the physicians to burn him out. He would enter a river port or town like a conquering hero with crowds cheering and bands playing (his own bands), acrobats walking on their hands and cartwheeling down the street.

He raked in so much money that he had armored wagons travelling in his wake guarded by mounted Pinkertons; when he wasn't traveling by boat. There was such an avalanche, he accepted only gold or silver coin, that he sometimes curtailed his tour to return to Chicago laden with his treasure; he owned his own bank; but its furthest branch reached only to Chicago.

Kleinsinger's father and grandfather both lived to an old age but never seemed to age. You would think that a man who was over a hundred but looked fifty would garner a great deal of attention and would receive insistent inquiries and accolades from government officials and heads of state. They were leery of him. One politician complained how "disruptive" it would be if the average person never aged. What about the doctors they complained. Do you want to put them out of business? Close down the medical schools?

> "Sickness is always with us. It is essential to the
> human condition. Disease allows us to cull the
> weak. It is god's threshing board"

one of them philosophized ridiculously.

People are grudging of even the appearance of a personal tribute. The fact that most of the health gurus today are overweight and look like shit doesn't seem to faze their devoted adherents who follow them like blinded sheep guiding their own herded way over the cliff to the tune of deafening bleats.

Kleinsinger's grandfather was killed by a runaway beer wagon pulled by huge draft horses with hair draped hooves who had been spooked or so the story was let out. But the truth is that he too was probably murdered; the murderer, protected, had connections.

His own father was shot in the back through the heart without warning by a deranged small-town doctor, a religious fanatic, who he showed up by curing the doctor's wife of an "incurable" disease. The doctor had painstakingly persuaded her, prepared her to peacefully accept her fate as god's holy will, to look forward to her wonderful journey into heaven and place her faith in "the Lord, our Savior, Jesus Christ". He not only embarrassed the doctor he up-staged the Lord, at least in the doctor's eyes, who was thoroughly indoctrinated with this stupid priest drivel. He seemed to be looking forward to her death so she could go up to heaven, get her reward and watch over and pray for him, his own private intercessor, a lock on the inside track.

Edward Winslow

How Edward Winslow got through the heavily protected perimeter of the Gatsby Estate is still unexplained. His pickups and deliveries, the extensive walking trips, his reconnaissance through the neighborhood gave him the lay of the land, imprinted the topography of the loaded on his sick brain. His repeated transport of Nick's patched up body work familiarized him with what amounted to a back door, the soft vulnerable underbelly, concealed by thick bushes, which was Nick's backyard; the barrier weakened, compromised by the habitual prying of the less than harmless gatecrasher. The guard dogs had grown accustomed to the strange, panicky smell of Carraway, and Winslow exuded that identical dull enervating fear. The ever-vigilant gatekeepers, those grim heavies with their bulging roscoes, should have followed their instincts, escorted Nick to his appointed rendezvous, that boat ride on the Sound that very first night, for a moonlight swim in concrete galoshes.

Miranda inserted the long nozzle into the receptacle and with spur of the moment enthusiasm rushed out into the dusk, waving her hands joyously, shouting a friendly hello to Gatsby's car. She loved Gatsby and was accustomed to gush like a girl at the sight of him; she had been pumping gas but the gas could wait.

Daisy had swerved in to fill-up, but seeing Miranda, hit the gas hard and... then... barreled back into the highway. Daisy, forgetting what car she was in, thought Miranda was mocking her, jeering at her in such high spirits, wearing an ecstatic grin. Daisy knew exactly who she was: Tom's woman. She had no idea she was a prostitute, the woman he would rather be with. But I think it was her extraordinary beauty and overt sexuality that enraged Daisy to this level of madness.

Winslow was inconsolable and cradled the ruptured Miranda in his wiry arms, ineffectually closing her gaping wounds with his bloodied, grease-stained hands, clumsily trying to put her back together again, sobbing convulsively like a little boy.

Winslow knew what Gatsby looked like; his coming and goings were no secret in this neck of the woods. He knew his extravaganza of a car; everyone knew it. At the first scene of slaughter, Tom insisted, unnecessarily protesting suspiciously:

> "... that big cream car I was driving this afternoon wasn't mine... it didn't belong to me... Listen to what I say. I was bringing you that coupé I promised you, that you've been wanting to buy."

A day late and a universe away, harrumphed Winslow in a murderous pent-up fury. He could easily kill this man now and loose nothing; but that might slow him down. As much as he would have liked to have brought them all down in one fell swoop, he would bide his time for the primary kill.

He slinked through like a wounded animal on the prowl; an ashen fantastic figure floating surrealistically through the diaphanous trees, through the undergarments of obscene goddesses hanging from anachronistic wash-lines in the leaden sky. The sun was in his eyes; he was over a hundred feet away, when Gatsby's heavies started unloading on him. For the first time in years, he stopped sweating. He instantly dropped to crouch on one knee, back in mortal combat, took careful aim, holding the gun with both hands and let loose his one shot, one shot just as a cloud brought back his sun-blinded sight, long enough to know he had killed the wrong man. All the shots rang out in less than three seconds. Blood began to fill the pool, dyeing it a deep ruby red, which soon enough turned brown. Who would have thought the man would have had so much blood in him.

If Kleinsinger had been alone by the pool, as was usual, Winslow would have passed him by. It was Gatsby's praetorians that fooled him, made him think that it was Gatsby in the water. The armed guards protecting him were a dead-give-away to a lie. They had received a warning call from neighbors that a crazy man was running loose in the neighborhood; run down by a burly grounds-man up the road, narrowly slipping his captor's grip. The grounds-man didn't know how lucky he was to let slip death, as if by propitious accident. They stood picket as a prudent precaution. They hadn't counted on a dead-eye marksman; or the dogs inured; or the weakened worn spot through an habitual gatecrashers yard; or that Kleinsinger would be a sitting duck in the pool, powerless to extricate, to make a swift escape; the water a molasses trap in the split second he rose like a primordial god snapping chains, sticking to the earth like glue, clutched by its tentacles, the surface tension of the artificial sea, a rich man's marble pool, only to meet his death with one clean well-aimed shot from one of life's left-outs. About to break free he fell back into his blood and drowned in it.

But the right man would have been the wrong man too. Sad dumb Winslow got it all wrong, as he did most everything.

It turns out that Kleinsinger was ten years older than Gatsby, though everyone assumed he was the baby brother. Kleinsinger's three sons, mostly grown, showed up at the abbreviated services and played their part, grudgingly, resenting the ruse, pretending to be other than who they were. There could be no crowds. They inherited the house, Gatsby's house, as a negotiated settlement, the least Gatsby could do; empty solace and they and their heirs own it to this day, the hub of subdivided estates and a small real estate empire and of course there is the drug company, the supplement company, the drug stores and a small interest in industrial abrasives and a chain of jewelry stores, all closely held corporations first with Gatsby, then his heirs. However, the golden goose slipped its' noose; the trick to making perfect diamonds died with Gatsby, just as the pearl business dissolved with the death of Wolf (the nuns went back to China). They keep the big house mostly for nostalgia's sake which considering its history seems to make no sense. The house is open to daily tours during the Spring, Summer, and early Fall. During July, August and September into Labor Day it is open to all night catered affairs; the ghostly revelry rings out into the night, all night and in the private rooms, which some say don't exist, Rot-Gut Ferrel rolls the dice and finally wins. And a man who looks just like Gatsby did in 1922 and never seems to age, greets all comers at the door with a winning smile which disarms even the most cynical with its inviting charm. And in the background, we hear Rachmaninoff, which no one interrupts.

Simple Headstone 1896- 2000

It has been duly-noted that Gatsby's epitaph, which he penned himself, was a joke; that his immediate heirs found it on the great man's big mahogany desk and being stricken with grief inexplicably lost their sense of humor and took it seriously enough to have it carved in stone; which in its own way is bizarrely appropriate; that his earthly remains should be marked by a final flippancy, an over-the-top witticism from the master's own pen. There has been talk of replacing it with a more fitting memorial, but level heads have prevailed; the concluding joke remains on top of his empty grave.

His simple headstone, more a marker, no cross, no star, no hammer, no sickle, no crescent, no swastika, a tall white granite obelisk polished to a high mirror sheen, simply says, anachronistically:

> "Here lies James Jacob Gatsby, sometime known in life as 'The Great Gatsby', a great magician, aerialist, tight rope walker, unmatched master of the flying trapeze, who spent the better part of his life in the circus and on the stage; a renowned Shakespearean actor,

celebrated for his Hamlet; a skilled sea captain of sailing ships who had circumnavigated this small globe many times, who went down bravely with his sinking ship while trying to evacuate every last passenger to the lifeboats in an ice-packed sea."